THE POWER

IAN WATSON was born in 1943 and raised on Tyneside. After graduating from Oxford University, he lectured for several years in East Africa and Japan before taking up a post lecturing on Futures Studies at Birmingham Polytechnic. He resigned as Senior Lecturer in 1976 to become a full-time writer, and has since published many sf and fantasy novels. These have won awards in Britain, America and France, and have been translated into eight languages. An active member of CND and the Labour Party, Ian Watson has twice stood as Labour candidate in county elections. He lives with his wife and daughter in Northamptonshire.

Ian Watson
THE POWER

HEADLINE

First published in Great Britain in 1987 by
HEADLINE BOOK PUBLISHING PLC.

HEADLINE BOOK PUBLISHING PLC.
Headline House
79 Great Titchfield Street
London W1P 7FN

ISBN 0   7472   3041   2

Typeset by Rapidset & Design Ltd., London WC1
Printed & bound by Collins, Glasgow

To all those past and present at Upper Heyford Peace Camp who have devoted valuable parts of their lives to opposing the evil of nuclear war.

Diabolus

If the world is a living creature with forests of hair and baldy deserts, with skin of soil and breath of air and sweat of sea, if the earth is a beast with ribs of rock and mineral veins, stomach of oil and lungs of gas, heart and bowels of hot deep magma –

– then a diabolus is a boil, a cyst crammed with filth, a rotten appendix, walled off by tissue, but festering inside.

If it's poked it can erupt, as a wasps' nest erupts. Squeeze the cyst and its powers emerge like some hallucinatory poisonous pus which can grant desires (for a while) and accomplish curses, which taints and torments what it touches.

A 'bolus' is a good old doctors' name for a large medicinal pill. Pills fight disease, or are supposed to. That other sort of bolus – diabolus – causes mortal sickness, madness, terror. It destroys like a tumour of the flesh, cancer of the mind.

Diaboli lurk in definite nooks in the world's skin. Equally, they are fiends inhabiting the psyche of the planet; things of will-power, nightmare, hatred, lust which certain passwords can awake, which certain rituals, symbols, states of consciousness can unbind.

Mostly diaboli lie dormant, walled off by the health of the world. A few shamans sought the passwords in paleolithic tongues back when word and object seemed to be the same, when people and the world were one. Dire names of diaboli were handed down. Magicians, witches would hypnotise and drug and starve themselves. They would pledge their souls. They would sacrifice babies and virgins. They would torture prisoners. All in order to nudge a diabolus, hoping to control and channel it – for a while, till it mastered them and dragged them screaming into itself.

Some people can never leave power alone – any more than other people want to avoid building thermonuclear cysts to burst the heat of the sun and poison breath over battlefields and cities. In the flesh of England hides a diabolus, appendix of black, corrupting power. . . .

Or did those crazy shamans and warlocks, and all that agony, rage, and lust, *put* the diabolus there in the first place? Gradually, through the long millenia from the old dream-time, did it gather its power from the sicknesses of the human heart? Did the conquering, domineering, two-legged creatures who had sprouted brains actually animate all the malady into a slumbering entity, one among many?

PART ONE

One

Jeni glanced up, and the spire of St Mary's was toppling upon her.

To squash her flat and messy as a cowpat, hamburger her body, hammer her into the turf littered with sheep turds. She staggered, gasping.

The sentinel-spire was still in the same position, was still tumbling.

Rising from a chunky, Norman-style tower, the steep pyramid of blue slates was patchworked by green replacements. Louvred belfry windows were inset under double-curved ogee arches. The stone summit-ball clasped a spike where a golden weathercock perched, twitching in the wind . . .

She realized that the little white cumuli rushing overhead were making her see the spire heel over upon her. St Mary's, Melfort Parva, wasn't moving – just the clouds.

Several of the hugely pregnant Masham ewes in the churchyard bleated in unison. Had they smelt her panic on the wind, read it in the jerk of her body?

Above the clouds the lazy dart of an F-111 drifted. Its hushed thunder had made her look up, but the noise of the fighter-bomber wouldn't have bothered the sheep. Too familiar. She hated the American jet and wished it would fall, then hastily unwished her wish. At the base, ten F-111s were always kept fully loaded with nuclear weapons in the high security, quick response area, codename "Victor". Given the international news, who could be sure that an F-111 on ordinary patrol didn't have nukes aboard? If it crashed, its bombs wouldn't explode, of course, but casings might split. Plutonium could disperse on the wind, a single grain enough to poison a person.

Supposing a warhead did explode five miles away due east – a direct hit on the Kerthrop base – the tower and spire of St Mary's might shade Jeni briefly from the light, the heat. Moments later the entire church would disintegrate, hurled westwards.

Yet she stepped from the shade of that spire which wished to crush her, into bright sunlight and the cutting March wind. As she hugged her anorak to her a few flakes of snow flurried by. Like radioactive ash. No, ash wouldn't be so white. Catching a flake on her fingertip she tasted it, pure and cold. Perhaps not so pure! Now that the F-111 had passed over, angel of death, a feathery contrail frayed and fluffed out. The snowflakes might be children of a previous jet's exhaust, or of the same one, circling round.

Along the boundary of the churchyard a line of eroded headstones stood shoulder to shoulder like Roman shields of rock locked together against an enemy. The older graves, from which those stones had been pulled, formed a humpy sward knobbed with sheep droppings. In the stones' lee, snowdrops dangled bunches of waxy white bells; crocuses showed purple tips. A church-size shadow hurried by, dulling colours; just as swiftly the curtain lifted.

Jeni spied the vicar emerging from the south door. The Reverend Jeremy Partridge, in his Dracula gear: voluptuous velvety black cloak with soaring collar and silver chain across the breastbone. How much had Partridge paid from his meagre stipend for that magnificent garment, which surely wasn't any standard item of ecclesiastical regalia? Though only a rural Anglican vicar, Partridge dressed like some prince of the church, a cardinal in exile.

But Partridge wasn't married; no wife or kids to support. It was the part-time home-help, goiterous, intrusive Mrs Enid Jackson ("You got a neck, Missus!") who directed Jeni up here this morning. Naturally Mrs Busybody knew where the vicar was. She probably knew by telepathy what Jeni wanted to ask Partridge.

He had mannerisms, that one. When he dropped in to the White Lion for a G and T or two the vicar could become quite ultraviolet in his act, his voice fluting in high scales of self-parody. Was he a repressed homosexual? ("No choirboys for me, thanks! I have Christ – but how about another itsy-bitsy splash of Gordon's?") However, the vicar wasn't always foppish. Partridge had a sharp satiric tongue when he cared to use it, in defence of faith, virtues, and his church.

Hereabouts, virtue included poshing up the vacant school house next to the C of E endowed primary school to rent to a USAF family from the base. When Old Donaldson retired as headmaster after umpteen years, new headteacher Miss Samuels hadn't wanted the big, tatty pile. She was buying her own place. The advantages of renting to the US military were twofold. With their lavish housing allowance, Americans would pay well over the odds; and they would sign short-term agreements unbound by British tenant law. The house had to come up to standard, but you could easily get rid of your Americans and milk them meanwhile to top up the diocesan coffers.

Whenever a church needed repairs, how curiously empty the coffers seemed to be! – leading to innumerable pig roasts, barn dances, raffles and other modern forms of medieval tithes. The Church Commissioners, amongst the richest landlords in the realm, recently cashed the imposing Melfort vicarage in for a cool quarter of a million to a scrap metal dealer, shifting their vicar into a convenient little bungalow; this windfall seemed to have no earthly connexion with church repair bills.

True, the *Church Times* had spoken out against American military adventures, and the Archbish of Canterbury himself had criticized the US bases in Britain. To what real effect, when the church was busily renting property to US personnel?

As County Council governor of Melfort's primary school – the Labour Party nominee – Jeni had spoken out six months ago against the rental scheme. Already there were a couple of other American families living in the village. Proven decent folk! The people who lived off base usually were the cream, the adaptable ones. Chirpy Captain Ron Diamond was, for God's sake, an F-111 pilot; with wife Sheri and little boy Felix they'd run a popcorn stall at last summer's village fete, decorated all over with the Stars and Stripes. Quiet Ed and Mary Kuzka had lived in Britain for years and were half-way anglicized; he was a civilian employee in charge of transient billeting, though he'd formerly been on active service in Vietnam. The Kuzkas' youngest daughter, teenage Carol, still lived with them and hung out in the White Lion with the local teenagers – she never wanted to go back to the States. But but but.

During the governors' meeting, Jeni had enquired pointedly whether Melfort's tender infants should be taught cheek by jowl with somebody whose basic business was nuclear war, next door to some possible Rambo from Little Rock; nowadays the base was sucking in extra personnel from the States and siphoning them around wherever spare housing existed. She'd speculated whether the rent was thirty pieces of silver. Partridge's tongue had lashed her – momentarily. The other school managers thought that renting to the American military was a fine, sensible idea.

Old Donaldson wouldn't have countenanced it, if he'd had any say. But Miss Samuels, bright spark though she was, was no match for the vicar. What a good idea Jeni had thought it at the time to appoint a go-ahead young woman headteacher to work with the two part-time teachers, Mrs Braithwaite and Mrs Vanderzee, instead of having another man in charge. Parental squeals as to how their male off-spring would learn proper football had struck her as ludicrous, reactionary. However, Miss Samuels was a prac-tising, obedient Christian, the consequences of which Jeni had rather left out of her calculations.

At least now that so much barbed wire sealed off the Ker-throp base there wouldn't be any more merry school trips there; not now that all minor gates were blocked and armed guards ran 100% ID checks at the sandbagged open gates, causing morning tailbacks. Ever since Libya.

"Vicar!"

Jeni hurried over, wondering how in heaven's name the vicar could refuse a request to support peace. A few local churches had already agreed to cooperate in the Easter fes-tival, but Jeni suspected Partridge's answer – though she would never have foreguessed his reason.

"*Miss* Wallis." Partridge stressed the "Miss". "Such a pleasure, on a fine spring morning."

Jeni was thirty-five, and unmarried. And why should that be? She was sultry-looking, smouldery. Quite slim and dark; not tall. Jet hair trimmed to her shoulders. Wild sloe eyes. A gypsy lass, her Dad used to say in offended be-musement. Passionate – about certain things.

Yet not wedded, not a mother. Not properly adult. Im-mature . . . politically. Too hectic. Not quite a full or re-sponsible member of society; that's what the "Miss" said to her. Never mind that she'd been a schoolteacher for years, was a governor et bloody cetera; that's what local Tory worthies thought of her.

"It's freezing, Vicar. And there's snow in the air."

"Matter of perspective. The sun shines, and the bulbs push up. God's earth renews itself. Don't be a pessimist, Miss Wallis. Pessimism tarnishes the heart."

"And the war planes cruise overhead."

Another distant soft drum of thunder had reached Jeni's

9

ears. St Mary's stood on a modest eminence; thatches and steep-pitched slate roofs descended in several directions. Miles east beyond farmland and the far knoll of Hobby Hill she spied another dirty dart lift itself into the sky from RAF Kerthrop. As the jet climbed it rolled steeply northward to avoid overflying the market town of Churtington, which was out of sight by day but aglow by night, though the glow from the base housing and perimeter floodlights increasingly eclipsed it.

F-111s usually went up high quite quickly. Low-level flying – contour-hugging down valleys, over chimney tops – that was the prerogative of the noisier, exhaust-spewing RAF Phantoms. Those kept clear of the immediate Kerthrop patch; American air space. Small mercies.

RAF Kerthrop. Royal Air Force – what a sick joke. Half a dozen British officers to answer the phone amiably, and five thousand members of the USAF zillionth Tactical Fighter Wing. With dependants, fifteen thousand?

During the "Day of Disruption" last year when CND members had pledged to tie up the phone lines all day long, for her part Jeni had begun ordering a whole menu of Chinese take-away food the moment the phone was picked up. ("I'd like number 23, Shrimps Chow Mein. Number 44, Special Foo Yung. Number 68, Roast Duck with Beansprouts. Two helpings of number 88, Egg Fried Rice. . . .") The RAF biffo had chortled with amusement. Damn him for a fool, he should have been furious. But hadn't she been just an itsy-bitsy . . . politically immature? (Oh no. Immature politics all happened ages ago. In that frantic, fervent Trotskyist time at Oxford.)

"Maybe," said Partridge, "you should ask the Kremlin to give its poor, overworked pilots a well-deserved rest?"

"We do support Soviet nuclear disarmament."

"Ah, but does your average Ivan enjoy the freedom to support anything?"

And in Jeni's head the fading voice of Trotsky's heirs chorused, "Not likely! The Soviet Union is a state capitalist bureaucratic tyranny. A fossilized statist oligarchy."

"Shut up," she told herself, "that's robot-talk. Chicken with its head chopped off." She wasn't going to get bogged down in some stupid, point-scoring debate which would all be water off the vicar's Dracula-cloaked back. So far as he was concerned, the Soviet leadership were atheists who put the boot into practising Christians.

She shrugged. "I want to ask you something."

"Maybe we should step inside?" Partridge swooped back to the wire-mesh door which kept invading pigeons out of the porch, and thrust it wide. "It *is* a teeny trifle frigid, out."

Two

As the wire mesh clashed shut on its spring, the stout main door of battered, blackened, worm-holed oak yawned inward to the vicar's push.

The nave felt refrigerated, though at least the wind-chill factor was absent. This could only be the second occasion that Jeni had set foot inside St Mary's. ("Mustn't encourage the buggers.") Since her "tourist" visit of four years earlier she'd quite forgotten the interior: of white plastered walls inlaid with brass memorial plaques, fine vaulted timber roof, great arch separating off the altar end. Vases of early forced daffodils stood about. The stained glass was mostly mediocre. Oh yes, and there was the relic.

Mounted on the wall at head height next to the pulpit there jutted a padlocked iron cage reminiscent of a sprung man-trap. Inside was a worn stone reliquary which consisted of a miniature turret with a gabled lid. This object had been dug from inside a wall during Victorian renovations. It held, she recalled, a throat bone supposedly from some martyr. A larynx bone; the silenced, skeletal voice of St Somebody, identity uncertain. Maybe St Boniface. Bonny Face.

How highfalutin' and quasi-Roman for a rural Anglican church to house a relic! The reliquary must have been hidden away during the Reformation.

Was it the relic that had attracted Jeremy Partridge to the parish of Melfort? If indeed vicars did choose their destinations. Jeni remembered hearing on the radio that a good number of vicars these days were refusing to accept inner city slum appointments. ("One must heed the welfare of one's family, mustn't one?") If vicars were able to reject a billet maybe they could also request one, particularly if they had connexions; as Partridge, with his airs, surely did.

If St Mary's had indeed been a Catholic church the relic would have been enshrined more nobly, in some golden vessel studded with gems – not stuck in a stone ashtray inside a rusty man-trap. The sight of it made Jeni feel creepy. Throat-bone, stone, dust. Did its presence exalt the vicar?

"Easter," she said to him. "Festival of the Prince of Peace."

"To be sure. Three weeks come Sunday. Then I can down my next ginnypoo."

She stared at him, baffled.

"*Lent*, you know. One gives up things."

"Yes, well on the subject of giving up things, as you know there's a peace camp outside our local base."

"Oh, I heard they were being evicted."

"They're on a thin neck of land just alongside the bridle path, and as it happens nobody can prove ownership. Not the MOD, or the farm next door. It's free land." In fact, a token attempt had been made by the council to declare the camp a nuisance so as to evict under the Public Health Act;

an enforcement notice had been posted, but never enforced.

"Don't they rather clutter the path, even so?"

"They've a perfect right to use the lane, since it's on the definitive map of the country. The right of way has never been abolished or extinguished."

"Dear me, how technical."

"In fact the base fence is illegal because it cuts the bridle path, and there ought to be a five-foot wide gate in it for the public."

"To picnic on the runway?"

She ignored this. "If the campers were 'cluttering' the lane the police could do them for obstruction of a public highway – just as they ought to do the MOD." She glanced at the concealed fragment of martyr. "I think those campers are modern saints, Vicar. The today equivalent. In the cold, in the mud. No mains light or water."

"Nor sanitation," Partridge tutted.

"They dig deep latrine pits, and they bury all their rubbish. Saints, Vicar. Poverty willingly embraced. Lack of material possessions and comforts."

"Don't they draw dole money, then? I heard there was some trouble at the Crown in Kerthrop. Your campers were drinking up their unemployment pay, weren't they? Apparently there was a fight. A broken arm. Your friends got themselves barred."

"That was the fault of some redneck Yanks and local yobbos. Plus the landlord."

"Deplorable."

"I mean it. Those rednecks terrorize the camp at night, when the weather's warm. They get tanked up and chuck stones. When they get a chance, they swerve their cars at the campers. Not the blacks from the base; they're laid back. But the whites do. The campers face the forces of Herod. As it were."

Partridge smiled ruefully.

"Those aren't sanctimonious saints, Vicar. They're practical, down-to-earth ones."

"I'm sure they're extremely down-to-earth."

"A lot of respectable people visit them, you know. People who care. A Dominican monk stayed overnight last week. And last month a curate who's in Christian CND –"

"Brought them a basket of eggs?"

"Anyway, there's to be a big peace festival at Kerthrop at Easter. Blessed be the peace-makers, hmm? We thought how appropriate it would be if the local churches were willing to . . . offer a stable overnight. Leave the heating on. The Rector of St Bartolph's in Churtington already said yes."

"Barty's? That doesn't surprise me! Old Rodney would welcome a congress of Zulu transvestites."

"And the vicar of St Thomas's too."

"You amaze me."

"Sleeping bags. There'd be no mess. None."

Partridge massaged his brow as though faced with an actual crisis of conscience.

"The PCC are proud of St Mary's, Miss Wallis. Its upkeep, its traditions."

And the Parochial Church Council was . . . parochial in more sense than one.

"How much do you know of the history of this church, and Melfort Parva itself?" Partridge started to stalk up and down as if dictating a sermon. "I always believe that people who wish to rearrange history should first know some history."

Jeni frowned. "I *am* a history teacher."

"Of course you are – at the comprehensive in Churtington. Rise of the trade unions; causes of the Russian Revolution, or whatever. I'm talking about the history of this parish."

Fortunately there had been a visit to the John Clare School by the president of the County Antiquary Association.

"Melfort Parva means Little Melfort," replied Jeni. "Presumably the name Melfort is Norman French for stiff, or strong, honey."

"Indeed?"

"Produced by monks at the earlier site of the village, down by the base. The Black Death wiped out the ancient village, so the survivors rebuilt up here – bringing the old church door along with them. And the wishbone over there."

"So they did a moonlight flit, like squatters?"

"Quite a lot of villages relocated themselves after that particular plague. Get away from the imps of illness."

Partridge nodded. "A mile or so; I'm well aware. Four or five miles is a fair distance to flee, don't you feel?"

"Nearest hilltop, presumably."

"Hmm. Accurate records are so scanty. The new Melfort didn't fare too well in the Civil War. The Parish Register went totally astray, thanks to Cromwell's men – they pitched camp in this churchyard and dossed inside St Mary's, generally wrecking it. Just as they ruined the village."

Oh, so that's where this history lesson was leading. St Mary's had been desecrated by campers once already. What a dreadful precedent.

"Maybe the Roundheads had heard about the relic?" suggested Jeni.

"And presumably that was when our reliquary was concealed, not during the Reformation at all?"

"Why not?"

Partridge smiled pityingly. "Maybe this, maybe that! You presume too much. I've come across ambiguous references in one old monkish Latin chronicle which indicate that something ghastly happened to the original village back in the fourteenth century."

"Bubonic plague, right."

"I fear the mass death and chaos of the plague is a convenient camouflage in this case, Miss Wallis. A red herring. It hides what really happened."

"Which was?"

The vicar's cloak swirled as he paced to and fro. "The ecclesiastical scribe spells the name of our village as Mal-fort, with an 'a'."

"So? Shakespeare's name was spelled eight different ways when he was alive."

"*Mal* means 'evil'. Thus Mal-fort is 'powerful evil'. The monk hints at demonic activity. Why else should my unknown predecessor have gone to the lengths of obtaining a blessed bone of a martyr to protect his church? There's no mention of a Melfort in Domesday. The village may have gained its present name only subsequent to the devastation of the old site. With Parva tagged on; that's Latin for 'little'. "

"I know that."

"A diminishment of the evil force."

So. This ever-so-elegant rural vicar toyed with the notion of demons and evil. Was that merely predictable – par for the course – in view of his ritualistic affectations? Jeni sighed.

"There's genuine evil in the world today, Vicar. The evil of nuclear weapons. Help us combat it."

He ceased his marching and stood still, as if defending faith against vandals.

"One wouldn't wish anything noisome to besmirch St Mary's, or this village – as in Cromwell's day, as in medieval times."

"Damn it, peace isn't evil. CND isn't evil."

"Damn, indeed? Do you truly understand damnation?"

Partridge strayed towards the cage and touched the grim iron bars.

For just a moment in the shadows Jeni saw a severed head inside the cage. A head resting on the raw-meat stump of its neck. Bulging eyes and swollen, protruding tongue – the head of some medieval criminal or heretic. The tongue was almost bitten through in agony. Yet the head was . . . *trying to speak*. To beg. The head inside the cage was still alive!

Brusquely Jeni shook her own head and the phantom vanished.

"Do you understand salvation?" continued Partridge. "The church has thought about these matters for a very long time."

Had she seen such a thing? No, of course not. The vicar had spooked her with his mumbo-jumbo. Of a sudden her flash of hallucination brought to mind a college room in Oxford with a flowering chestnut tree outside the window. . . .

It hadn't even been a hallucination, damn it! It had been no more than a moment of heightened suggestibility, such as when you see figures dancing in a fire.

(Or wheels and whips in the boughs of a chestnut tree. . . ?)

"Wiser minds than mine, eh?" she muttered.

"Wiser than Marx or Engels. Certain things endure; certain things are merely fashions."

Jeni glared at the Dracula cloak.

"This house of God once suffered some . . . evil devastation. The door, and the martyr's larynx, endured. Yet that's all that is needed: a way in, and a voice."

"I thought you said the bone came later? Oh never mind! If devastation's the game, how well do you think St Mary's would stand up to a few megatons five miles away?"

"Russian megatons, Miss Wallis. One might say that's why the base is there: to protect St Mary's and Melfort from such brutality."

17

"Oh shit this," she said to herself. Since she was getting nowhere very fast she smiled – sarcastically, she hoped – and left the church. She walked to the lych gate, outside which she'd left her Mini. Next stop, the peace camp.

Oh double shit it.

A pair of horses came clopping along Church Lane, bearing devotees of the hunt in full regalia. One was Mrs Parkes from the Manor. Stout, beef-faced Mrs Parkes, black-booted and jacketed, chin-strapped into her black riding hat. Whip clutched in her fist. The woman's greying hair was bound in a bun as tight as the corn-rowing of her grey mount's mane.

Jeni didn't recognize the hatchet-faced fellow who rode alongside, on a big black beast. Narrow head, harsh watery blue eyes, jutting jaw and chopper of a nose, cheeks that looked flayed – he seemed all the uglier because of his impeccable outfit.

Jeni felt like some medieval smocked peasant cowering before a charge of armoured knights. Or a peace protester faced with police horses. She took refuge in the sky-blue Mini as the riders advanced, towering high and both ignoring her. The horse power of her little tin box on wheels struck her as puny, compared with them.

The veins of the black horse, which was shaved naked from the ribs downwards, stood proud like exposed electrical cable, wires of blood. Stupid, servile, massive, hysterical animal. If it crashed through brambles or hawthorn, nature's barbed wire, surely a few veins might be slit.

Down where Church Lane joined the High Street a Range Rover drove by, horsebox in tow, followed by a larger mobile stable the size of a furniture van. The Thrushby Hunt was on the move this morning – meeting where?

It wasn't on account of a few foxes being hounded to death that Jeni loathed the hunt; to her mind drag hunting would be equally pernicious. What she hated was the uni-

18

forms, like rural SS gear – the strutting of power and privilege, the fascist ceremony of it.

Mind, even if it did cost a bomb to keep a hunter, fox hunting wasn't entirely a class phenomenon. Jeni had canvassed enough local villages on behalf of the Labour candidate during the last election to realize that some working class council tenants rode to hounds too; no doubt flush from cowboy building enterprises on the black economy. What's more, the rural proletariat would be out in their cars blocking the roads, gawping admiringly at the chase.

She gladly obeyed the country code for ordinary riders, and girls on ponies, even if some girls on ponies grew up to become Mrs Beef-Face, dressed to kill. But it stuck in her craw to slow down for hunters and hunt lackeys. Hoping that the route wouldn't be too "cluttered", she tugged out the choke and roared the engine.

Three

Oxford, yes indeed. Fifteen, going on twenty years earlier – the best of times, worst of times.

Jeni went up to Somerville during the brief hangover from the Swinging Sixties into the Sour Seventies, during the two or so year appendix of freedom, protest, and joy which finally festered.

The underground press were still churning out their wares: *Oz, Frendz*, and *IT, Black Dwarf* and *Red Mole*. But Jeni's main subterranean reading matter had been the *Workers' Press*; for a while she'd been a slave to the then Socialist Labour League. A busy chicken with her head chopped off, to a fair degree.

Then there was all the Glastonbury stuff: the Incredible

String Band, Yes, and *Close to the Edge*, and communes
. . . which wasn't quite Jeni's scene, though it was headily
in the air, like dope fumes.

Dope and acid and acid rock, Jim Morrison, Jefferson
Starship: not exactly her scene, though the sounds thrilled
her.

And police were merely pigs back then, who busted
people for pot. They hadn't yet got their trotters into riot
gear and stocked up with CS gas, plastic bullets, real
bullets. The Angry Brigade had only set off a few amateur
bombs; which Jeni knew was sheer adventurism with no
solid theory, no industrial base.

Oxford . . . and Trotskyism . . . and Donna the Domi-
nator who wasn't a member of the SLL at all. . . .

Looking back, Jeni reckoned that she'd mostly wasted
her time at Oxford, though some might argue that was Oxford's *forte*: to find your own way of wasting time, which
later on might pay unpredictable dividends.

How proud her Mum and Dad had been when she won
that scholarship from grammar school. And how she'd re-
belled at their assumptions, their bourgeois complacency.
Not that she quarrelled openly, at least not for long, with
her insurance-broking Dad and her plump, fey Mum. Perhaps she quarrelled with herself instead. That was when she
stopped being Jennifer, which was such a well-bred, twitty,
cuddly, Young Conservative sort of name, and became
Jeni, or Jen. That was when she joined the SLL.

Her weekly college essays were thin and doctrinaire,
heavy on Marxist theory often culled directly from SLL
publications, short on pragmatic historical facts, but she
ended up with a Third in History. In those days before mass
unemployment a Third was good enough for teacher-
training, quite good enough to net her a post in the history
department of a Reading comprehensive, a factory-like
shambles of buildings with a housing estate catchment

area. She could well have aimed for a swankier grammar school, but that comprehensive was her choice, a political commitment even though by then she'd quit the SLL.

People who end up with a Third from Oxford usually have some fun en route. Drama, societies, sports, the Union. In retrospect Jeni hardly had *fun* as such, though she smelled the early Seventies in the air and heard the sounds; even though she was drunk on vodka at 6 a.m. in a punt below Magdalen Bridge once, along with the best of them, to hear the choirboys pipe out *The Merry Month of May* from the top of the tower. Much of the time maybe she was incapable of "fun", since fun was a frivolous symptom of capitalism in crisis. What had Donna Hodges said? That Jeni's was a rigid personality; that she wore Reichian character amour.

Mad Donna was a disciple of Wilhelm Reich, author of *The Function of the Orgasm* and *The Mass Psychology of Fascism*, founder of the Socialist Society for Sexological Research – though would Reich have agreed that Donna was a disciple? That terrible evening when Donna. . . . To break through someone's armour erotically, by force. . . . Don't think of it, not just now!

During a good two-thirds of her student years Jeni had worked hard. Not at history as much as on behalf of the correct historical cause, Trotskyism – which was, in retrospect, the wrong cause. Yet this prepared Jeni for sane politics in the actual world, now that she was more realistic. Now that she was wearier – though still energetic. Now that she was less hectic – perhaps! Sometimes she fantasized herself as . . . not a terrorist, oh no; the Trots had taught her that was adventurism. But something more than a snipper of Ministry of Defence wire in some Snowball action; more than a human sack of spuds blockading a gate, till the sack got hauled aside.

That ghastly evening when Donna. . . .

Urgent, conspiratorial days those had been in the SLL! The coach trips to Digbeth Hall in Birmingham to hear Gerry Healey orate: a charismatic hobgoblin with the brawn of an ex-merchant seaman and a shiny bald head stabbing the same finger over and over again at the ceiling, as if telling all capitalists to stuff themselves. No luxuries such as fish and chips were allowed on the return journey.

Fellow history student Michael Berry, whom Jeni mentally christened "the Whipmaster", would thump on her door demanding, "What did you think of the paper?" just two hours after delivering it as though she should have learned the *Workers Press* by heart in the interval. At that time the paper was hailing Solzhenitsyn as a true critic of the Soviet state capitalist system: Solzhenitsyn who would soon call for that yellow atheistic Genghis Khan horde of Chinese to be nuked by a future Holy Russia. Burnt out early like so many SLL activists, the Whipmaster had a nervous breakdown. He packed his trunk and fled to Gerry's bosom in London. No word from him ever again. . . .

High times, being lectured by a Leyland convenor. And even higher times getting acquainted with the working class, which meant tramping round blocks of flats in Cowley preferably during a snowstorm to pester pissed-off men who'd just got back from the car factory or Pressed Steel for their tea. Ironic that "trots" was a name for diarrhoea; she and Michael and Phil and Carol and Len and Steve had been selling something as welcome as verbal diarrhoea, diarrhoea of the mouth.

And that zany evening when Donna. . . .

No.

Yes!

Donna Hodges was a mature student, who'd previously been at Ruskin on a trade union grant. When her Somerville servant was urged to address Donna by her first name, the servant replied patronizingly, "Ah, I see: a young lady trying to better herself!" Thirty or thirty-two, Donna was built like a tough little tug-boat, but a well-manicured one, spick and span. She was reading PPP, with philosophy tacked on to psychology and politics rather than economics. Prior to Ruskin she'd been a psychiatric nurse. Apparently she'd shed any family or relations. She still spent the vacations working and lodging in mental hospitals.

Years before she had also spent time as an inmate in these same institutions. Teenage schizophrenia accounted for a curious lump on the end of her nose (kept neatly powdered). Donna had tried to cut her proboscis off, requiring plastic surgery.

Jeni thought it was clever, though sinister, how Donna had managed to swap roles from prisoner to wardress of the insane wards. One side of the keyhole or the other, a mental hospital was her only constant home. Home was a wardrobe full of strait jackets, beside power points ready to deliver electroshock, a bathroom cabinet stocked with chlorpromazine and LSD. Set a thief to catch a thief; set a loony to look after loonies? Donna had theories about how to unzip mad people's character armour.

And that bloody evening. . . .

Because Jeni was young, Donna fascinated her. Many were the cups of cheap, tarry Camp coffee she sipped in Donna's room late at night, hearing tales of asylum life, chewing the fat about the psychology of politics, or telling Donna resentfully about her own parents just as if Jeni was visiting her own private psychiatrist. For Donna dominated her, rather as did the SLL.

"So how's your sex life?" Donna asked Jeni one midnight. "Ah, you've tensed! That's *armour* in action. Have you had a man? I don't think so."

"I haven't. Not yet."

23

"You should. It would loosen you. So do you masturbate? Nothing to be ashamed of! Sexual energy demands release, otherwise it cramps you up."

In a poem by Sylvia Plath Jeni had come across the line, "Every woman loves a fascist." This was a line that Jeni felt she fully understood; for she masturbated to the image of authority figures. In her early teens those had been blond Nazi officer types in black uniforms. Now it was Trotsky, as head of the Red Army purging opposition. Gerry Healey; the stabbing finger like a stiff penis. Donna might tell her, incorrectly but forcibly, that these figures represented Jeni's own father. Jeni didn't want simplistic explanations.

So she nodded, and lied. "I think of tall dark Latin types. Italian hairdressers. Waiters in tight trousers. Bull fighters."

"Do you reach orgasm?"

"Of course."

Donna's teeth clicked like knitting needles coming together. "Bull fighters wear uniforms and stick sharp tools in the flesh of victims, yes?"

It was June, and hot. The Whipmaster was becoming more robotic week by week, conversing like a Speak-Your-Politics machine. On a Friday evening Jeni and spotty Carol and the Whipmaster were driven to Cowley in Phil Daniels' banger of a Morris Minor, which Phil flogged up the Banbury Road then along the ring road far too fast and carelessly. After a fair effort had been made to sell the paper and the other two had been returned to St Giles, Jeni invited herself back for a coffee to Phil's digs in Parktown.

Phil Daniels enjoyed dark good looks, wild shoulder-length hair, a Zapata moustache and ever-stubbly chin, soft large liquid eyes. His political commitment was becoming as erratic as his driving. Jeni guessed that Phil was on the brink of graduating out of Trotskyism, decently prior to graduating from the university. After all, he'd been educated at a minor pubic school, his parents were flush enough to present him with a banger, and he roomed in upmarket Parktown, not half way along the Cowley Road.

Jeni's blouse clung to her breasts. She was wearing a long light Laura Ashley skirt in pastel blue from the shop in Little Clarendon Street, and tan boots from Oasis Trading over the way. The Whipmaster had torn her off a strip for this unrevolutionary outfit (which actually sold a record number of papers); Phil had eyed her with interest.

She set down her china mug. Lenin's head on the outside, genuine percolated Arabica within. She uncrossed her legs. Commenced, "One hears talk about making *revolutionary love*. . . ."

Though Phil had ejaculated rather quickly and it seemed ages till he could enter her again – and despite his Mexican moustache he was no fantasy authority figure – she at least left her virginity upon his sofa.

Naturally Jeni reported to Donna – who shocked her by lunging and grasping Jeni so tightly that she could hardly move. More like a strait jacket than a congratulatory hug. But before Jeni could protest, Donna had released her.

"You're still much too armoured, Jennifer. You're still *Jennifer*. I have some LSD – you ought to take some with me. Not for adolescent thrills, understand? For therapy. It'll help you know yourself, free yourself from the armour."

So the next day after lunch, in Donna's room, Jeni took a tab of acid. Not a home-laboratory microdot, but a proper tablet from some mental hospital's pharmacy – she supposed. Donna explained that she herself wouldn't take one. Her job was to guide Jeni through the experience.

Four

In the event Jeni opted to go the long way round. The direct route to Kerthrop looked like being choked. So Meg the Mini (named from the letters on the number plate) buzzed along a lane between pastures and ploughed acres. Would that soil be under oil-seed rape again this summer – painted an alien sulphur yellow? She passed the odd ironstone farmhouse with accompanying barns and a silver silo or two. Meg startled a pheasant.

Just short of Higham at the gravel pits a robot conveyor belt soared from its scooped-out lake like the start of some big dipper ride. A grading gantry shat hillocks of pea shingle and ballast. Next, the hamlet of Higham itself, and Higham Hall in its railed beech park – home of the local Tory county councillor since forever for this blue hole.

And then Thrushby Wood: two square miles of fir trees managed by the Forestry Commission, a slice of Norway. Jeni ended up approaching the peace camp from Churtington direction, along the main road which bisected the base.

Residential side, operational side. On the latter, reinforced hangars humped like beached whales which had been dipped in a lake of rusty concrete. Huge concrete tail-flukes jutted out of the rear ends. A radar dish rotated atop a squat tower of girders. Distant grassy mounds topped with ventilators gave access to storage bunkers for warheads presumed to be chemical as well as nuclear and conventional. During the previous decade five hardened sub-levels had been excavated under the base, with the work split among a number of contractors so that no one would get the complete picture. The Officers' Mess, a piece of 1930s redbrick mansion architecture, cut off her long view, then many other buildings: billeting, welfare, security. . . . Behind the wire fence further bales of razor wire concertinaed across lawns. Sandbags and bulldozers protected gates.

On the other side of the road a car dealership had yielded to more masses of wire guarding Smalltown, USA, though it wasn't all that small. Kids cycled American streets, but rode on the left. Disco music blared from a hall window. A dozen junior children were working out at karate with a black instructor, wearing a black belt, on green practice mats out in the open.

Meg was tailing a Chevy Camaro; in the mirror was a Mercury Cougar with Texas plates. As the cars approached green traffic lights the Camaro slowed, winking broadly to turn off through the main gate on the residential side. Several vehicles were waiting on ID checks. The Camaro blocked Meg; the lights went red. Jeni sat watching a USAF guard who seemed about eighteen, with casually slung M-16, as he glanced at pieces of plastic and waved cars through. He pulled a pack of Marlboro from a trouser pouch and lit up. A gangly companion who looked every bit as callow handed his good buddy a can of Bud for a swig.

The lights changed and Jeni drove on. The Cougar behind peeled off.

The next gate was monitored by an asiatic soldier in steel helmet, backed by an armoured car and MOD Land Rover. Two WASP Yanks in caps, fatigues, and heavy gloves were gardening the neighbouring barbed wire, tying in a new roll like bizarre rose pruners.

Beyond, the line-up of Sky High Bowling Center, Run-in Chef, and the busy Main Exchange. Opposite these: the Keesler Credit Union building next to some permanent portakabins housing British businesses – Waterways Holidays, Antique Boutique.

"Prostitutes," Jeni muttered to herself. She patted the

big envelope lying on her passenger seat as if this might have flown out of the window in the wake of the American cars.

The peace camp was just beyond the western fence where trees and hedgerows flanked chain-link with a simple barbed wire topping. Jeni pulled over on the verge by a speed restriction sign, from which a plastic dustbin lid painted with a white CND logo hung on twine.

Over the way, beyond the main road, a full multi-track set of high barbed wire and razor wire stretched away into the distance, ploughed field to one side, turf on the other yielding to concrete and rows of green-painted Nissen huts. The grassy fenced acre adjacent to the peace camp itself was a guard dog compound with kennels a hundred yards back.

Three caravans stood, Indian file, just off the earthen lane. One lacked wheels but was painted in rainbow colours. The others were beige and battered. Windows facing the main road were missing, blocked with boards. There was also a derelict-looking yellow bus with boarded windows, Nell's old white VW, and a couple of tarpaulin igloos. A pow-wow parliament of tree stumps and deck chairs and a rickety aluminium table surrounded a campfire of sawn branches.

The lane was walled by skeletal elders and hawthorn. Ground was still winter-firm and mightn't yet be a quag by Easter, but space here was tight. For the festival Jeni had managed to rent a huge pasture from a semi-sympathetic or economically hard-pressed farmer about a mile away. That would take the coaches, portaloos, inflatables, hot dog vans, and such. The marchers, including the usual clowns, stilt-walkers, jazz band, banner-bearers, and saffron-robed drum-thumping Buddhist monks from Milton Keynes, would tramp along verge and highway past the peace camp and right through the midriff of the base, like some motley medieval crusade of innocents invading Middle America. Then they'd follow the perimeter on the residential side all around the American housing before returning past the peace camp to the festival field.

Ideally. Jeni hoped it wouldn't rain on the day. She also hoped that the Class War anarchists wouldn't venture so far from their city haunts to start fights, provoke the police, and cause a bad press. How the media loved to bray about twenty arrests when twenty thousand other people had protested peacefully. With the Mediterranean and Near East trouble hotting up, and all the other hot spots blowing their lids like volcanoes, the cause was too urgent, too important, for those adventurist anarchists to stick their oar in and stir a mess.

Already she could visualize the banners: Christian CND, Punks Against the Bomb, Labour branches, maybe some beautiful trades union lodge banners, Ex-Servicemen's CND, and Young Tories Against Trident well in the vanguard for the benefit of TV cameras. Sure as hell, you wouldn't see that wretched Cessna circling overhead towing some besotted sky-sign such as WELL DONE, YANKS or CND LOVES MOSCOW – not unless the base commander deliberately invited the Freedom Through Security crusade into his air space for the day. No, he'd want his Chinooks up in the air to keep watch and intimidate and take photos. All to the good. That would look better on TV.

"Hello, Jeni!"

Mitzi rose from the fireside, quitting Big Mal and Jack, and ran to greet their visitor. A skinny, short blonde girl in her late teens, Mitzi was dressed in dungarees, sandshoes, and a loopy purple sweater. She wore a cluster of sparking plugs dancing from a chain by way of jewellery. Mitzi had spent time at Greenham and she now treated her visitor to what Jeni thought of as Greenham grooming: a quick, primate-like patting of the cheek, stroking of the hair. New forms of female tenderness-bonding had evolved at that other all-wimmin peace camp. Momentarily Jeni was reminded of Donna clutching her, and stiffened.

However, Mitzi who was a defector from a working class household in Swindon had quit Greenham after six months. She'd confided to Jeni how she found its emotional togetherness liberating at first but then increasingly exclusive of the outside world, of non-initiates. Greenham seemed a specialized club, almost as though a separate sub-species was evolving psychologically. ("Mind, that's only *my* reaction!") Jeni thought she understood the reasons: the fierce commitment of Greenham, the continual discomfort and hassle and drain on energy. Mitzi retained some of her learned behaviour, which was really an unlearning of male impositions.

Jeni knew exactly how it was to be imposed upon, to welcome being imposed upon. The SLL – and Donna, hmm? Nowadays Jeni imposed duties on herself, duties to the peace movement and the Labour Party, so that people could live free of fear. Yet didn't she sometimes in a sense obliquely court her own fears, at the same time as she fought them? Didn't she woo her own horrors, of the hunt, and Tories, and the American bases? *Every woman loves a. . . .*

No! She'd thrown Donna off!

(Had *she* thrown Donna off?)

Jeni squeezed Mitzi's hand, as Mitzi told her, "There's lots of activity on base. Engine tests. Pick-up trucks dashing around. They had a *black* alert yesterday. We heard it all over the tannoy. 'Mortar attack on Gate Ten. . . !' 'Hostile activity still in Zone Ruby.' They stepped it down to red at tea-time, then relaxed."

Jack's black labrador, Bess, had woofed and lolloped to meet Jeni and was now thumping a rudder against Jeni's thighs. A big dog, but fat. Labradors were designed to jump into freezing seas to rescue drowning sailors. Leaping into the Atlantic every day and hauling a body half a mile kept them in trim. Otherwise they turned into barrels of lard. Bess looked like a burly enough watchdog but she would only tackle marauding rednecks if they actually advanced up the lane. The main road scared her since an American car had finally managed to side-swipe her. Despite a vet's care the labrador's thigh was unreliable.

At least Bess was on site. Before Jack and his dog arrived a tiny office caravan had been burned down containing the campers' records of aircraft movements and their log of which contractors delivered what supplies to the base. Even the civilian police conceded this was probably arson. But directed from on base, or off? They never knew.

"Fancy some tea, pet?" called Jack. A big blackened kettle balanced on the burning branches; he shifted it further on to the flames.

Jack was from Tyneside, and just turned thirty: a stocky redhead with curls of ginger beard and orange peel freckles. He'd been a joiner till the dole queue swallowed him. Even before that happened, he'd been sent south time and again with the lads by night in the backs of rattly vans, squashed in with tools and timber, bags of sand and cement. Tyneside wages were low enough for firms to put in almost half-price tenders against southern builders and still turn a profit, so long as they trucked all their materials south as well. Down to the very last nail – their craftsmen mustn't even buy a two-by-four from a local southern supply yard. Jack had grown profoundly sick of canny buggers using him as a modern form of paid slave, cheaply cartable to any foreign building site. But by the time employment weaned itself from him, he'd weaned himself from Geordieland.

"Yes please, Jack!"

Skin peeped through the knees of Jack's jeans as he rose. He headed past the brewing-keg of water to bring tea bags from the rainbow caravan. Water was lugged daily a quarter mile from the nearest standpipe in a field below Hobby Hill, where a spring freshened a cattle trough.

In the doorway he collided with Gisela, their guest from the German Green Party. Gisela squeezed past impatiently.

"Have you that information?" she called to Jeni by way of greeting. Gisela's hair was a spiked punky green; she wore loose leather trousers and a bomber jacket to bulk out a spindly frame.

Jeni flapped the envelope by way of response.

"Where are Nell and Andy?" she asked Big Mal, hunched in that old Crombie of his which would have cloaked anyone else's toes.

"Gone walkies up the hill. Plane spotting." The bridle path was blocked beyond a bend where it curved east to follow the contour line, but you could walk six abreast into the neighbouring field that sloped uphill and penetrate the tangly hat of Hobby Hill from the west. The campers had trampled their own path through the upper thicket to their look-out post.

"We'd better wait."

"No, let us hear the worst," said Gisela. "They may be half an hour. You will leave copies, yes?"

"I made two spare xeroxes."

"Fuck off," growled Mal. "We'll wait." His chin was stubbled black, but he shaved his head scrupulously. The better to butt you with. . . . Mal's right index finger was still in plaster, but he had broken the local yob's jaw. Presumably his own injury was what prejudiced rumour had transmitted to the vicar as a broken arm. Pity Mal hadn't taken out one of the Yanks; dislocated a redneck. Mal pulled a black corduroy cap from his pocket and jammed it on his skull. He looked like a Marxist bargee sitting in judgment. "We'll wait."

"They can read," retorted Gisela.

Mal had a point, though he seemed to be in one of his moods. Big Mal from Brum was the longest-serving camp resident, preceding these others by, oh, a couple of years. He'd seen volunteers come and go. One winter he'd been completely alone for three months. That was truly heroic, but at the same time Jeni wondered whether Mal had suffered (or had *invited*?) some psychological warpage. His was the life of a tramp – the same shrinkage of needs – without a tramp's mobility. Mal could react to stimuli effectively enough – he'd broken that young sod's jaw – but sometimes he'd curl up in his mental shell like a hermit crab . . . with claws. Without Jack and Mitzi and company the camp could have collapsed by now, but Mal didn't always appreciate their bustle. Jeni could never feel certain of his reactions: utterly realistic and clear-sighted one day, better genned up on news than anybody, at other times lost in his own world, which he defended guilefully, abusively. He'd caused problems, and perhaps had driven some volunteers away. Still, he had to be admired. He was the backbone, even if the backbone was a bit askew.

And Gisela *was* bloody abrupt. Maybe not her fault – she was wrestling with a foreign language.

Jeni sat on a copy of the *Guardian* on a tree stump and waited. Gisela produced a notebook and biro as if to take dictation.

Five

Jeni took a last swallow of Jack's strong tea. Since Nell and

Andy still hadn't turned up, she emptied her envelope on to the table.

"Right. This has all been hushed up till now. Hospital administrators were told nothing. Even the government's own health service defence planners were kept in the dark. That's just for starters. Government ministers have deliberately misled Parliament about the Emergency Powers Bills. 'Who can predict what these might contain?': that's been the official line. It's a lie. The three bills are already in print, stockpiled in safes in Whitehall and all the regional offices. Luckily we had a mole-for-peace in the Cardiff office."

"Wey man, this could torn oot to be Cardiffgate!" Jack exchanged glances with Gisela, for whom he had also made a cup of tea, and been rewarded with a smile.

Mal shook his head. "Us Brits don't have the calibre of journalism the Yanks have. Most people are too busy goggling at Sammy Fox's tits on page three."

"You don't have the American Freedom of Information Act," said Gisela. "Can we please have the details?" Pen poised.

Jeni shuffled pages.

"In the event of crisis the first bill is to be rammed through Parliament within twenty-four hours. This bill lets the Secretary of State designate half the sodding country as 'ground defence areas' – where everybody and everything is subject to the military, whether British or American. Householders can be kicked out, their homes bulldozed for free-fire zones. Roads closed. Any quote subversive protestors can be rounded up without charge or trial. . . ."

"That's worsels," said Jack. "So we'll aal be stuffed behind wire at gun point, to wait to be incinerated."

"It means almost anyone you please! Labour Party members, union convenors, half the electorate."

"Half?" Mal laughed harshly. "You could be in for a sad

surprise. Would your own good neighbours lift a finger?"
He wagged his own plaster.

"I know! I've thought of that. Cowardice. Latent fascism."

A squirrel scrabbled half way down an elder. At once
Bess rushed over, barking. Foiled by the squirrel's instant
vanishing trick, the labrador sniffed the air then trotted off
up the trail.

"Can we proceed?" asked Gisela.

"With the second bill, the entire country becomes a
GDA. Total control of transport, fuel, and food. No
strikes; wider internment powers. Full censorship."

Mal raised his finger again. "Who needs censorship?
There's already a secret agreement between Government
and the BBC."

Jeni nodded. "Bill number three will be made law by Order in Council. Piss off, Parliament. This brings absolute
rule by decree. Bye-bye, British Medical Association. Bye-
bye, Law Society. Anything can be requisitioned. Summary death penalties. Conscription of adults and children
into labour gangs. Detention for so-called suspected disease carriers; that's a good one! Permanent imprisonment
for protestors. And they'll set the normal criminals free."

"Knaa who yor friends are, eh?" Jack nudged Gisela.

"They'd put criminals in the labour gangs," Mal said to
Jack.

"Wey aye, as overseers."

"This whole package is a lot more swingeing than when
Hitler was poised to invade the UK," Jeni went on. "Now
here's the jolly jackpot. While all this is going on, the whole
British army – Territorials included – gets shipped to
Europe, and massive American forces arrive to take over."

"Where do these Americans arrive?" asked Gisela.

"Merseyside, Clydeside, Barry, and South Wales. A
joint logistic plan signed secretly in '83 agrees to hand over
most British military and civil resources."

35

Mitzi smiled in a sickly way. "Child labour gangs included."

"Up to thirty major hospitals will have to empty all their beds for possible American casualties – much to the surprise of those hospitals."

"What if the nurses threaten to strike?"

Jeni told Gisela, "The UK and USA haven't quite yet decided whether to force doctors and nurses to stay on, at gunpoint, or simply bring in US medical reservists. Oh, and the US National Guard have tickets to this hoe-down too – every redneck sheriff's deputy from Alabama. With absolute power of life and death, plus total immunity from British law. That's what's known as a host nation support agreement."

Jack thumped his fist into his palm. "The enormity of it! We're no more than a pinch o' shit."

"Meanwhile," said Mitzi, "there are more than twenty *American* protestors actually in US prisons already. The Plowshare People. One fellow in Connecticut's serving eight years for banging on a Minuteman silo lid. Another is locked up for *eighteen* years."

"Never mind about those," snapped Gisela.

"But I do mind. That's pretty permanent imprisonment, happening already in the land of the free."

"It is irrelevant when we are discussing the British situation. Naturally I regret for those people."

"That's generous," said Mal. "Seeing as you aren't British either."

"In Germany the terrible battles will be fought."

"Not the way the news is gannin' noo, pet. But ye might be right."

"Using Britain as the fortress. So peace must be international."

"Quite," said Mitzi. "There are the American peace heroes too, braver than us."

36

"They had no chance. Here is different."

"A pinch o' shit," repeated Jack. (Could Gisela really follow his dialect?)

"I'm sometimes ashamed of the little we do," said Mitzi.

"Never act out of shame! That's bourgeois. Act out of –" Gisela didn't say what.

"You all do an enormous amount," said Jeni. "You devote your lives."

By now the sky was clouding over thickly and rapidly. It might snow heavily. It might sleet, to make some nice slush. But it probably wouldn't hail bullets of ice to beat up the camp; hail liked to crash down by surprise out of bluer skies.

A jet up aloft on exercise sounded as though it was skidding across the clouds, actually squealing along them. Every time an F-111 took off, the operation cost over £30,000. High technology, indeed. Expensive technology, all designed for death.

Yet there were idiocies about the base too. Despite all the wire and floodlights, dogs and armed guards, five wimmin from Greenham had virtually strolled inside a few months earlier. Technicians servicing an F-111 in one of the sacred hangers finally noticed the wimmin decorating another jet with peace messages in felt-tip pen. Result: an absurd trial in Churtington Magistrates Court for criminal damage amounting to exactly £343 and one penny, being the cost of special chemicals used to remove felt-tip graffiti. Not eighteen years in prison. Mitzi had a point. Maybe Gisela did, too; more was possible here.

Again, only last autumn Nell had found a detailed military plan of the base in a dustbin by the bus stop near the main gate. And earlier, a sergeant with a sixteen letter Polish name, all "C"s and "Z"s, had dropped his passport in a gutter in Kerthrop village; this had been returned to the base commander via CND with ironic comments.

And the campers had torn down whole sections of the fence, which remained unnoticed by the eagle-eyed guardians for a day or two.

Also last autumn, to Jeni's chagrin, a class of catering students from the John Clare School had paid a visit to the base. The teacher who led the outing, Brenda Galloway, was no left-winger but she related afterwards to the common room how sloppy she thought security was. This was after Libya, so she needed an escort to take her troop in, but no guard ever bothered looking in the luggage boot of the minibus which could have been filled with banners – or bombs. What most amused her, and curled her lip, was the array of gambling machines in the Raven's Nest pub attached to the Officers Mess – "Raven" was the codename for the EF-111 electronic radar jamming jets which also flew from Kerthrop, just as the ordinary F-111s were "Aardvarks".

"Walk into any pub in England," Brenda had said, "and what do you see? Machines that you almost need a research degree and a course in touch typing and an elephant's memory to play. And what do you have there in the Raven's Nest? – which is for top brass, the brains of the USAF! You have one-armed bandits where you can only stick you money in and jerk a handle. No holds or nudges or spins or gambles or whatnot. They were brand-new machines too – built like 1950s Cadillacs with great chrome bumpers. I do wonder about our allies' intellect at times!"

"They're trained for one thing," Jeni had said. "Otherwise they get confused. And their war computers crash every fifteen seconds on average. Roll on Star Wars – that only needs one jerk of the handle. By the machine itself."

And what did the USAF think was the use of an exercise pretending mortar attacks on Gate Ten? Who was going to attack with mortars? CND? Special Russian *spetznaz* saboteurs disguised as local yokels? The Libyans? When any terrorist could drive right through the centre of the base and lob grenades at the Main Exchange?

Perhaps one day the British army might have to attack, if a British government disagreed violently enough with what a US base was about to be used for – and the US didn't like being disagreed with?

Bess returned back down the lane at an ungainly lollop. Behind strolled Nell and Andy. Plump, gold-pigtailed Nell in duffle coat and wellies, and black lace fingerless gloves. Tall, trim Andrew Lascelles looking smoothly well-bred in dirty trainers and a frayed donkey jacket, even with the butt of a roll-up stuck between his lips like a displaced tooth. Andy waved a casual hand, and Nell beamed.

"Hi, Jen," said Andy. "Your very own hunt's out, other side of Hobby Hill. Charging around like the old SS on holiday."

Six

A sunny afternoon in Oxford. The chestnut tree outside Donna's window was lavishly in leaf, with candles of waxy pink blossoms uplifted. Birds twittered and warbled.

As Jeni sat there on the sofa, wondering whether anything unusual was ever going to happen or if Donna had only given her a joke cachou to swallow half an hour earlier, the effects washed over her symphonically, bejewelled, and for some reason tasting of glycerine of thymol mouthwash which her Mum used to give her when she was a toddler to gargle with for a sore throat.

That long-lost taste linked her intimately to childhood, as though childhood had never been lost, but only occured the day before. From then until now her life was suddenly whole and continuous, joining up uninterruptedly by way of some shortcut through time and memory so that she felt like weeping and giggling at paradise regained – there outside the window in the midsummer Christmas candles of chestnut blooms that multiplied and copied themselves across her vision like a wallpaper design by Laura Ashley, but larger.

So the window was a wall, yet the wall was also a window: profound insight. *Words* were walls and windows too, since they all began with W-S, just as her own name of Wallis did. . . .

Time drifted away. She shut her eyes. Her own personal windows became walls, of eyelid skin. Yet still throughout that tree, as in a cabbalistic Tree of Life, walked and waltzed all sorts of W-S, pink and green and golden. Just as in a kid's first spelling book these letters were shaped from dozens of little whales. Then dozens of wagtails. Then wheels, then whips. She felt a surge of paranoia, terror. Wellington boots – more fear and excitement. Wasps and witches and wine bottles. And witches.

But that was only the very beginning. She lost count of how many times she had lost count. Of what? Of each high wave of amusing weirdness – the amusement always teetering on the brink of some cold abyss, like a gaudy clown capering Blondin-style over Niagara. Of the troughs where she remembered herself – before she remembered a previous remembering and thus lost herself again.

When the strongest effects were subsiding an hour or more later, Donna took her out for a walk to the Parks, holding Jeni's hand while they crossed the zebras at the top of St Giles. How patient of Donna.

But no. Donna wasn't the patient. Donna was the nurse, the matron. Jeni was the patient. Keble College with its brick patchwork seemed to be a hospital. A don in a penguin gown, a doctor. Some wit had chalked on the hospital wall, "This isn't a collage; it's a Fairisle sweater." This cosmic truth filled her with hilarity. Hospitals knitted bodies back together, stitching with needles. Everything connected. She had a bad cold; her nose was running. No, it wasn't. She was merely aware as never before of her normal nasal mucous.

At the Round Pond squabbling mallards quacked at her, knowing in their bird brains that her brain too was flying high.

Along she and Donna went to Parson's Pleasure, where nude men might be skinny-dipping in the willow-curtained Cherwell behind the high fence. They watched a punt race down the rollers bound for Mesopotamia. Poles splashed in the glycerine water; angrily a swan shook out its wings.

Although time had melted, somehow it became evening. Jeni was back in Donna's room, curtains closed against the gloaming. She balanced on Donna's bouncy bed. For hours she'd been aware of cramps in her stomach, though the stained-glass illumination of the outside world had distracted attention from these. The cramps weren't severe, just noticeably present. Maybe she should eat? Go out to the Dildunia for a cheap egg curry? The Dildunia seemed ten miles away. She'd never find her way there, or be able to read the menu inside of an hour.

"I've a pain," she told Donna, who'd been her companion all her life.

Months later Jeni would realize that the tab must have been bought from a dealer, not filched from a hospital drug cupboard. Thus the acid would be cut with a pinch of strychnine.

"Ah!" exclaimed her nurse. "That's the armour in you. You must relax. I'll massage you." Bustling Donna pressed Jeni back upon the bedspread.

"Hey!" Jeni flailed.

"Don't *fight* me!" Donna pinioned both of Jeni's wrists in

41

one strong hand. Muscular from restraining homicidal loonies. All built like a beautiful tug-boat.

"Don't resist. I'll soften your armour."

Donna's free hand was massaging, groping up Jeni's legs, rucking up the Laura Ashley. Firm fingers between her thighs. ("Dress light and loose," Donna had advised.) "Let me bring you to orgasm," the heavy nurse ordered.

Jeni could only remember fragments of what happened after that. Donna . . . staggering aghast as though she'd been struck by a plank. Her nose blooming blood. Donna's eyes had gone mad: bulging, piggy eyes. The woman crouched into a wrestler's stance, rocking to and fro. Panting, "You're insane! Dangerous! You should be locked up!"

As Jeni hauled herself from the bed . . . *how had she thrown Donna off?* Donna flinched as Jeni darted to the door. Jeni escaped, fled along corridors, locked herself in her own room. She sat up wide awake half the night with her light on, confused and mortally scared. Of what Donna had done. Of what she herself had done – *but what was it?*

Plainly she was in imminent danger of burning her fuses just like the Whipmaster. At this rate she'd take her degree in the Warneford.

So she quite the SLL and joined the Labour Party – one must still *do* something. She collected her Third, and moved to Reading for the next eight years.

During her stint at that city school occasionally she went out with fellows – aside from union or Labour activity – but she never committed herself to a man. Maybe a woman needs a man like a fish needs an umbrella.

Besides . . . something awful had taken place that evening in Donna's room, although she wasn't sure what it was. Something to do with domination and refusal and the mind

42

unbound. Something violent from the depths – over which the clown danced.

Finally she needed a change. She was tired of graffiti and smashed windows, condoms in the corridors, juvenile dope pushers in the toilets, pregnant schoolgirls, delinquents from broken homes. A friend and comrade, Nancy Abbott, had reached the same decision – along with her live-in boyfriend Gareth Jones. Nancy and Gareth both taught sciences and didn't believe in getting married.

A school in a rural area ought to be less hot-wired to heroin and crime and violence. Nancy and Gareth both netted posts at the John Clare School in the market town of Churtington. Nancy told Jeni of an upcoming opening in the history department there. While house hunting, she and Gareth had fallen in love with a cottage in some village called Melfort Parva. The property included a stable converted into a spanking new granny flat. Even with two salaries and no pressing desire for kids, Nancy and Gareth would need to rent out the granny flat to afford the mortgage. Why not rent to Jeni who needed a change of air, if she could snare the history job?

Jeni weighed the notion of paying a slice of her comrades' mortgage for them. A naive move, perhaps? On the other hand, she'd always rented. She had no ambitions to be responsible for bricks and mortar.

So she hauled out a road atlas, found the right page for that county, and closed her eyes. Briefly she had experienced a flash recall of a huge chestnut tree aflower with furled whips and wellies and comic witches. Opening her eyes, she found that her finger had descended within an inch of Melfort Parva. A sign – to the unsuperstitious. That decided her. She even felt an uplifting sense of mission: time to export a dose of socialism from the city to the fields.

Actually her fingertip straddled the edge of some air-

43

field. That didn't mean too much to her just then, beyond the possible prospect of aircraft noise. The country couldn't be any noisier than city streets. If so, then Nancy and Gareth were stuck in the mud, not our Jeni.

RAF Kerthrop was named – she peered – after a straggly hamlet to the east of Melfort, five or six miles short of Churtington itself. Melfort was some ten miles to the west of the market town, easy commuting distance. A largish village north-east of Melfort was called Thrushy; she found a tendril of river labelled the Thrush.

Where she'd first touched the map closer inspection revealed tight contour lines around "Hobby Hill," like her own fingerprint left on the page. Ah, so planes most likely took off to the east and landed from that direction. No bother.

Jeni hadn't lived long in the countryside before she realized that behind almost every other herd of cows there seemed to lurk some item of the next world war. A radar dish, a forest of aerials, a microwave relay tower. An airfield, or camp in mothballs, or storage depot, or maintenance facility, or American township. At the latest count there were an amazing one hundred and sixty US bases and facilities in this country which was tinier than most American states.

To city dwellers the extent of doomsday packaging was virtually invisible. Not in the green and pleasant land, once you looked beyond the scenery. On the drive to school by that main road which bisected RAF Kerthrop, and in Churtington itself, Jeni often saw almost as many Pontiacs and Dodges as British cars. Presently she had also joined CND, which was swelling out of its doldrums of the Seventies thanks to the advent of Cruise. She marched to Molesworth through the mud, from the Embankment to Hyde Park. She organized.

And the diabolus waited to be nudged.

Seven

"The Social Security?" enquired Gisela.

"Stormtroopers, Kamerad! Never heard of those?" Nell didn't seem entirely fond of the punky German; but then, it was often hard to tell what Nell was really thinking.

"Ah, *Schutzstaffen*, yes. I thought you meant. . . . But I am not a *comrade*. I am a member of the Greens. You know that!"

"She's just kiddin', pet," said Jack. To Jeni he explained, "Wey, some reporter bugger came pokin' roond yesterday durin' the alert. Askin' Jiz what side o' the German border she comes from, an' can she prove it? She showed him her borth cerificate an' aal. Put up to it by MI6, Aa'll bet. Can't ye see the headlines? 'HOW MANY EAST GERMAN SPIES IN PEACE CAMPS?' "

"But this might harm the Easter festival!"

"Wey, that'll be the notion."

"Maybe Gisela ought to take a trip for a few weeks."

"Had away!" Jack flushed indignantly. "She's not gannin' off. She's me canny lass."

Was she? Had Gisela been having it off with Jack up Hobby Hill? The red draped over the green?

"I do not wish to leave," stated Gisela.

"Though of course," said Nell idly, "any decent spy would carry forged documents, wouldn't she? Maybe only spies have their birth certificates in their back pockets." Belying the innuendo, she grinned.

"That is not true!"

"Keep your sense of humour, love."

"Oh come along," Andy broke in amiably, "she's okay, she's kosher." He wrinkled his dainty snub nose like a rabbit sniffing for dandelions. "Listen, I came up with some hot new chestnuts for the guide." Andy was compiling a satiric "Rural Survival Guide" full of off-beam definitions, aimed at urban activists who fancied taking up residence amongst the hedgerows and byways. Printed and sold through CND, it ought to raise funds for the camp.

He pulled out a notebook. "How about this one? '*Railways*: Very long narrow fields used to store rotting straw and rusty machinery.' "

Nell clapped.

" '*Farmers*: Always do better under a Labour government. Always vote Conservative. Thus usually in debt. Despised by Conservative governments.' "

"It's true, it's true!" Nell shook with laughter.

"*Ja*," agreed Gisela.

"Here's one for you, Jeni. '*Fox Hunt*: Has absolute right of way across all fields or gardens. Farmers welcome it as an alternative to ploughing.' "

Jeni had to grin. Quite a few small farmers hated the hunt because of the damage it did, compensation or not. They would only ever grumble quietly, and pocket the handouts. "One smashed gate, Mr Wilkins? Rotten old one; call it twenty quid? Two dead sheep; bolted in panic, stifled in a ditch? Seventy apiece, deadweight price? Chuck 'em in the back for the dawgs' dinner." After every meet a Land Rover toured the route handing out cash.

Jack hawked in disgust. "Yer bugger!"

"What's up with you?" asked Nell. "We run out of vege-burgers?"

Jack jerked a thumb. "Jeni brought us some readin' matter."

Just then from up Hobby Hill way they heard a furious baying and yapping. Moments later a russet missile came streaking down the lane – and a large fox rushed heedlessly through their midst, almost hitting Bess. The labrador lurched about, barking excitedly, uncertain exactly what was happening since the fugitive had reached the main road already. Almost, the quick brown fox jumped over the lazy dog.

Hot on the scent and the sight of the fox the hounds erupted down the bridlepath. Thirty, forty baying brown and white beasts; a slavering panting stampede of bared teeth and straining limbs. The campers scattered to the sidelines, ducking behind caravans and under trees – with Mal managing to grab hold of Bess's collar; Bess was raving now. Mitzi had snatched up a spade; to do what?

The avalanche crashed through the camp, toppling table and chairs. Jeni's documents flew, to be trampled and shredded under clawed paws.

And then the first riders came, heads ducked to avoid low boughs as their mounts thundered down the lane – massive mounts. Calls and halloos rang from the field to the west. Most riders had kept to the open ground. But four – no, eight – chased the pack down the bridlepath. Black hats, flushed red faces, boots and smart jackets and whips.

"Out of our way!" as the first hunter smashed by.

The next rider's distorted features looked like a case of polar frostbite. The man who followed sported open duelling scars welling thinly with fresh blood where twigs had whipped his cheeks; he seemed oblivious of the wounds.

And here came beef-faced Mrs Parkes – who glanced at Jeni with blank indifference as though she had never seen her before in her life; blood-lust blinded the woman.

"Control that dog!" a rider bellowed at Mal, who was struggling with Bess.

"Frigging bastards!" shrieked Mitzi. A stinging flick of a whip made her drop her spade.

"You're blockin'! Damn this tinker trash!" A caravan window shattered – thanks to whip butt or gloved fist.

47

No more riders. The site was a churned-up wreck.

"Damn well ought to *pay*," vowed Mal, reluctant to let Bess loose yet.

Pay? Oh yes, thought Jeni. Paying peace campers for smashed glass and crocks and a buggered-up site might be a different kettle of fish from compensating farmers. Very likely!

Pay.

Pay.

She and Jack – and Mitzi, Nell, and Andy – ran along to the road. Mal was left trying to shove Bess inside the rainbow caravan. Gisela had disappeared; she must be sheltering in one of the vans or the bus.

Hardly quarter of a minute had passed since the last horse. A blue coupé with Idaho plates stood slewed across the mid-line. Other traffic was backing up – a milk tanker, cars – as the scarlet-coated MFH imperiously held up his whip while riders poured across the road.

Two hundred yards down the field the fox was thrashing, tangled inside razor-wire. It must have despaired of out-distancing the hounds, had tried to burst through into the base. Was that torn fur, or its flesh in tatters? The red body squirmed, half-way in, contorting. Hounds seeking entry bounded, pawed, and nosed, and howled at sudden wounds. The vanguard of huntsmen and whippers-in were trying to force the pack off the concertina of razors.

Pay!

Jeni experienced such a wash of hatred, as if she'd tapped some deep hot, foetid spring inside herself, or stuck a knife into a bag of boiling filth under pressure, which now splattered her, staining body and mind.

Donna. Domination.

Not a fresh-water spring! One reeking of sulphur, rotten eggs, foul farts. A well of bubbling blood-streaked mud. She felt giddy.

48

A pit had opened at her feet. Her friends couldn't see it. Mitzi was standing right upon it, staring over the ploughed furrows. But Jeni saw. Except that the pit couldn't be there, otherwise Mitzi would fall deep down. Down there where something moved . . . but didn't, couldn't.

"Jesus Christ!" yelped Andy.

Along the concrete-staked wires where horses and hounds milled, suddenly soil erupted. Blinding phosphorus brilliance razed zig-zag among the coils, jaggedly along straight strands. The fence opened. A mass of razor-wire unravelled – sharp steel whips lashed out at the hunt.

One black hunter tossed its rider under hooves. Mounts were hysterical, with blood-lines on buttocks and bellies. A bay mare collapsed, as if hamstrung. As its head jerked up, mouth wide open, little razor blades ripped right through, tearing out its tongue in a red gush. Whinnying, howls. Screams, cries!

The MFH lashed his horse, shouting orders. Just as a whipper-in was hauling and booting his own blood-dripping horse away, a flail of steel blades wrapped around the man's neck. When the fellow clawed at this noose with ribboning gloves and fingers, his mount bolted. The man's body jerked back in the saddle. For a full twenty yards the horse carried . . . a headless rider, upright. His stump of neck spouted a mane of red liquid. Then the corpse fell backwards over the animal's buttocks. His sliced-off head was being kicked to and fro. All at once the lashing wires collapsed inertly.

"They electrified the fence!" Mitzi shouted at Mal, who had just caught up. "The Yanks or MOD electrified it! And it just popped off."

"Garn! Without any bloody warning notices?"

"I'm telling you. The fox hit some live wire."

"Yor bletherin', woman," said Jack. "Where are your in-sulators, eh? Only a feul'd put volts through that tangle.

Your current would short straight to earth."

"So what the hell flashed?" asked Nell.

"Hell itself," mumbled Jeni. It had looked as if the electricity came upwards *from* the soil itself.

"Eh?"

"I feel sick." She held her head. What had made the earth boil? She felt as though some great malign snake had surged through her guts en route from the peace camp to the fence – by way of that pit in the road, which no one else had even noticed.

The Thrushby Hunt blundered about the field, wounded and shocked – an ambushed band of cavalry. Two fallen horses screamed. Or was one cry of animal agony a man's? Now that the wire lay lifeless, helpers were bending over the first rider who'd been thrown and trampled. The MFH dismounted. After a moment's hesitation he stripped off his scarlet jacket and went to lay it over a blooded rugby ball, which was the whipper-in's head. And then the Master vomited.

Part Two

Eight

To Gareth's sorrow the All Whites, playing at home at Swansea, thrashed Cardiff that afternoon. As soon as the rugby match was finished on ITV, he pecked Nancy on the cheek.

"I'm just popping along to the Kuzkas. Occurs to me Ed's bound to have a power drill."

Nancy wanted a pine shelf put up in the kitchen extension above the work top. Awkward angle for using a hand-drill; a right sod of a job if there were breezeblocks behind the plaster.

No such modern stuff in the lounge, of course! The big wall had been stripped to the ironstone, which had been smartly repointed in relief. Ancient beams were exposed. An authentic inglenook nursed a smouldering wood fire next to a depleted mound of split logs. Furniture was new, on credit from John Lewis.

Nancy looked dubious.

"If it's an American drill, you'll need to lug a transformer back with you." Behind her large round glasses – white-framed and slightly tinted – her weak blue eyes swam liquidly in a wide face like two small vulnerable bowl-dwelling fish.

Gareth reached to pat her blue-jeaned rump. His lady with the yellow, strokable curls and full sensual mouth was putting on a spot of fat. Country air syndrome; he didn't mind. All the softer; Gareth didn't fancy bones digging into him.

"Be faster, even so."

"The Kuzkas, though. And it's snowing."

"So it is. Bloody hell, what a climate. Never mind, it's only down the street. Look you, it's neighbourly to borrow." (And to lend, but other people were unreliable

53

about returning your own things.) "It's communal. Don't want to go round putting people's backs up."

He spoke as though the American had already volunteered to lend Gareth his power drill and would be offended if he wasn't taken up on the offer.

"*Especially* not if I'm going to be secretary of the village hall," Gareth added. "That's your Jeni's whole trouble, to my way of thinking. She's into socialism out of, well – venom, not love of your fellow man. I'd say the way to convert people is to rub shoulders, not dig elbows in. Charity: that's the ticket. Don't you think?"

"Oh yes."

These was a meeting of the Village Hall Committee that evening, a pre-AGM get-together, and Gareth had been putting in spadework for months. Not that he needed to exert himself excessively, since anyone willing to lend a hand with village activities was quickly co-opted and soon liable to be proposed as an officer. Jeni was on the committee too, and Gareth hoped that she'd become his minutes secretary at the April AGM – an extra job which she insisted she could surely do without. He felt confident Jeni would succumb, since it was a good thing if Labour Party members were seen to be serving the village with a will.

In his heart Gareth had his sights set beyond, upon the Parish Council, and here Jeni had offended him by dashing cold water. "Hardly a great putsch becoming V.H. secretary!" she'd said the other week at school in the common room. "If you imagine any of *us* will ever be elected as Parish Councillors just because we do the dog work, you're deluding yourself." "Oh I don't know," he'd temporized. "Journey of a thousand miles and all that? The cunning Chinese water-drip can wear away even Tories." "After a thousand years?" she asked archly.

Yes, it was a good idea to borrow something from the Yanks, and he'd keep his CND badge on too. Ed and Mary

Kuzka had been in the village for years. Likewise Carol Kuzka, who was a sexy minx with just the right curves in the right places. The Kuzka daughter obviously "dug" the British, perhaps provided they were ten years Gareth's junior. Maybe Carol Kuzka would answer the door; *not* that Gareth harboured any ideas there. A teacher was wise to immunize himself to nubile seventeen year olds. Otherwise, trouble! Still, Miss Kuzka was the other side of the coin to those English lasses who hung around Yanks in the Kerthrop and Churtington pubs, letting their bums be fondled as if they were Bangkok prostitutes. Carol was a Brit-groupie.

Thought of Bangkok reminded Gareth that Ed Kuzka had served a stretch in South-East Asia before he joined the civilian side. Any of it spent visiting those famous massage parlours for R & R? Exploiting Thai girls? Knowing Ed, probably not. Still, appearances deceive. He might have. Serve him right if. The biter bit.

"Right?" he asked Nancy.

"Carry on, comrade."

He laughed, climbed into his wellies, and stepped out of Old Roses Cottage. Half an inch of snow lay on Jeni's Mini, parked further along.

The name – Old Roses Cottage – on an ornamental cast-iron oval – had been Nancy's inspiration. Previously the place had simply been known as The Cottage, Green Street. Now it sounded as though some lovable village character called Old Rose had once lived there and was now memorialized. ("Should put another grand on the price!" Gareth had excused Nancy's notion to Jeni, whose address was being changed too. "Not that we go along with this godforsaken property exploitation, you realize? But where's the sense in losing out?") Actually, some woody old roses – Else Poulsons and Anne Poulsons – grew in the strip of front garden.

As Gareth hurried down Green Street he whistled the pop song which, with one amendment to the words, had become a joking anthem of the common room back in Reading: *When the going gets tough, the teachers get going. . . .*

He'd certainly got going, to a saner and gentler billet. Not that some of the pupils at John Clare weren't stroppy no-hopers in their own way – who could blame 'em nowadays? They were still a soft touch after Reading.

He was glad of the excuse to wear the wellies. The green boots looked businesslike, like a farmer. Thick Fairisle sweater and old brown cords completed his image; a briar pipe stuck out of his back pocket. Gareth's curly, coaly hair was receding prematurely just as his Dad's had done. However, this only made a broad open face seem even friendlier and more guileless. And he knew that his dark eyes had a twinkle in them.

Alas, only Ed was at home in Eagle House, his cream Saab Turbo outside; Mary and Carol had gone shopping in the Maestro. "Eagle" had nothing to do with the Kuzkas being American – the square, heavy building used to be a pub back in the days when even little villages could keep a number of pubs ticking over. Eagle House had nice gardens behind but presented a grim countenance to the street.

Ed invited Gareth in, so he stepped out of his boots like a courteous countryman. On his feet, thick fisherman's socks. Ed showed him into the Snug, which still kept its old half-panelled walls with a cushioned bench-seat along one of them. Otherwise the furniture was what Gareth thought of as gothic-colonial. Two massive dark armchairs faced a TV cabinet built like a mahogany safe. A huge oval mirror framed in ornate brass veneer attempted to buck up the light. These were ex the billeting quarters for transient officers, which was Ed's pigeon, and were imported from the USA by the furbishments office in Germany. Elsewhere in the house less troggish, overbearing furniture made inroads. Mary collected Chippendale, real or copy, as well as Staffordshire figures.

"How about a beer?" Ed had the softest of accents, dilute transatlantic. "Or something stronger?" He was tall with greying hair cut short, slatey eyes, thin nose, almost invisible pastel lips, and a neat salt-and-pepper moustache without which his face might have looked as though an eraser had been at work on it. Ed rarely got worked up about anything and was very literal-minded. Equally, he was hospitable in his quiet way. He was wearing slacks and a brown jogging top.

"No thanks, I had a can during the match. And there's a village hall meeting this evening – pub afterwards."

"Match?"

"Swansea versus Cardiff. Rugby, man!" At least it hadn't been snowing *there*, even if the All Whites had behaved like a blizzard.

"Of course. You're a Welshman."

"Rugby and the Labour Party: both in my blood." Not that Gareth, coming from Cardiff, could speak a word of Welsh. He was no mountain-man.

He recollected Jeni telling him something that had ruffled his feathers. If he challenged Ed, that would be research. Jeni should approve.

"What's this I hear about your chaps going round telling the Brits they buy from not to vote Labour, then?"

"Doing what?"

"When your USAF chaps spend some money in an antique shop or whatnot, they tell the owner not to vote Labour or he'll go out of business."

Ed said vaguely, "Oh, I guess they have political education classes on base. It helps the new arrivals cope with culture shock."

57

Jeni had got the story from the man who ran Treasure &
Trash in Churtington. "The Yanks *hate* Labour," he'd told
her. "They're being told that if Britain ever kicks out the
nukes, then everything will go, down to the last paperclip."
Businesses such as antique shops relied for eighty per cent
of their turnover on US personnel; not that the Americans
were squandering money or being rooked – they could
easily resell whatever they shipped back to the States for
two or three times the price.

"It's a bit interfering, I'd say."

"I don't really know about that," replied Ed, "but you
could ask Melfort's own new arrivals. I hear a family moved
into the school house yesterday; though really they're instructed not to talk about what happens on base."

"You and Mary'll be helping these new ones get their
bearings?"

"Us? No, not specially. Billeting isn't housing management. We just live here. I don't know them. Of course, if
they want to *ask* anything of us, or the Diamonds –"

"Ah. On the subject of asking for things –"

However, Ed lacked a power drill. Gareth got back to Old
Roses in time to catch the five o'clock news headlines on
local radio, which Nancy was listening to in the kitchen.

A suspected terrorist bomb explosion near the peace
camp at RAF Kerthrop; there'd been one death and serious injuries to members of the local hunt. Gareth's heart
sank.

He hardly heard the items which followed: more about
the closure of the Suez Canal to Western shipping by the
militant Islamic coup leaders in Egypt; Soviet protests at
the strafing of their anti-submarine cruiser by aircraft of the
US 6th Fleet; that sabotaged tanker still ablaze off the
Cape.

Hadn't Jeni said she was going to the peace camp today? Her car was outside. Should he call round?

Knowing her, if she hadn't heard the news she might rush off to Kerthrop and miss tonight's meeting. That would be a damn shame so close to the AGM.

What if hunt members from Melfort had been among the casualties? Even if not, committee members might well be acquainted with the victims. His stock and Jeni's could nosedive by association with the outrage. He needed to know the details.

Ten past five. Tom Tate usually opened the White Lion up promptly at six, unlike certain other village pubs. Eager for trade in tight times.

Nine

The phone crackled as if pigeons were prancing on the wire. Jeni banged the ear-piece.

"Say that again, Mal. I can't hear."

Outside, dusk was gloaming, but the inch of snow that had fallen had mostly melted. Jeni had fled the peace camp shortly after the . . . incident. She'd spent all afternoon at home. At first she'd sat numbly, feeling lost, then to distract herself she'd begun to mark a heap of history essays. These had to be done in any event. On Monday John Clare resumed after the half-term break.

The essays were about the British Revolution of 1805. No such revolution ever took place, yet there were umpteen reasons for a revolution then – as good as any of the reasons for the French Revolution of 1789, which did occur. Jeni had dreamed this theme up as a stimulating exercise for the Fourth Year. For once she had tuned her radio to an offshore pirate station playing pop. Every hour on the hour there was still news of multiple crises, mainly in the Med and Near East. For once she tried to blank the news out.

More pigeons on the line. "What did you say earlier, Mal?" (*Thump*.)

". . . MOD police *and* USAF security police. They turned the camp over. Did as much damage as they reasonably could."

"Oh no."

"Looks worse than it is. Took Jizz away for questioning. Took our visitors' book."

Jeni's stable had been tastefully converted: exposed beams, whitewashed stone walls, stripped pine floor and staircase leading up to bedroom and bath. Slim storage heaters, wrap-around techno-kitchen. She'd furnished the living room with a second-hand tufty wool suite in dark brown, an old roll-top desk, a glass-fronted bookcase. No need for a table and dining chairs; she wouldn't be hosting dinner parties. Guests could eat buffet-style. Nor had she rented a TV. TV bathed you in images and opinions, but somehow she understood information better from a radio. From Radio Four, anyway, her usual broadcasting tipple. Or perhaps she was prejudiced because TV captured you, immobilized you, stopped you from doing anything else but drink it in, submit yourself to it.

On the floor sprawled a large numdah rug from Oxfam, showing a naively woven tree with a score of doves perched in the branches. Mostly this reminded her of peace, occasionally of a chestnut tree in Somerville College gardens. On one wall hung a blow-up of the famous photo of Lenin addressing workers from a wooden stand – famous because Trotsky's image, just below, had been obliterated from later printings of the photo.

"They arrested Gisela? On what charge?"

"To assist enquiries, eh? They seem convinced the wire was dynamited. Bombed. How else could it have blown up? They're still out there in the floodlights sifting the soil. Couple of plain-clothes blokes followed me down to the phone box. You'd better steer clear for a few days."

"At a time like this, steer clear? You need support. Solidarity. I've every right to visit –"

Oh, this was Mal's peculiarity acting up again. Events were overloading him, so he was trying to scare people off till he could cope again. Mind, she'd fled the scene herself – otherwise she felt she might fly apart. Maybe Mal was trying to protect her.

"Don't tell me about rights. You brought us the truth about our rights, all nicely typed out – at least till the hounds and gee-gees shredded it. Not that our friends didn't scrupulously pick up every scrap. Just in case it's a commie explosives manual."

Crackle-splatter-piss. Now a gang of doves were pecking the line.

"I can handle it," she thought she heard; then she was listening to the buzzing of a put-down phone.

Had someone – Gisela? – really stuffed explosives under the wire? Set them off bloody-mindedly to coincide with the hunt?

Had the fox in its agony and terror bitten through some booby-trapped fuse wire?

Jeni remembered the snake which had writhed through her own entrails, and the imaginary pit in the road. As she shuddered with the recollection, a twitch of movement caught the corner of her eye. The branches of the numdah tree were asquirm with curled-up slippery venomous vipers, giant millipedes, coiling worms, vile black creatures –

No! Doves. White doves. Of peace.

61

The air stank of rotting, wet, mouldy wood buried underground for centuries, as though the room was floored with coffin boards.

The rug had rucked up and slid towards the phone. She must have skidded it as she was hurrying to answer Mal's call. She advanced to stamp the numdah back into its proper place – and stopped, terrified that if she stood on the weave right now there might be nothing beneath. Just a dark hole. With something at the bottom of the hole. Something big and simmering and foul. Or a pool of liquified dead flesh that was still alive.

Oh there was foulness, all right! The evil of M-16s and F-111s, the nuclear evil!

Skirting the rug, she stooped quickly and tugged it back again. It lay obediently on clear-varnished pristine golden pine.

She stirred the bowl of pot-pourri on the window sill till her room smelled sweet again. The pot-pourri was a present from Nancy; the dried petals came from Else and Anne Poulson and other roses with women's names that grew in the back garden. Jeni sometimes fancied that these roses contained the women in spirit, imagined that the women, when dead, had been burned to ash and buried under the first hybrid plant, magically to nourish the namesake bloom.

"Why don't they like pot-pourri in Ulster, eh?" she asked herself aloud, and answered her own question in an Ian Paisley boom (played on the windpipe organ): "No – Popery!" She laughed. Even to herself her laugh sounded sick.

The MOD had taken away the visitors' book, but that needn't bother her. Meg the Mini had been logged time and again by the MOD. Whenever any vehicles called at the camp, a Transit van would cruise slowly by. It occured to

Jeni that her phone might well be tapped. Probably was. Perhaps she ought to be grateful to Telecom for all the static? How could an eavesdropper understand conversations when she had her own work cut out half of the time?

It was Gareth, rather than the police, who rang her doorbell at quarter to eight. Jeni grabbed her pink anorak from the peg and stepped out.

"You've heard about that business at Kerthrop?" he asked.

She simply nodded, not quite wanting to tell him that she'd been present.

"I nipped up to the White Lion earlier. Village is humming about your camp, and the hunt."

"*My* camp? It's yours too, Gareth. What are people saying?" – as they headed up the street of cottages towards the green.

"Chap from Thrushby, dead – head sliced off. Jim Jackson-Thorpe, brother of our beloved County Councillor'll never walk again. Minor injuries galore. Several horses destroyed on the spot. Sounds like a ruddy massacre. A bomb."

"No, it wasn't."

"How do you know?"

"Mal phoned."

"Sounds like a bomb to me. That's what the news said. Mrs Parkes had her cheek cut open by flying wire. Another inch, and she'd have lost an eye. John Touchbrook had his leg slashed and his horse all cut up."

John Touchbrook was on the village hall committee. . . . Had Mrs Parkes recognized Jeni on the bridlepath?

"A bomb's bad news, Jeni. Terrorism. We should dissociate ourselves. They'll come down on that camp like a ton of bricks."

"Mal says they already started."

63

"What price an Easter demo now?" She fancied she detected an edge of relief mixed with his anxiety, which prompted her to wonder who else a bomb might gratify, for other reasons. Not that it had been a bomb at all.

"Neat way of aborting the festival, wouldn't you say?" she asked. "Department of Dirty Tricks strikes again."

"You surely don't think – !"

"I don't know. Don't forget the Greenham microwaves."

Radiation had been beamed out of Greenham at the peace camps on occasions when police and troops were conspicuous by their absence for hours. That started in the winter of '84-'85. A radiologist brought in by the wimmin at Green Gate had measured microwave levels a hundred times normal background. Result: nosebleeds, confusion, irregular menstruation, headaches, sun-burn at night. The wimmin were being "cooked".

"If that story's true," grunted Gareth. "*New Scientist* said the National Radiological Protection Board were able to reassure the Greenham women. I showed you the article. You've never dug out any confirmation about this radiologist of yours. I think it's like those stories about yellow rain in Asia. Bee shit, actually."

"I remember that article! Photo of 'Red Ken' Livingstone 'with reasons to thank the NRPB', and not a word about why. Photo of Greenpeace, given a clean bill of health after they'd been checking on radioactive discharge into the Irish Sea. Their dinghy didn't make the geiger counters buzz that day; whoopee. Photo of the wimmin who were so surprised to find that the NRPB employs top females. Fine reassuring stuff. Moral: even the loony left loves the NRPB, so obviously it needs more funding."

"Come on now, *New Scientist*'s not like that. It's always opening cans of worms. And Tom Dalyell writes for it."

He seemed disposed to argue; and she realized why.

Technicalities. To distract her.

"Our friends could use some moral support, Gareth. I'll phone round tonight to see who can get there. Will you and Nancy drive down with me tomorrow?"

"I suppose we *ought* to. Though if it was a bomb . . ."

"If! And whose bomb was it?"

"Mm."

They walked in silence across the green towards the long wooden shingle-roofed hall where light glowed and a few cars already stood on the forecourt. Other cars and a Land Rover were drawn up outside the White Lion, illuminated by a string of coloured fairground bulbs and by the floodlit inn sign. Other lights, or blue TV glow, showed in steep-roofed ironstone cottages. Dingy white ducks sailed, squabbling, on the pond. A lone goat, tethered on a long chain to the mid-way lamp post, cropped coarse grass. The sky wasn't too doleful now; stars winked through open rifts.

Could the wire possibly have acted as an aerial to lure ball lightning? Gareth taught physics . . . he ought to know the answer. Why bother even asking? The lightning had burst out of the soil.

Right now the peace camp seemed no distance away at all, as though shifting the site of the village all those hundreds of misty years ago had made not one scrap of difference . . . to whatever had squirmed beneath her rug. To the thing which might burst out wherever the pressure and the irritation mounted – wherever the flimsy surface was punctured.

You needed to scratch an itch. You even needed to make it bleed. You couldn't stop yourself. What was the greatest irritant hereabouts? The US base, of course. That's why she had to go there as soon as possible – so as to release the pressure there and not here. Unless . . . it was already too late to choose where?

She almost halted in her tracks. What on earth was going through her mind? Just now she could hardly follow her own thoughts. These weren't thoughts at all. They were more like visceral surges, ugly tensions as if she was about to have a period. A bad period.

"Won't you be coming to the pub after, then?" She caught the pleading note in Gareth's voice. Generally about half of the committee adjourned to the White Lion following the meeting. "You could phone round tomorrow morning. Saturday; catch people in."

Aha. Often a spot of idiot banter was directed at the two resident "reds". "If you're true Socialists why don't you go and live in Russia" – that sort of thing. Tonight, the mood might be ugly. Gareth was on edge.

Ten

Gareth wasn't sure whether to feel relieved or peeved at the poor attendance in the village hall that evening. Apart from Jeni and himself there were only five others. There was Chairman George Vaux, and their current secretary Marianne Bennett – Gareth knew she wasn't too anxious to be re-elected. Shy Clare Fox was blinking at her minutes – Jeni could do better than Clare any day. Plus there was Betty Gibson representing the WI, and Bert Morris.

Apologies from treasurer Ralph Underdown who was on business in Scotland; but he'd already given George copies of the balance sheet for distribution. Apologies also from Ian Yardley, a fuddy-duddy church stalwart who wouldn't have dreamed of going drinking afterwards (never mind that the vicar drank). No other apologies, but Marianne mentioned that John Touchbrook was tragically indisposed. Nuff said. The atmosphere cooled a few degrees.

It warmed gratifyingly as soon as Gareth suggested his solution to their financial dilemma. Income was way down due to a moratorium on disco lettings to outsiders. There had been too many brawls, too much vandalism, and even a stabbing outside Thrushby village hall.

"I should like to propose a wine and cheese evening," he said. "By way of a farewell to winter! That'll bring everyone out of the woodwork. How about two weeks from tonight? Nancy and I will gladly organize it, and I'm sure Jeni'll pitch in."

He expounded to general approval on which volunteers he would persuade to do what.

Jeni darted him a pained look. "How about beer and sausages instead? You won't get the council house people turning out in droves for wine."

"Oh, we'll lay on some canned beer."

Was she going to object again? He could guess why. "Wine and cheese" meant that Tories would turn out en masse, whereas the working class would stay at home. But this was a matter of fund-raising. Wine and cheese made money; you had to face facts.

Fortunately Jeni just nodded and sat hunched into herself. The meeting ambled on for an hour and a quarter in all.

The bar was crowded. Darts board busy; skittles table likewise. Standing room only. A suntanned nude wearing a skirt of peanut packets simpered at Gareth as he got the first round of halves in.

"Met the new Yanks yet?" he heard Bert asking Marianne.

Bert was the only "genuine" working class member of the committee, though he would never hint how he voted. Stocky, grizzle-haired, with mild blue eyes, Bert worked for farmer Vaux and lived in a tied cottage. George Vaux himself, with his ex-RAF handlebar moustache, was stout, florid-faced and gentlemanly but not prosperous. His place could do with a lick of paint, and he'd recently got rid of half of his milking herd because of the quotas. Bert and George mucked in together on first-name terms, though there was still an edge of social difference. George was also chairman of the Parish Council, and Gareth cultivated him when he could.

Marianne Bennett was plump, permed, and fussily efficient. With her husband Eric she was co-director of a mail-order fashion accessories and cosmetics business based at Churtington Industrial Estate. Though Marianne had access to cut-price gewgaws and face-powders she went very easy on these. She wasn't a walking advertisement for Bennett products (or repackagings). Her perfume was a subtle French one.

"Did you say more Yanks?" Jeni butted in. "Moved into the school house, have they?"

Bert knew everything almost before it happened, though he was generally unobtrusive in his omniscience – and basically gentle and kindly, unlike Jeni's bane, the dire Mrs Enid Jackson. In fact Bert was one of the friendliest villagers, amongst whose numbers could also be counted Ralph Underdown, George Vaux, though he looked like a right-wing codger, the Chases of course, and the Haverstocks, and – oh quite a few. Gareth did hope that Jeni wasn't going to sour the renewed cordiality. As he waggled a fiver to attract Tom Tate's eye he noticed that the pilot, Ron Diamond, was playing darts with the lads.

He hadn't spotted the pilot till now because the man was quite short. No doubt you didn't want giants in a jet. Trim, tanned, and olive complexioned, Diamond's sturdy black hair refused to look scalped even by a close crew-cut; Gareth couldn't help feeling a slight twinge of envy.

Dressed in jeans and red lumberjack shirt, Diamond grinned boyishly as he retrieved some neatly aimed arrows. He was a companionable type – though not with Gareth, thanks to Jeni – but he didn't seem to have any new protégé in tow.

"Name of Harper," said Bert. "Jim and Glory."

"Gloria?" queried Marianne.

"Glory, as in Hallelujah. With a bumper sticker saying, 'I love Jesus.' They're negroes."

"Oh."

"Tall skinny chap; looks like a basketball player. She's pretty tall too." Bert smirked. "Got a couple of piccaninnies."

Gareth heard Jeni tut loudly at the good old racial prejudice rearing its head, however gently.

"I'll call on his wife tomorrow," declared Marianne, who was by way of being the village welcoming committee.

"This should appeal to you, Jeni," teased Bert. "He's a mechanic, but *she's* a soldier."

"What?"

"You know: bang, bang. The Yanks are very liberated."

"You're joking."

"God's truth. Saw her driving back in battledress this evening, looking proud as punch."

"That's *obscene*. Right next to our school! I feared something like this."

Jeni took her half of Flowers from Gareth's outstretched hand and swallowed most of the beer immediately.

"Damn it," she whispered to him as soon as he joined her, "did you hear that? The first black faces in the village, and they just had to be – !"

"One of life's little ironies." Gareth sipped his Heineken discreetly. He was a lager man.

"Hmm! Our patriotic rural Tories were getting all steamed up after Tripoli was zapped from Merrie England,

69

right?" she went on intensely. "Selfish cowards, the lot of them. Maybe they would suddenly be a target for some Abdul with a bomb." Fortunately the din in the pub muffled her remarks.

"As at Kerthrop today?" he murmured to sidetrack her. "A bomb?"

"Now I suppose it'll be 'Welcome to Melfort, Mrs Glory Killer,' even though half the Near East's in flames."

"Um."

"Not to mention the trouble in East Germany. That's dropped out of the news."

"Oh yes, those SED cadres being purged." Keep to technical details. "It *is* the SED, isn't it?"

"Sozialistische Einheitspartei Deutschland, right. Did you say purged? You must be joking. They're resisting Soviet pressure to back-pedal links with West Germany. Naturally that's all part of an American-backed attempt to destabilize the DDR. Snarl up the Russians with their old bogeyman of a united Germany, distract them from the Arab mess. Some people have ten minute memories," she went on, reverting to her theme. "Tories vote like sheep."

"No solid political education," he agreed temperately. "That's the trouble. Tories have instincts, belief in their own values. Whereas *we* always need to apologize for ours."

"Oh do we indeed?"

"Well, no, we're in the majority. On the whole. But not hereabouts. This isn't Liverpool or Glasgow." If only she didn't cause a fuss!

The way she had caused a fuss when they first met Captain Diamond. . . .

That had been in the pub too; and while Gareth didn't approve of the USAF, one could surely still be friendly. Engage in dialogue, softly softly.

"Mustn't be shrinking violets, must we?" he'd remarked to Jeni, with a nod at her CND badge – he wasn't wearing his own at the time. "Bert'll introduce us, won't you, Bert?"

Mine-of-information Bert had been there. Gareth aimed to become just as *au fait* as Bert with the ins and outs of Melfort; though of course one mustn't degenerate into a gossip the like of Énid Jackson, who seemed possessed of X-ray eyes so that she knew whenever you changed your bed linen.

Even Nancy had uncharacteristically conceived a fair dislike of Mrs Jackson on account of her prying, sociable questions, all with the kindest of intentions. Questions about the new name of Old Roses, of which Mrs Jackson rather disapproved, about the exact marital non-status of Nancy and Gareth, not to mention their friend Jeni in the granny flat, and whatever else came to mind. As skivvy to the well-heeled, as well as to the vicar, Mrs Jackson was a dead ringer for a Tory supporter, not that she would confide anything about herself or her own little clan; that was private. Such people sold their loyalties along with their labour. Didn't have to, but they did; so the Labour Party must be anathema. Gareth had successfully suggested to Nancy that she should simply treat Mrs Jackson casually and vaguely whenever encountered; but you could never suggest anything of the sort to Jeni, which had been Gareth's mistake on that night a year and more ago.

Ron Diamond could have been a graduate from a charm school, crossed with a dose of bouncy hot-diggity.

They'd chatted a while; or rather Gareth and Ron had chatted.

"It's a big base, Kerthrop," Gareth had said.

"Not as big as some. Mildenhall's a *giant*."

"So what do you do, Captain?" Gareth asked presently. "Jockey a jet?" (That was the jargon, wasn't it?)

71

"Well, I'm rated for F-111s."

"Those can carry nukes, can't they?"

"Sorry, sir, I'm not allowed to say."

"Fair enough. Though it isn't exactly a dark secret."

Captain Diamond shrugged and smiled.

"Why is it fair enough?" demanded Jeni. "America could launch a nuclear war from this island without our own Parliament or people having any say, and we aren't even supposed to ask about it?"

"Frankly, ma'am, if I was the President I'd nuke some *Arabs* I could name." He laughed self-deprecatingly. "I guess that's why I'm not President."

"You'd nuke some Arabs. Just like that. One whole city? Or two?"

"That would be an operational decision. Pentagon, White House. I just fly where I'm sent."

Gareth remembered intervening fussily. "Don't you think it's a trifle disconcerting that America is the only country which ever actually used nuclear weapons in anger? On Japan, I mean."

"Not in anger, sir. Those two birds did the job. Brought peace. Should have dropped one on Hanoi, in my opinion."

Gareth could tell that the Captain was growing leery of this conversation, though pleasant courtesy still held him, a point to which Jeni wasn't oblivious, either.

"I don't wish to be rude, Mr Diamond," she asked, "especially as Americans are mostly so polite. But the way we see it, you Americans are naïve at heart. Trusting in God, saluting the flag, apple pie values. Your national naïvete's dangerous. You never experienced the ghastliness of total war the way the Russians did. You never really got hurt. Look how you swept the Vietnam veterans under the carpet! Nowadays you police the world to protect Mom's apple pie from gooks and wogs. You view the rest of the world as full of gooks. Us too, when the chips are down. We're gooks as well."

"All apples have gooks in them," joked Gareth. "The cores, eh?"

"So therefore collectively you napalm kids. You sponsor filthy dictatorships. You sabotage peasants struggling for a decent life."

"There's an *element* of truth," Gareth tried to moderate. She cut across him.

"You elbow right up against Russia then you squawk if the red rooster shows a feather within a mile of your own sacred back yard."

"Want to know why the Commie chicken only got half way across the road?" Ron asked Gareth. "It was a Rhode Island red!"

"No, listen to me, Mr Diamond. You might destroy the planet with your deadly, God-fearing, sanitized innocence – and to keep the mice from your apple pie, which is anywhere and everywhere. Better dead than red. Nuke the bastards. And a fifth of all Americans are looking forward to a nuclear war with positively biblical fervour. All those born-again Christians, right? How more lethally apple-pie innocent can you get?"

"*Hey, Ron!*"

"Excuse me, I got to buy drinks for those guys." He turned away. Soon Ron Diamond and the lads had been laughing and telling jokes.

The pilot had avoided Gareth since then, though in the aftermath of Libya, Gareth had felt indignant enough and confident enough to buttonhole him. "I suppose you people'll all be retreating inside Fortress Kerthrop soon, eh? In case some death squad decides on a vacation in England."

"No way," Ron had said. "I'm not bothered. No one's calling olly oxen free." Whatever that meant. "Fact is, with all the extra personnel arriving, there'll be *more* of us living off base, enjoying your British hospitality."

"But a *pilot*'s a likely target, isn't he?"

"Yeah, well I'm not moving house unless I get ordered."

"His family too."

Ron's half-smile had vanished. "So who's telling the Libyans my address? I warn you, buddy. *Don't. Ever. Threaten. My. Family.*"

"No, of course not! I didn't mean –"

"Don't think of any funny tricks."

"Don't think, is it?" Gareth had nerved himself to mumble. "Must be nice to be immune to world public opinion."

"Aw . . . stick a sock in it."

However, after her initial muted flare-up Jeni seemed unusually subdued, and concentrated on her next half of Flowers which George had already got in. Harry Blesworth from Church Hill Farm joined them, and conversation shifted to lambing and drainage, courtesy of that rural deity, the JCB. Then some farmer arrived, whom Gareth didn't know – from Thrushby, he soon gathered – and the talk was suddenly all of the explosion at Kerthrop. Gareth hastily guided Jeni and Marianne aside to discuss wine and cheese arrangements.

. .

Eleven

After Gareth had let himself in through the front door of Old Roses, Jeni stood alone for a while in the night.

No, not quite alone. Quiet thunder rolled overhead. Two black darts close together eclipsed star after star. Moments later another pair of jets traversed the sky. F-111s never normally flew by night. This must be a crisis exercise, even a full alert.

Those swing-wing warplanes were each burning up the annual income of an African village every half-hour. In her entrails Jeni felt a sluggish surge, bilious and baleful.

All hyper-modern fighters were unstable in the air, so she'd read. They could only keep airborne if an onboard computer trimmed them constantly. If only she could poke a finger up into the sky.

She must be drunk. The idea that you could magic away bits of the war machine! Instead of organizing politically, building towards a true socialist government which would expel all US bases. Even Labour only pledged to get rid of the *nuclear* weapons. Phased withdrawal; there's a good get-out clause. Phased over how long?

Really to succeed, Britain had to quit NATO. Whereupon the US would start destabilizing Britain, via the money markets first of all. . . .

No, one must have faith.

What, faith, with a nuclear war maybe brewing overhead right now? With those Emergency Power bills just waiting in the wings to stifle any dissent and give foreign armed forces the run of the whole land? Even if they did speak English.

If it wasn't faith that she felt as she let herself in to the granny flat, it was a sensation quite as powerful and consuming. This sensation wasn't exactly familiar. It neither echoed her period of trust in Trotskyism nor the exaltation of subsequent CND marches through London when, for a few hours, you experienced the illusion that you owned the streets. The feeling wasn't even familiar from her distant girlhood when a God had existed, and when she had (for approximately a month) contemplated becoming a saint who had visions and wrote ecstatic poetry. The sensation was a *little* like that. Perhaps because it was the opposite.

She had given no more thought to saints once she discovered how to manipulate herself. Black-robed inquisitioners were more potent figures – powerful, bullying lords of the land, armoured Captains, masked executioners, and all their modern kin.

She hadn't wished to remember this! Such feelings were so foreign to the comradeship of socialism and the peace movement, so alien to the fresh, liberating sisterhood she saw reflected in Mitzi. It was as if something was making her remember.

That night she dreamed she was in the stone chamber of some ancient monastery. The vicar was searching inside a stone coffin, desperately tossing out bones which crumbled to dust as they hit the flagstones. She knew that he was hunting for the key to the reliquary cage. Two hounds, which had formerly guarded the foot of the coffin in marble effigy, had come alive. They had mutated into a pair of slavering Alsatians. The dogs were wolfing food from a platter which the vicar had put down to distract them, a wooden plate piled with floppy white . . . what? Chapatis from an Indian take-away? Pitta bread? Or slices of drained human veal? The dogs would clean the platter in a trice; that's why the vicar was in a hurry.

She had to get out of this chamber! Moments earlier, there'd been an archway giving exit through the thick stone wall. This had now shrunk to a mere crawlspace. The room was sealing itself. If she tried to creep through the gap the stones might clamp on to her.

The vicar swung round. Eyes of blood stared at her.

He asked, in the fluting ironic voice of Jeremy Partridge: "Does the hate wake the power? Or does the power wake the hate?"

A riddle. If she could solve it, the doorway might open again.

The Alsatians licked their chops and glared at her. But then they turned towards the vicar, and she knew that he was their appointed victim.

She awoke refreshed. Almost nine o'clock. Bright sunshine poured through a gap between the pink Dolly Mixture curtains, Nancy's choice, co-ordinating with the bedroom wallpaper. The bedroom looked more nursery than granny. A peace poster blu-tacked to the wall seemed stupidly jolly, as if the H-bomb mushroom was no more than a big bad wolf.

For once the decor exactly matched Jeni's mood. She herself felt sunny and innocent. Hopeful. Had she dreamt something vile? How could she have done, and now feel so renewed? In the morning perspective all of yesterday's events appeared containable. She had work to do; phone calls to make. But first, coffee!

She padded naked to the little bathroom to empty her bladder of last night's beer. Pulling on jeans and jumper, she hurried downstairs humming to herself, to flip on auto-jug and radio.

Washington announced that the US Sixth Fleet would blockade the Suez Canal until free passage was guaranteed for ships of all nations. The Soviet Black Sea fleet was moving into the Aegean. The UN Security Council would meet in emergency session later that day. Israel's Defence Minister threatened that if its Arab neighbours tried to launch "a new Holocaust", his country would have no choice but to resort to "ultimate force" to protect itself. The Warsaw Pact was scheduling large-scale manoeuvres along the East German border. The oil tanker had sunk; a twenty-mile oil slick was threatening South African beaches . . .

That should turn white beaches black. No mention of any NATO alerts last night. Surprise, surprise! The jug boiled; she made herself a mug of instant Nicaraguan coffee which, unusually among coffees, tasted to her nearly as good as it smelled.

Here it came now!

". . . Experts admit they are baffled by yesterday's mystery explosion outside the American air force base at Kerthrop, in which one member of the local hunt was killed and several riders and horses were seriously injured. A Ministry of Defence spokesman said that apparently no bomb was involved, and as yet no other cause can be confirmed, but investigations are continuing. . . ."

So. And they'd have used a fine toothcomb. Even plastic high explosive should leave chemical traces.

No cause.

What, then? The force that through the green fuse drives the power . . . that blasts the roots of razor-wire is thy destroyer. So said Dylan Thomas. Almost.

A cramp clutched Jeni's abdomen and wrung it like a dishcloth, paralysing her for half a minute. God, she must need a giant crap. As soon as she could move freely, she hurried up to the toilet in the bathroom again. Scarcely was her bum on the mahogany seat than all came tumbling out, in one long unbroken surge, on and on.

When she could leap up and look, the shit lay neatly coiled like a yellow mound of sausage underwater. Odd. She didn't usually do craps that colour. The toilet tissue was clean after a single wipe. She balled the paper up tiny.

Before she could touch the flush lever, the rounded head of the shit rose up, questing like a water snake's. It surged into the U-bend, followed by the entire uncoiling sausage. Away it swam! Up through still water, before she could flush it!

It must have hit the bottom of the bowl with some sort of

– ha, energy of motion! An almost muscular energy which had bounced it back up and away.

How could. . . ?

The water wouldn't really have been still. She'd already flushed the toilet after peeing. The currents in bath water circulated for hours after the taps were turned off; hadn't Gareth once mentioned that? Likewise water in a toilet bowl.

So small a pool could whisk so much crap away like a leaf?

She felt fearfully sick. If that thing could swim away of its own accord, mightn't it swim back again? Maybe . . . rear up out of the bowl?

She pressed the flush. Waited. Pressed again. Then she fled downstairs.

Strangely, she still felt desperate for a crap. Pressure mounted in her bowels. Pain cramped her abdomen. She didn't dare go up and sit on that seat again so soon.

Carol – Oxford Carol – had worked part of one long vac as a chambermaid in the Randolph. She'd told Jeni about one loony woman guest who stayed shut in her room for weeks and wouldn't let the maids in morning or evening. "Seen to it all myself!" she shouted through the door when anyone knocked. Well, no maid was going to fight for the privilege of extra work. Finally a smell began to slink into the corridor.

It turned out that the woman had shat into newspapers. She'd rolled up her turds and filled drawers with them, drying.

Jeni wouldn't have thought of a solution otherwise. As yet she hadn't opened any curtains. Feeling like a mad-woman herself, she spread a copy of the free paper, the *Churtington & District Advertiser*, on the amber lino. Jerking her jeans down, she squatted.

None too soon. Soft dark brown crap rushed out, smelly

chunks with bits of day-old peanut embedded.

It took three sheets of kitchen roll to wipe herself clean. Quite a load she'd dropped. A steaming heap. Utterly unlike the other.

It was then Jeni realized that the long coil of yellow matter which had swum away earlier – that *thing* like a yard of pale unsegmented sausage in a butcher's window – couldn't possibly have come out of her anus. . . .

It had come out of . . . her other opening.

Terrified, she folded the *Advertiser* over, slid her parcel into a plastic bag and hurried it out to the dustbin.

The sewage downpipe was gurgling, endowed with a voice: the voice of something inside the pipe, slurping and glutinous. Presently the noises transferred themselves to the drains underfoot.

It was as if she'd become fully pregnant overnight with a deformity, child of a nightmare she'd forgotten. She'd given birth that morning to a pale boneless limb. Now the limb was loose in the village. By way of the drains, it could slide anywhere it wanted.

"What nonsense! Nonsense!" Jeni's cry startled a blackbird from the fence. She'd been hallucinating. Could some of that acid still be lodged in her system after all these years, locked inside brain cells? Unlikely.

Maybe the acid had unlocked a door in her mind which was now a swing-door. A strong enough wind could blow the door open at any time; such as the wind from an F-111, such as the wind of rage.

She hurried indoors to drink more coffee, char a slice of wholemeal toast, make phone calls.

Twelve

It was four that afternoon before Jeni drove up to the peace camp; Nancy alongside her, Gareth penned in the back seat.

A series of POLICE: NO STOPPING signs lined both sides of the verge but there was still room to squeeze Meg the Mini into the mouth of the green lane behind several other cars which she recognized as belonging to supporters.

A white MOD Police Range Rover waited over the way, with a couple of watchful officers inside. Part of the churned field beyond was cordoned with white tape. A new half-moon of razor wire bulged a few yards behind the wrecked part of the fence. A mobile multiple floodlight, like a vaulting horse on little wheels . . . a vacant jeep . . . two men in suits consulting in a wood-panelled estate car. Half a dozen Americans in battledress slouched at ease, armed with M-16s, a couple smoking cigarettes. One soldier was a sharp-faced woman with bright red hair spilling from her cap; she looked like trouble. The only soldier wearing a steel helmet was oriental, stocky and expressionless.

"That one could be Korean," Jeni told Nancy. "Korean-American. Did you know that's the only foreign language they hold religious services in on the base? Korean. Must be enough of them to have their own chaplain. Maybe some of them are barbecue chefs."

"He isn't."

"No. Fancy being shot by a Korean in the heart of Merrie England? Kim the Killer."

Nancy glared through her glasses. She ran a hand through her yellow curls. To Jeni's eyes Nancy Abbott could well be Gareth's brother, a negative photo of him even to the fleshy fat lips. No doubt that was why the two had gravitated together. In loving each other Nancy and Gareth loved themselves, anima and animus without any chance of animosity. No wonder they didn't feel the need to get married formally. Or to have kids; they'd already reproduced, become twofold. Jeni occasionally felt jealous of her friends' mutual identity, yet mostly she felt safe with it, consoled and sheltered. Above all, they didn't dominate her. So what if she'd moved her home and job at their prompting? Something else had urged her to make the move. So what if she paid them a fair rent, with which to buy themselves Old Roses? So what if she became minutes secretary? Village activities and socialism notwithstanding, Nancy and Gareth were ultimately self-involved. They would never try to invade her head the way Donna or the Trots had done. She was simply their comrade who lived next door.

"It's cooled. No panic." Mal sounded offended to see Jeni.

"How about Gisela?"

He shrugged. Actually he looked a bit catatonic, maybe due to lack of sleep.

If only there was a "safe house" in Kerthrop where a camper could wallow in a bath, catch a film on TV, spend the night when feeling sickly. Yanks rented or owned fifty per cent of the village, yet surely there must be a dissenting British household who'd be willing to help out. Mal had overruled this idea. A camper must camp, not swan off to the lap of luxury whenever the weather turned foul. For then the camp would fail. They would blow it.

"We needn't have come," observed Gareth.

"You don't think so?"

"There's nothing going on, is there, Jen girl?"

"Except for twelve thousand Yanks getting ready for Armageddon."

"That's counting wives and kids. Mind, I agree." He stared broodily through the wire at the runway's huge expanse of concrete partly masked by those concrete whales; he pulled out his pipe.

Jack pointed. "Don't knaa if ye can make it oot, but yon's a Rapier missile contraption."

"Won't it be wonderful," asked Nancy, "when all this is restored to farmland again?"

Gareth sucked on his pipe. "Don't know whether we'll see *that*. Can't do without a conventional defence policy on the Swiss or Swedish model, can we? We'll probably use the base as a base."

"Oh don't fudge before we've even won!" exclaimed Jeni.

"I'm not, I'm being realistic. What, more farmland? With all the grain mountains and milk lakes?"

"*Aid*. For the Third World, Gareth."

"We overproduce as it is, without adding hundreds of extra acres. Do you realize, this base could make a perfect low security prison? Relieve overcrowding no end, it would. Fine recreational facilities."

"Is that what ye think, ye daft bugger?" Jack butted in. "Wey, if army camps is wanted as spare prisons they'd used some shithouse in the north. That's where yor workin' class yobs without jobs is, what gans roond commitin' outrages."

"A proper revolutionary government would dynamite this place," Jeni said hotly, "because it's a symbol of power against people. Sod its bowling alleys and burger bars."

"It could be a leisure park," suggested Gareth. "A liberated US base, hosting freedom holidays for Czechs and Poles." Was he joking?

"Have you any news of Gisela?" Jeni asked Jack.

"Bit soon for that, pet." Jack didn't look as distressed as he should if he and Gisela had been flattening grass together. Maybe her suspicions were ill-founded.

Mal had sunk into a bent, torn deckchair and was gazing vacantly into space.

The supporters from Churtington had all driven away by six. A civilian police van had collected the NO STOPPING signs. All the perimeter spotlights had come on, providing free street lighting for the peace camp. USAF guards on the far side of the wire were down to three, plus Jeep.

Mitzi strummed a guitar, singing softly to herself. Jack had taken his dog for its evening walk up Hobby Hill. Nell was playing portable Scrabble with Andy. A calm mackerel sky; there might be frost later that night, or a fog.

Gareth paced restively, pipe long extinguished.

"We going soon, Jen? Nance and I have things to do."

"I've decided to stay overnight." Jeni suddenly didn't wish to go home just yet. The toilet-creature . . . that hallucination. She needed company. "You drive Meg back, will you? Pick me up some time tomorrow morning."

"Surely." Gareth promptly stuck his hand out for the keys.

"I'll get my sleeping bag." Jeni always kept it in the car. A bad snowstorm could quickly block country roads; and a Mini had tiny wheels. Twice that winter she had stayed over in Churtington after school rather than risk the ten miles.

"Jeni!" called Nell. "Are you insured for a second driver? The MOD tailed me last week, then a few miles further on the civilian fuzz flagged me down. Said they'd had a report of an unroadworthy vehicle. I think it pissed them off as much as me, since the beetle's quite okay. I finally got them to admit it was the MOD."

"Did you get the full works?" asked Jeni, while Gareth fidgeted. "Pennies in the tyre treads?"

"Absolutely. They weren't too happy with the shocks, but they let that go. Pissed off, they were."

"I'm fully insured."

Nell winked. "To live outside the law, you must be honest, eh?"

*

Supper was vegetable stew cooked over the open fire, and slabs of wholemeal bread. Wispy mist began seeping from the ploughed land over the road, from the lawn of the dog pound, from those parts of the airfield which were still field. If anything, the wall of floodlighting surrounding the base seemed all the brighter. The residential side was a city of lights. Had Jeni been back home in Melfort she could have seen a dome of radiance that smudged the stars away.

Towards nine, pairs of F-111s roared skyward in unison, each with twin exhausts aflame. In all a dozen jets took off. Their meteor-fires disappeared into the east.

"Maybe they're shifting them," hazarded Mal. "Perhaps to Turkey."

Mist thickened. A guard dog howled, though dogs usually patrolled quietly. Bess whimpered softly. Jeni shivered one instant then found herself unaccountably sweating. The night air was playing tricks; there was a fever in it.

"At least if they pull the plug," said Nell, "we're in the right place to die fast."

"They're trying to pull it, aren't they?" murmured Mitzi. "Come in, human race; your time is up."

"Damn them!" swore Jeni. "Damn them to hell."

Hooves drummed down Hobby Hill.

For a moment everything was frozen.

Then the first horse burst into view, side-lit by blurred arc lights, its rider ducking over.

Thoughts flickered through Jeni's head. The hunt was coming for revenge. Rednecks had formed a company of the Ku Klux Klan. As yesterday, the campers scattered – Jeni ducking under a hawthorn which tore at her hair.

A second horse . . . now a third. This was a total echo of the day before.

Except, as the first beast leapt the campfire, the smell of it hit her. Except, the rider's clothes were all rags and in his haggard face the eyes squirmed like egg-white loose in a pan of boiling water.

Thirteen

The next rider who thundered past on a putrefying nag wasn't even properly human. Never could have been. Sprouting from his or her shoulders was a hound's head, which gave cry.

The third horse was flayed raw. A dog, stretched into human shape, rode it.

The fourth and last hunter was an X-ray animal. Hardly any flesh still hung on it. Its internal organs were visible as bouncing bags and tubes of jelly in a cage of bones and ropy muscle. In the valley of its neck vertebrae pulsed a leathery football which seemed to be its rider. A free-loading tumour, a giant toad. The creature passed by.

Andy was shrieking in a high-pitched way, till Nell ran and slapped his cheek, then hugged him. Mal was jerking his plaster-cast finger after the nightmares; his jaws worked but no words came.

"Yerbuggerinhell!" With this cry, Jack took off for the road in pursuit. Jeni rushed after him on quaking legs which threatened to dump her in a heap.

Already the beasts had reached the scene of yesterday's explosion. They galloped full-circle in the foggy glare of lights – American voices were shouting – then the dog-ridden horse charged at what was left of the original fence.

As soon as it touched wire, the beast popped like a bubble. Where it had been an instant before, darkness swelled. A short black tunnel repelled all light.

The X-ray horse charged next. It vanished into the blackness . . . and emerged beyond, to hurl itself headlong at the inner ring of razor-wire.

Flashes. *Crack-rack-rack-rack* – at least one of the guards had opened fire. Bare bones and dripping entrail bags hit the steel bales, and vanished. The black tunnel leapt out almost to the spotlights.

Rack-rack-rack.

The rotten nag pounded into the tunnel, pursued by the fourth beast.

Rack-rack-

The spotlights went out. Night gulped that area, though it didn't muffle the screaming.

. . . On the TV set in Old Roses Jeni had seen infra-red videos on the News filmed from an F-111 as it targeted its laser-guided bombs. Grainy shadow-images of apartment blocks, cars parked on avenues, barracks, compounds.

As she stared into the guzzling darkness she now saw her own personal infra-red video. Not of a Jeep and those USAF guards, not of the horses from Hades. She was seeing a muddy, rutted earth road, thatched cottages with vegetable gardens.

Few of the cotts were built of stone. Most had clay walls speckled with chopped straw. Pokey windows were either sackcloth, which had been ripped, or lattice smashed through as if by fists. No: one cott's windows seemed to be of polished, cracked horn. Doors were only hard burlap curtains, torn aside. So many trees loomed behind!

A child's naked matchstick corpse lay in the road, near a dead hound. Crows were hopping close.

Beyond the cotts she saw a stone-built manor with outhouses of wood and clay. A man's crumpled body, wearing tunic and hose, lay in the manor gateway; and more than the manor's chimney was smoking. Grey tendrils seeped from the whole tiled roof, soon to flare ablaze.

Oozy blackness hung over the village. Not night or low storm cloud or smoke pall . . . a sort of aerial rot or inky fungus.

Opposite the doomed Manor was the timber lych-gate of a Norman-style church. From the church itself strode a monk in dingy brown robes, whose head was concealed by a cowl. The monk held out before him a heavy brass cross, pointed at the ground like a divining rod. Or like a sword. The tip glittered and flickered. Behind the monk capered a line of nude men and women, boys and girls, sniggering, leering, and goosing. Hands thrust to clutch the bum in front, hands groped behind to clutch whichever genitals.

As the monk led his followers through the lych-gate on to the road the mud squirmed as if thousands of worms were writhing in the dirt. Now the naked people were grimacing as much as grinning, groaning as much as sniggering. It occurred to Jeni that they *couldn't let go* of each other. They were glued together sexually.

A woman clad in russet gown and white wimple ran from the Manor, screaming soundlessly at the procession. The monk jerked his cross at her. No sooner, and she was spinning round, burning like a pitchy torch. Her screams now were of agony, and of a despair greater than agony. When she collapsed, the mud bubbled about her greedily.

A soldier rode into view, half-armoured in breastplate and pointed helmet with chainmail tails. In his mailed fist, a broadsword. He'd arrived too late to save the lady, if that had been his intention. To Jeni's eyes his mount was a giant, prancing carthorse. The warrior – maybe he was a knight – spurred at the monk, swinging his sword. The glittering cross rose to meet the blow . . . and the broadsword incandesced like phosphorus dipped in water. The attacker's studded gauntlet glowed red hot. He howled unheard anguish. His steed bolted clumsily. Tearing at that terrible, flesh-cooking glove with his other hand, the man unbalanced. He crashed to the ground. His weapon had already fallen; quenched by the mud, the metal had warped into a sickle shape. The man lay still. The fall must have snapped his spine.

The monk gestured to his flock. They fell upon all fours, to root at the mud like snorting swine; and then to abominate each other, mounting, squealing.

Jeni shook, appalled. Was this something which had actually happened once, at the original Melfort? Here, hereabouts. Desecration, evil indignity, death. Which she was suddenly seeing re-enacted in some mirror of the past?

Or was this an insane degraded parody of the present? Of the earthy peace camp and the military . . . and who could that monk be but her own twisted subconscious version of the vicar?

The manor house was well ablaze, cascading sparks. The polluted church was shaking as if an earthquake shrugged its shoulders beneath it. Cracks forked the walls. Coping stones fell.

And then the monk marched purposefully in Jeni's direction. For the first time she could see the head inside the hood.

A thing, part skull, part waxy flesh, part polished black idol. She recognized the blood-red eyes from her dream, the equine teeth. Those eyes stared at her, to tell her something awful which she ought to know. Or remember, or anticipate. Something entirely awful.

Blackness closed around her.

Fourteen

Sunday morning. As Jeni sat in Meg's passenger seat, Gareth steered the Mini back into Melfort. The bells of St

Mary's were calling Tories to the 11 a.m. service, and no doubt some disgruntled SDP sympathizers.

Off-the-peg suits of funeral charcoal, natty bespoke grey suits, ladies' tweeds and flowery flocks plus woollies, some floral hats begotten at Ascot, boys in Fauntleroy gear, stout girls in white dresses with white cotton sashes and even straw boaters; that was the Sunday morning fashion scene. Home, afterwards, to a roast which was sizzling away even now in the oven – *somebody* had to be supporting the beef industry – or perhaps a cockerel.

Jeni hadn't felt able to drive safely. Sleepless, wrung out and strung out, who knew what she might see darting across her field of vision or rising out of the road?

In the back seat Andy hunched wearily, nursing an ill-made roll-up, his duffle and sleeping-bag beside him. Their satirist had quit the peace camp. He couldn't take another night, not after seeing . . . those things. The four horsemen. Of. An unimaginable apocalypse. Andy was taking events a few words at a time now. A bit, a puff, at a time. Otherwise the avalanche might bury his mind. Jeni had thought Mal would come unstuck, but it had been Andy instead. Maybe Mal would crack yet, and Andy was wisely getting out in time. Whereas Nell and Mitzi had become stubborn. Or were utterly brave. And Jack was gormlessly . . . enthusiastic.

"I think," said Andy. (Puff.) "Last night. Maybe they tried. Hallucinogenic gas." (Puff.) "Loony gas. Experimental. From Porton or Edgewood. Stuff like BZ, LSD. Turn us into mental cases." (Puff. His roll-up had gone out.) "Scare us off."

Jeni said nothing. Let Andy believe that if it helped. To bail the boat of his brain, the capsizing ship of his soul.

Of course there'd been no gas attack. Nor had those Americans over the way been exposed to some of their own loony gas, so that they emptied their M-16s into the generator and the Jeep's fuel tank, causing unheard explosions which had wrecked the lights and the Jeep and torn two of those same guards apart . . . their screams had been noisy enough.

Nor had some ingenious terrorists or peace-commandos sneaked up in the night to project a horror movie on the fog. . . .

"You saw *what*?" the MOD officer had bellowed at Mal and Jack.

Ambulance lights strobed the ruins of wire, Jeep, and generator. Two armoured cars were covering the gap. A truck had towed a replacement generator and spot-lights on site; suddenly these flooded the area brilliantly. There must have been a score of armed soldiers on alert, with officers.

"Wey, the four bloody pit-ponies of the Apocalypse, man, what de ye think?"

"Funny buggers!" The MOD man had come with a colleague and a black American guard; their faces were set grim. "There are two men *dead*, Geordie. Torn to shreds. So what was it, eh; grenades? A mortar shell?"

"Why not ask the other Yank?" growled Mal. "He'll tell you."

"He's in shock," purred the black. "He can't talk."

"More like catatonic," muttered the other policeman.

"Shell-shocked," his superior corrected him. "So what was it, then?"

"Spooks and ghoulies," said Mal.

"Come off it! I *know* you. We've talked before. Do you want me to get unfriendly?"

No telling with police, Jeni had thought. Some were bastards. Others were very affable. Last year, at the Hiroshima Day vigil at the main gate with candles in coffee jars, some jars had got dropped in the road and the police said not to worry, they'd clear up the mess themselves afterwards. A young American with the procession was mind-blown. "Do you mean your police'll bring out brushes and pans? And put *aprons* on?" Of course, there was always the old trick of the nice policeman and the nasty policeman. One to act as prisoner's friend, the other as bullying interrogator.

"Wey man, what was it rived yor wire the forst time? Did ye find any bits o' bomb?"

The MOD officer glared at Jack without comment.

"Ye won't this time, neither! What's rivin' yor fence is somethin' *paranormal*, man. It divvent like yor base no more than we do. But *we* divvent gan roond killin' folk. How'll ye like it when some enormities hoy theirsels at an eff-one-eleven as it's takin' off?"

"Is that a threat, Geordie?"

"Na it ain't. This ain't any ov wor doin'. If ye had any gumption ye'd be consultin' an exorcist."

Isn't it any of our doing? thought Jeni. *Isn't it?* Earlier she'd fainted at the end of the green lane. She'd fallen in the dirt. Nell helped her back to a seat in camp, and she still felt woozy. Jeni hadn't said anything at first about her own vision of the ancient lane, degraded villagers, devilish monk – if the person was even human. No one else had mentioned seeing that.

After hunting through caravans and bus and VW and even shining a torch down the latrine pit at the rubbish bags and shit, the visitors departed, back to the confusion over the road.

"Aa'm not kiddin', man, it's paranormal," she heard Jack telling Andy.

"Look, I'm sorry. But. I'm leaving tomorrow."

"Bugger it, man, we're winnin'."

"*We* are? Something might be . . . doing things. It's vile. Foul. It isn't us."

"Wey, so's the base a clarty thing."

"At least that's natural – I can cope with it."

"What's natural aboot a nuclear war base? Was a hair of wor heeds harmed? Na! Somethin's on wor side, for once."

"Something ghastly, Jack. I feel contaminated."

"Wey, it's better than radioactivity. Maybe this is happenin' on account of us. Wor hopes, wor passion. Maybe we're on one of them ley lines Nell blethers aboot, an' there's a geat big power in the earth."

With her pigtails like corn dollies and her ample harvest ripeness, Nell *was* a bit of an earth mother in appearance; but this was the first time that Jeni had heard Nell was interested in ley lines and all that nature-magic nonsense. Maybe Nell confided her beliefs only to her fellow campers because she was embarrassed, and could be wounded by scepticism or derision. The peace camp on this rural lane was a way for her to express such private feelings under a "sensible" banner, to fight for them under another flag.

Nell seemed too . . . healthy . . . to be responsible in any way for what was happening. Yet maybe she had noticed more than the others? And wouldn't confide? It was Nell who had come to Jeni's aid.

Jeni got up and walked over. Mitzi hurried to touch her supportively, and stroke Jeni's cheek. The labrador's wet nose nuzzled Jeni's hand for reassurance. Momentarily Jeni recoiled as though a branding iron had touched her skin.

"I. . . . Did *we* see anything else apart from those . . . four beasts?"

Nobody admitted.

"Nell, did you?"

"Why me?"

"I just heard Jack mention how you're interested in stuff like ley lines. Well, if you're sensitive to . . . certain things . . . Personally I'm a political animal, but –"

93

"If you're asking whether I'm psychic, the answer's no. Sorry! Wouldn't have *minded* being," she conceded, "up until tonight. Oh no, I think what came through here is no friend of the earth. It isn't to be courted."

"Aa don't knaa aboot that –"

"It isn't, Jack. But we shouldn't let it scare us, either. The goodness of the earth is stronger. Those Yanks were hyped up – for war. Servants of death, poor things. Maybe that's what attracted . . . whatever. We mustn't be like them. We mustn't rejoice in what just happened. We must be ourselves, firmly and strongly, in key with . . ." – she gestured at the leafy lane – ". . . life."

Impatiently Jeni said, "Well, I saw something more." And she told then. She also repeated what Partridge had told her about the "evil" in the old Melfort. Yet she kept mum as to the reason why she hadn't wanted to return to her own home that night; that seemed indescribable.

"The vicar put ideas in your head," Andy said. "That's why you saw –"

"It was real."

"To you."

"I saw the past."

Mitzi cooed soothingly; and Jeni thought of that opaque, confused moment in Oxford when . . . when what? When a force smashed Donna backwards.

A far stronger force had punched through the perimeter and ripped two living bodies limb from limb.

At that moment the main runway lights came on.

"Maybe they're checkin' it for monstrosities," said Jack. "Ye knaa, Aa wes havin' a crack wiv an electrician lad from Churtington. Met him in the Crown afore wor bit o' trouble. Anyways, he wes once called in to do maintenance work on the cables for them roonway lights." Jack told his story so as not to have to dwell on the recent horror. "So he got his pass with his photo on it, though they wouldn't let him drive his own van. Ferried him oot there wiv his box o' tricks, they did. They wouldn't torn the power off either, an' that's twelve thoosand amps we're talkin' aboot. If ye touch the wrong bit you're a gonner. So he's workin' doon this pit off the runway when he hears a click, an' somethin' hard gets jammed up his back. He torns roond slowly, an' finds a couple o' young Yankie soldier-boys coverin' him. 'Ye want te eat your rifle, sunshine?' he asks. 'Cos there's twelve thoosand live amps doon here. If Aa even nudges this, yor gun'll be rammed doon your gob.' "

But his story was interrupted. Wing and belly lights of an aircraft dipped from the eastwards. . . . With a roar and scream of throttling back, a giant transport jet came rolling along the runway.

"Grief, that's a *Galaxy*," said Mal.

Scarcely had the great jet finished taxiing, than a companion plane touched down.

"They're beefing up the base." Mal's voice was calm again. "They're sneaking in stuff to control subversive Brits with. I feel it in my waters."

Activity on base continued all night long, and Sunday morning too. It was a relief when Gareth eventually drove up in the Mini. A relief for Andy as well; he was jittering.

Jeni gestured at her sofa. "You can sleep on that tonight. Should I drive you into Churtington tomorrow? To the bus station? Shall I see if somebody in town has a spare room? You might want to go back to the camp."

"I don't know." Andy relapsed on to the sofa, still clutching the *Observer* which he'd picked up from Jeni's doormat. "I can't decide. I feel. Like a coward. But." Dropping the newspaper, he took out his Old Holborn tin and began, all thumbs, to make a cigarette. The *Observer* lay askew on the durrah rug. The main headline was: US WARNS SOVIET FLEET OFF SUEZ. A photo showed a sea streaked black, and for a moment Jeni thought she was seeing the aftermath of a naval battle; but those must be South African waters. The news seemed both urgent and out of date. She felt no desire to read it.

"I can't take it." He lit up.

"I'll make us some coffee. Let's go to the pub at lunchtime, hmm?"

Through in the kitchen she switched on Radio Four. Pick of the Week. Johnny Morris was telling faintly xenophobic anecdotes about funny Balkan foreigners. He faded in midflow.

A different, grim voice interrupted. "We break into this programme for an important newsflash. A nuclear weapon has exploded over Damascus, the capital of Syria –"

"Andy!" she screamed.

Fifteen

Gareth held Nancy's hand as they watched Weekend World from noon on. News from the Near East was chaotic, save for the certain fact that Damascus had been annihilated and a fire-storm was raging. No pictures of this, not even satellite ones. Not yet. Parliament would meet in special session throughout the night to consider an Emergency Powers bill. Any MPs visiting their constituencies for the weekend would be hurrying back to Westminster.

"Do you think Jeni's all right?" Nancy asked tonelessly.

"She has Andy with her."

"What use is he? You said he's having a breakdown. Maybe we should all get together."

"I know it's awful to say so," Gareth murmured, "but this ghastly news could have one good side. America or

Russia haven't been hit directly. Syria, instead. That's so terrible in itself that it might, well, haul everyone back from the brink. Scare them back to sanity. I've sometimes thought . . . maybe the world needed one new Hiroshima. One reminder, with today's much more destructive nuke. As an object lesson. Since it's only one bomb so far, it could save all our lives."

On the screen journalists debated hotly, their comments interspersed by confusing updates, maps, and film footage – of Damascus before it died, the Knesset, the UN, the Soviet and American fleets.

"Yes it must have been the Israelis," parroted Gareth. "Islamic Egypt and Syria were obviously planning a knock-out blow. If the Yanks intervened, and the Russians took the Yanks on . . . well, the chaps in Jerusalem must have said to themselves, 'It's time. Take out Damascus, and the boat will rock like crazy but it probably won't sink. We won't all go down.' Look you, nothing else has happened yet! If we can just last through today and tomorrow –"

"What's this Emergency Powers bill? Why's our government doing that? Jeni'll know!"

"I suppose it's a precaution."

"But isn't that preparing for worse?"

"That's what a precaution is, Nance."

"I wish we had a cellar. Why didn't we buy a house with a cellar? Do you think we should close the curtains?"

He cuddled her. "They might set on fire. *We* can't take any precautions that make sense."

"I'm going to ask Jeni in. Why hasn't she come round?"

"Let's eat something hot." Before the power supply goes off, he thought. And the TV, along with it. That might happen. Today. Next week. Today.

"*Eat?*" echoed Nancy.

"Do you suppose Jeni's had a *bean* since last night? She'll hardly be cooking now. Let's stick something special in the

97

microwave. How about those two moussakas?" Before the oven fails, before the freezer starts to thaw. . . .

"You're right. I'll fetch her. And Andy."

"Let *me*. You'll start fretting, along with her."

As Gareth stepped into Green Street a white VW cornered and raced past him to brake hard outside Jeni's door. He recognized yellow pigtails, ginger hair and beard, a girl's blonde crewcut. It was the peace campers. Nell, who'd been driving, and Jack scrambled out, followed by, what's her name, Mitzi. Also, the fat black dog, which started barking at him. Nell was already banging Jeni's horseshoe knocker.

"Hey there!"

"Gareth!" Jack stumbled towards him. "Mal's *dead* – a Yank shot 'im! He bloody murdered him like vermin. They came boilin' oot o' the base in Jeeps an' armoured cars an' aal. One squad told us te boogar off immediately. Wivvin a minnit. Don't stop te pack. Cos they're shuttin' off the main road – an' gettin' rid o' any folks they fancy for two miles roond, just like Jeni telt us. Hoying them oot o' their hooses, Aa suppose."

The door had opened, and Nell was telling Jeni.

"Wey, you knaa how Mal has a temper –"

"I didn't know him very well."

"He went berserk, man, an' this Yank kid shot 'im lots o' times. We just had to pile in Nell's car and *drive*, or they'd ha' shot us too. Mal's bloody deed!" Jack cried to Jeni.

"Bastards, bastards," swore Mitzi. "They were already starting on their road blocks, dumping sandbags round a machine gun."

Jeni's face was drained white.

"Come in, all of you."

"No," began Gareth. He was still on his appointed mission to invite Jeni, and Andy, for lunch; but then he counted heads. "No," simply sounded like his own protest against an atrocious situation; and he crowded into the granny flat along with the others. At least he'd had no wall-to-wall carpets fitted to be soiled.

"Wey, wit a smashin' home," he heard Jack compliment Jeni briefly. Mitzi was busy spitting out their story to a stunned Andy.

"I don't know if I can sleep four, and a dog," Jeni said.

Gareth performed a lightning calculation.

"I'm sure Nance won't mind Mitzi having our spare room."

Mitzi was really too scrawny for his taste, an anorexic punky fifth-year type, and he recalled Jeni saying that the girl had been at Greenham, so she would be part of the women's movement – of which he was all in favour so long as it wasn't taken to extremes. Nancy shared this view-point, which was the reason why he and Nancy hadn't entered into any domineering marriage bond complete with ring and ball and chain, but had become equal and friendly partners.

Nell, on the other hand, was well-fleshed; however he felt no gonadal response to her. Nell was too wholemeal, too bursting with bran, whereas he liked fluffy white bread.

Not that he visualized any hanky-panky with young Mitzi. Even so! She was a bit of a tearaway. Having her in the spare bed, and using the bathroom, should stimulate the old adrenalin and testosterone. In a time of crisis conventional behaviour often lapsed all round with nobody the wiser or culpable.

"You'll only take Mitzi? That still leaves me three people, Gareth. Your place is bigger."

"I don't mind kipping on Mitzi's floor," offered Nell. "I'm better padded, aren't I?"

"Or you could both take turns. Good, that's settled."

Settled by Jeni. Gareth pulled himself together. "Do you have enough food? There'll be panic buying tomorrow.

You should get on down to the shop first thing before everyone else thinks of it." The larder in Old Roses was healthily full; Jeni's was a different kettle of fish. Gareth was tempted to inspect it.

"But it's school tomorrow," she reminded him.

"Ho, ho. How do you get to Churtington with road-blocks in the way?"

"Go round by Thrushby, or further."

"Talk sense, Jen. It's not very wise to distance yourself from your home base. With these Emergency Powers likely to be law by tomorrow I bet there'll be petrol rationing, and teachers won't be a priority. Maybe the government'll shut the pumps."

"No, that's in the second of the emergency bills."

"Don't count on it."

"Don't tell us they're shovin' them bills through already!"

"It was on the news, Jack."

"The Yanks have obviously jumped the gun," said Gareth. "Act first, change the law the day after. We should top up our tanks at the garage."

"Join every queue we can tag on to, along wiv the other feuls? Ye'd have thowt as we could behave better warsels."

"Very laudable sentiment, Jack," began Gareth, "but –"

"Could we please have a minute of silence for Mal?" asked Nell. "And to get our heads straight?"

"Good idea!" seconded Mitzi. "I went to the Quakers a few times when I was a kid. Mum and Dad thought they were getting rid of me to the Baptists, but they never went themselves so what did they know? I always liked the silences. The peace. Wasn't much of that at home."

"Yor right," said Jack. "We should show wor respect. Whisht, everyone."

But of course, through in the kitchen the radio was still on. Desert Island Discs, by now. The guest on the show

100

seemed to be some classical performer or conductor since he was talking about the world's concert halls. His next choice of record, one of Richard Strauss's *Four Last Songs*, began – melancholy, goldenly sensual. Maybe it was the last song in the world.

It cut off.

"We interrupt this programme for a newsflash. Reports are reaching us at the moment from the eastern Mediterranean that the American aircraft carrier *Enterprise* has been destroyed by a low-yield nuclear weapon. Several support vessels in the vicinity were crippled or sunk. We are going over to Mark Tully in Nicosia –"

"That's for Damascus," Gareth said blankly. "One for one. Tit-for-tat, you see. It isn't actually escalation. They said *low*-yield."

"You don't use five megatons te wallop a boat!"

"The poor shits," whispered Nell. "Burnt, blinded, boiled alive. Hundreds of people. Thousands."

"Less than in Damascus," mumbled Gareth.

Sixteen

At five Jeni announced, "I'm going out for a breath of air."

No more news of actual hostilities had been broadcast, though there were threats and counterthreats by Washington and Moscow, plus much analysis and improvisation from studio experts and foreign correspondents. The Territorial Army reserve had been called up by Queen's Order and reservists should report to their units the following day. Even that wasn't totally ominous, though as a commentator observed events were happening faster than anyone had ever predicted. Would all British forces be transferred to mainland Europe? – hardly an overnight manoeuvre – when thus far the death and destruction had happened in the Levant?

Police reported a twelve mile tailback on the M4 out of London to the West Country, as well as major congestion on other routes such as the M5 south of Birmingham and the roads to North Wales. These routes had now been closed and motorists were being urged not to leave home unless their journeys were essential. No doubt Gareth, back in Old Roses, was feeling exonerated.

Ports and airports were still operating normally, though the latter were besieged by people clamouring to fly to destinations supposedly out of harm's way: the West Indies, Guyana, West Africa.

Jack volunteered to tag along with Jeni on her walk, since Bess would be needing to empty herself. In fact, they could all do with a stroll.

"Thanks, but I'd rather be on my own. To think. I'll take Bess with me."

"We're crowdin' ye outa house n' home, pet."

"No, no. Besides, Nell and Mitzi will be sleeping next door. Let's all go to the pub when it opens. Andy and I were planning to go at lunchtime, but. . . . The pub'll either be totally empty –"

"Or else every bugger'll be there. Unless they'd rather gan te chorch te pray."

She shrugged and clicked her tongue to the dog, who came willingly. Soon she was wandering aimlessly down Green Street in the direction of the brook, with Bess lolloping ahead.

Every bugger did indeed seem to be in the White Lion that evening. With similar instinct, Tom Tate had opened early, and bother the Sunday licensing hours. Old Tom already had extra volunteer hands behind the bar. This was the only

102

way most people would get served inside of ten minutes. At this rate he would run out of beer by Wednesday, before the draymen were due to call again. By then would breweries be allowed to use petrol or roads or trucks? Right now Tom was coining it. Occasionally he flicked a speculative glance at the notice pinned to the main oak beam: SUNDAY SNOWBALL NOW £40.

Some lucky sod was bound to walk off with the snowball tonight. He'd instituted this at a mere five quid to buck up what was invariably a thin Sunday night. Until now. Week by week the snowball had accumulated. With the attention of most customers on world news, maybe he should try to sneak the sign down. Fat chance, with this mob to squeeze through!

The most recent news before Jeni and party had headed for the White Lion – collecting Gareth and Nancy en route – was that Warsaw Pact forces had pushed their massive manoeuvres through into East Germany, according to ham radio broadcasts picked up in Vienna. Seemingly some DDR units were being obstructive and were being swept aside. With casualties. So much for doubts about reinforcing Europe.

The usual taped music wasn't playing in the White Lion that evening. Instead a transistor set was propped beneath the optics, tuned to Radio One to catch any newsflashes. Meantime, Bruno Brookes was counting down the last of the Top Forty, mostly drowned by chatter.

"Who are this lot, then?" Bert Morris asked Jeni, and for a moment she worried that the villagers were about to turn their backs on all outsiders.

"The peace campers from Kerthrop, Bert, that's who they are. The Americans saw them off at gunpoint. They *shot* one man dead for arguing. They're blocking off the roads and expelling householders from Kerthrop village. They shot a British person."

103

"*What?*"

"It's true," confirmed Gareth.

Immediately the group became a centre of questions, incredulity, and as their story was heard, indignant sympathy; for the most part. The local battery pig farmer, Dennis Ainsworth – a flushed, belligerent fellow – declared that the American allies would only be doing the necessary to protect freedom, we should be damn glad of it, and lefties could sod off. Jack started shouting, but couldn't get close enough to collar Ainsworth, who looked as though he was spoiling for trouble in any case. Gareth calmed Jack. Fresh arrivals – farmers – brought word of lanes and fields occupied by USAF troops.

". . . But I've got ewes *lambing* in that field. 'See the commanding officer,' says soldier boy. How do I see him, eh?"

". . . The Russians mightn't have blasted those ships themselves! Maybe some Arabs got their hands on a nuclear bomb? They've been trying for long enough. I mean, otherwise that red fleet's a sitting duck for retaliation."

". . . Bulldozers churning up his rape for missile batteries. Does he get compensation?"

". . . That's Tears for Fears, with the biggest jump to four. Billy Ocean goes up!"

". . . Num-ber Threeee!" sang the gung-ho chorus line.

". . . They shot one of those peace campers as if he was a dog."

". . . You're in charge legally, George. You're the chairman of the PC. What should we be doing?"

George Vaux dragged on his moustache, perplexed.

The Anne Nightingale Request Show had been running for half an hour when it was broken into. Tom Tate flapped his arms, and the pub hushed.

". . . two Emergency Powers bills have been made law by royal prerogative –"

"They didn't *wait* for Parliament!" Jeni cried. "They just rammed those bills through by fiat."

"More like by tank, pet," said Jack.

"Shut up, we can't hear!" snapped Ainsworth.

Time warped onward, seeming to slow down and speed up unpredictably. There would be a broadcast by the Prime Minister on all radio and TV channels at eight o'clock, followed by the Home Secretary outlining the detailed provisions of those emergency bills, with which Jeni was all too familiar. . . .

"We're going to be interned," she whispered.

"If anyone has time to," Jack pointed out. "Things is whippetin' alang."

"What do they mean, agricultural stockpiles'll be requisitioned?" someone was demanding loudly. "And *oil* too?"

"You'll have to wait till eight, Roger!"

"You'll notice," Gareth commented, "that broadcasting becomes subject to ministerial direction. Maybe that's the last real news we're ever going to hear. We'll just be guessing from now on. I'll bet you the government isn't in London any longer."

It was then that Sheri Diamond forced her way through into the bar: hot-diggity Captain Ron's wife. She was blonde, blue-eyed, snub-nosed, with a very strong jaw, as if an orthodontist had not only perfected her white teeth but had decided they needed a superb foundation of marble. She was also slight – no pyramid-hips on her – but her American accents cut through the noise, quieting it as though somehow she might be bringing them the genuine global bottom line.

However, what she cried out a second time was, "Can anyone *help* me?"

Take Two: her blonde curls were damply matted. Her white wool sweater was soaked, delineating breasts a bit large for her frame – a polar bear nymphette after a swim. The bottoms of her tight jeans and her once-white sneakers were brown with mud. She clutched a torch.

"Mr Vaux, can you help?"

George thrust through. "What is it, Mrs Diamond?"

"Our boy Felix hasn't come home for hours. I've been hunting all over. The Kuzkas too. Ed and Carol are still out searching. Mary's at my house in case Felix . . . Ron's on duty."

"I bet he is," said dumpy Eric Bennett. The little man sounded unfriendly for once.

"I tried the new folks at the school house, but they aren't at home."

"Too busy shooting British people, I suppose."

"Eric!" George rebuked.

Ainsworth barged through, swaying; he'd been knocking them back. "The lady wants help, Bennett, not your lip. Right! Who's going to turn out and search?" He glared pugnaciously, his face as red as if he'd just walked across the Sahara, though drought played no part in his condition.

Bennett licked his lips, and smoothed back sparse slicks of black hair from the top of his cranium. "Ah, so she'll be wanting a posse? While thousands of kids are burning alive in Damascus!"

Oh, the worm was turning. Ainsworth grabbed Bennett by the lapels of his dark blue suit.

"What's wrong? You land a fat contract to supply beauty cream to the Syrians?" Ainsworth wrung Eric Bennett, almost lifting him off his feet.

"Some Syrians'll need more than beauty cream," squeaked Bennett.

"*I* didn't do that," protested Sheri. "Please!" she squealed, clinging to Ainsworth's arm.

Ainsworth released the little man, with a, "You aren't worth it."

Bennett dusted himself off. Muttered, "The peaceful intermediary, hmm." Tried to order a Scotch.

"Come, come, this won't do," said George.

"I phoned the police but I just get the out-of-order tone –"

"Domestic subscribers have been cut off at the exchanges, that'll be why," said Gareth.

"Wey, if the bairn's gan missin' we should aal pitch in. The police'd be as much use as scalded cats."

Ainsworth eyed Jack, his flushed face twitching. "That's the spirit."

Seventeen

Morning had broken, like the last dawning. All red and orange stops were pulled out on the colour organ; must be extra dust in the stratosphere. Jeni had fled to the churchyard to be by herself. Today the serried old gravestones looked like a filing system for dead families of bygone years, as if a score of skeletons had been compressed into each of those weathered rectangles. The golden lichen was dried flesh or remains of scalp. Worn chiselled dates were inaccessible code numbers in this stony data bank. Sheep, like woolly erasers, had used the memorial markers as rubbing posts and sparrows were scavenging the tatters of fleece to pad their nests.

Equally, Jeni was fleeing from herself. . . .

Last night they'd all missed the eight o'clock broadcast.

No matter; it was also the nine o'clock broadcast – and the ten o'clock one.

Felix Diamond had been found along the lane beyond the brook. A ford for tractors and a footbridge led on to the lane. Rough-surfaced and hedge-hugged, it wended a mile through pastures, past an isolated cow byre, till it reached the embankment of the one-time railway line. Shadowed by stands of Scots pine, the line, long since stripped of its rails and sleepers, was now one of Andy's "very long narrow fields". Felix hadn't been quite that far along.

The little boy was dead. Of course he was. Would you expect a half-naked child, whose bowels had been hauled out through his devastated anus and knotted round his neck, to be alive? He'd almost been turned inside out.

Jeremy Partridge and Ainsworth had found the boy. It had been Ainsworth's idea to call the vicar out to do his duty. Ainsworth smelled as if he'd vomited all his beer, and the vicar was stunned enough to break his lenten resolution with a very large neat gin back in the pub, when those two checked in as arranged by posse organizer Ainsworth.

They'd be needing a wheelbarrow to use as a stretcher, and a blanket to hide the contents.

Ought they to shift the body from the scene of death? Or should they leave it out overnight, with volunteers keeping watch in the wet mizzle? Hardly – when no one looked like being able to phone for any police or ambulance in the near future.

The news would have to be broken to Sheri Diamond, who was through in the pub kitchen with Mrs Tate. Mrs T was looking after her, encouraging her. Mrs Diamond had to be told that her boy was dead – but not how. She mustn't be allowed to see the corpse. The vicar would have to talk to her. Him, obviously. He was the right person. After just one more gin, to blind out the devil's abomination he'd seen. . . .

Other search parties were returning as agreed, to rejoin those who had stayed in the pub to co-ordinate. The new arrivals heard the news in whispers. Jeni, who had stayed, listened blankly.

Ainsworth was cold sober now, pallid with a sudden all-draining sobriety.

"What I saw, I tell you it's physically impossible. Not that anyone could bring themselves to do such a thing – though that's hard enough to credit. But that it could be done *at all*! I've seen a prolapsed sow or two in my time, but . . . someone, something, must've reached right up inside the poor little bastard and . . . yanked everything out. You tell 'em, vicar! I'm not spinning a. . . ."

Partridge said, "I couldn't believe what I saw in the light of the torch. The boy wasn't murdered. He wasn't . . . buggered to death. He was martyred." He drank. "God forgive me." For what? For the gin – or for a lapse of faith at the sight he'd had to witness?

"Evil is abroad," he murmured. "Foul evil."

"I'll help you collect the body," offered Bert Morris. "Where shall we take it, though? If that's the state it's in, we daren't even tell the woman where. How about the church?"

"No!" howled Partridge. "That would be allowing an abomination in. Something may have hidden itself inside the boy. Perhaps that's why it tore out his – "

"Divven't be so – !" Jack checked himself. Doubtless he was remembering the ghoul horses and their riders; he exchanged glances with Jeni and friends. Jeni could only think about the . . . toilet thing . . . which had come out of her and swum away.

George began, "Surely the church should protect – "

"No, I forbid it."

Tom Tate leaned over the bar. "*First*, get shot of Mrs Diamond. If you wrap the thing up well, and it's sealed

109

inside a few plastic bags, you can stick it in our cellar temporary. Till an ambulance can collect it. It's cold down there. Chilly as a morgue."

"What, put it right next to the beer we're drinking?" asked a voice.

"That's in casks. The little lad won't sup any. And don't look a gift horse."

"That's an outstanding offer, Tom," said George.

"I've got an empty cupboard down there, anyway."

"What about the teleph – " began Bert. He bit off his words. George was shaking his head violently. Tom mustn't have put two and two together yet about the phones and the emergency services. If he cottoned on, he might take his offer back.

"Yes, Tom's cellar!" Partridge spoke with utter certainty. That would be far enough away from St Mary's.

"The boy might have been done in some place else, and taken to where we found him." Ainsworth was playing detective, to sterilize an impossible experience. "Lane's muddy. I noticed recent drag marks."

No murderer would drag a little boy, thought Jeni. A murderer would carry such a light burden, especially if the person in question was strong enough to . . . do what had been done. A *dog* might drag its victim. She herself had been down that way with Bess, hadn't she? Bess the bestial molester! – she almost laughed.

Such marks in the mud as Ainsworth described might be the work of a thin boneless disembodied arm pulling itself along the ground as it escaped from the scene. Supposing it had compelled the boy to go there by clinging to him like a lamprey to a fish, by biting into his nervous system to pilot him. They might have been made by a yellow muscle creature which could force itself up a child's anus as if up a waste pipe, and fasten on with teeth or suckers then contract fiercely enough to expel itself along with the intestine

110

it was gripping. She sensed this occuring almost as clearly as if she was dreaming it, right there in the bar.

"You all right, Jen?" Mitzi was touching her.

"Yes . . . but how about Andy?"

Andy looked on the verge of fainting; Mitzi diverted her attention to him.

"So now I must tell Mrs Diamond," Partridge announced to one and all. "And take her home, yes! Take her well away from here so that you can bring the martyr back."

By ten o'clock the butchered corpse had been stowed away in the beer cellar. They had heard the Prime Minister address the nation, followed by the Home Secretary.

And amongst much else, such as the requisitioning of the assets of all private haulage and transport firms, the closure of petrol stations pending a priority allocations system, the outlawing of any strikes in a swathe of major industries, the takeover of British Rail, of all merchant shipping by Royal Prerogative, all aircraft by powers under the Civil Aviation Act, and the closing of all major roads so that city fire brigades, excavators and many other categories of vehicle could be redeployed into the countryside, they learned that private telephone subscribers were being disconnected. Temporarily.

Smart idea, to neuter subversive groups, to stop rumours spreading, to prevent panic or protest especially if the rumours were truth. And of what use was your phone when the police were too busy to answer, when fire engines and ambulances were speeding towards quarries and woodlands? "Constable! The US army just dynamited our house – will you do them for criminal damage?" "Hello, I want to report a nuclear explosion down our street. . . ."

Who had killed the boy so terribly? This horror, stunningly closer to home, competed with all those scaring government announcements. Yet Felix Diamond's death also seemed like a projection of those announcements into their midst in the most visceral fashion. It was a foretaste. Police had ceased to be available; a bandage had been torn away from their lives, causing its own wound. From now on the law might be an M-16 or a British Army weapon, but it would be the law of summary execution. For hoarding a sack of potatoes, or driving somewhere in your own car.

In addition to the vicar and Ainsworth, Bert Morris and Jack had actually seen the body raw when they went with Ainsworth to bag it and wheel it back. The pig farmer still insisted that what had been done to the boy was a physical impossibility, as though this could somehow alter the facts. Partridge hadn't returned to the White Lion. He'd still be consoling, still preventing Sheri Diamond from searching for wherever her boy might be – in a barn? in the back of a van? – in such a condition that no one would let her see him. Had the vicar felt obliged to confide in Mary Kuzka?

Andy was lolling drunk in a seat. Jack had been silent a long time before he said to Jeni:

"This aal has te do with them happ'nin's at wor camp, eh?"

"Do you mean it's a sort of tit-for-tat for Mal's death?"

He looked surprised. "Na. Aa mean it's the same kind o' thing. A paranormal thing."

"Maybe. . . ."

"Aa divven't shake no hands with it when it rives a bairn. Nay bairn's te blame. Nivva! Nell was right."

Nell was sitting by Andy, with a glass of cider in front of her. Occasionally she dipped a finger in and drew wet lines on the table top. Playing tic-tac-toe with herself? Pretending the lines were ley lines?

Nobody, least of all Tom Tate, was interested in the other end of licensing hours either, though people were beginning to filter away by eleven. Gareth and Jack had to guide Andy back to Jeni's; he puked in Green Street.

Jeni had feared that she would dream about Felix's murder by the toilet thing.

She didn't. She dreamed that she killed the boy herself.

She met Felix near his home. He was a fair, slim, quiet lad who knew he should be polite to villagers he recognized. Their voices were a bit funny, but they were friends. In the failing light he was swinging to and fro on a tyre roped underneath an oak tree. Waiting for Daddy to drive home? But Daddy wouldn't; Daddy was in the sky. Mommy and Daddy had been talking not long ago – serious talk – and he'd overheard some, which was why he hoped Daddy could drive back, snatching the boy up when Felix ran to him so that Felix flew for a while like a bird, like Daddy.

As Jeni walked towards Felix, she found she was reading his thoughts. She was linked to him, which was why the boy wouldn't worry, at first. Even though he guessed that Mommy and Daddy didn't like this lady much. He thought that Daddy regularly flew towards heaven, where a starred, striped flag also flew, on a white lawn of cloud. And his Daddy made thunder, which was like God's voice. God was Daddy's father in the sky, and somehow Mommy's too. But there were devil airplanes as well, which his Daddy might have to fight. Of course Daddy would win because of superior techknowledgy. Which meant knowing you were right.

When it started raining, like now – though it wasn't wet under the big tree – Daddy would land on a cloud and haul down the flag to keep it from spoiling. If a flag got wet, the colours might run into each other, then you'd never know whose flag it was. It might even turn all red.

That big black doggie sure walked funny, as though its back leg ached.

"Shall I push you?" asked the lady with the dog. "Shall I make you fly?"

He nodded. "Sure."

She stepped behind him.

Jeni strangled the boy then she lugged his limp body down the lane, skidding like a skater. Bess gambolled alongside, pausing to sniff and cock a leg. The boy mightn't be dead, only unconscious, but they were out of earshot now. A cow bellowed from the byre like a klaxon starting up, like the siren on top of the school gym which had gone off accidentally a few weeks earlier, scaring some of the third year half to death. Gone off accidentally – unless the siren was secretly being tested.

Here was far enough. As she ripped off the boy's shorts and underpants to give him his cervical smear she couldn't help noticing that her own right arm was becoming – it shifted before her eyes – a pale yellow tube, an unsegmented sausage of crap, a powerful muscle like a thin eel. What had been her arm plunged inside the boy, and she woke up screaming.

She bottled her scream, but Jack came hurrying upstairs, flipping on the light. She persuaded him to go away. A nightmare, that's all. Who wouldn't be having nightmares tonight?

As she stared eastwards, trying in vain to telescope her vision so as to see the roadblocks and Rapier missile batteries poking from bulldozed fields, the sun appeared, ruddy and quivering, through the golden curtains of dawning. A trio of jets – Phantoms – screamed overhead bearing southeast. She felt herself shoved as if by their slipstream, by a hand of air, into the chilly lee of the church tower.

A moment later the shadow where she stood went quite black. By contrast. The tower was a seam of darkest coal, a column of ink, behind which the brightest floodlight ever was switched on. The eastern sky glared bright white as burning phosphorus.

114

A millisecond earlier Kerthrop – or vicinity – had been nuked.

Eighteen

So therefore all the missiles in the world had been launched, and were being launched. All gone, all gone forever. In that expanded instant before death actually reached her, it was as if she was sucked empty, empty of any hope, and possibility. In the belly of her spirit there was instantly only desolate cold void.

This was more than mere emptiness; this was ultimate despair, total sorrow. Nothingness draped an arm around her shoulders, and showed her the end of life – not only of her own, but of all life. Life past and present, life future. Life all over the Earth, and the memory of all past life. Perhaps the only life existing in the universe. It died, disappeared.

In that moment of stunning light the whole future ceased to exist, ceased to be possible. And the past, all of history, all art, all knowledge, all civilizations, all gone.

Together with all birds and beasts, all flowers and songs and dawns. All beauty or desire, every dream or hope.

All gone.

Nothing mattered any more. Nothing could ever matter again. There would be no "again".

Her life had become death, but her lungs still took one more breath.

Standing there in the shadow of the church she shut her eyes and still could see. As she stood there in the cool of the wall, reflected heat baked her skin. In another second trees and thatched roofs and woolly coats of sheep would incinerate.

Next the blast wave would come. She would be a splattered egg upon the fabric of the church hurled westward.

Momentarily she twitched a glance. Such furnace light! Turf was steaming, winter's dead weeds were crisping. In after-image she saw the tower wall start to stretch, stones begin to separate from each other like that Channel Four logo –

She lost all sense of weight as though she'd fallen down a lift shaft. Dank darkness, strange silence, engulfed her.

She squinted. Then opened her eyes wide. Seconds had passed. The tower still stood. She still stood below it, giddily. Thin black mist boiled out of the ground everywhere, dissolving into the sky which had become a grey blank without content. Beyond the churchyard she could see, dimly but distinctly, cottage roofs. The toupée of one thatch had slipped. Slates had slid, exposing battens. Some damage. Hardly any. Where were the raging fires? Where was the blast wind, the hot hurricane from hell? Why was she, a dead person, still alive? Unharmed?

An inch-wide crack had riven the tower, zig-zagging down like a shaft of lightning. Yet otherwise. . . .

She looked twice. Surely that crack emerged *from* the foundations, from out of the soil, and wended upwards to where stones and mortar were still firm? As if the finger-fracture was clutching the tower together instead of cleaving it.

A sheep lurched into view, and Jeni almost threw up. She might well have done if the smell wafting to her nostrils hadn't been so enticing. That hot juicy smell of roast lamb. Wool had gone from all along one side of the animal. Exposed flesh was fresh-cooked, bubbling, dripping fat and broth stock. The animal was a walking side of mutton. One eye was blind, a boiled egg. Yet the sheep walked. Yet it lowered its half-cooked head to graze. Some teeth fell out of its jaw.

116

Jeni ran into the open. To the east, where she ought to be seeing . . . inferno, a mountainous, convulsing dirty lurid mushroom cloud full of spores of Kerthrop or Churtington . . . *nothing*. Nothing but the same grey quiet blanket.

"Something's wrong – terribly awfully *wrong!*" she thought in cold fear. Now she had time for fear. Fear had a chance to enter the emptiness in her. Could anything conceivably be worse than the nuclear war which she had just seen begin? No! But –

But she was alive, genuinely alive. Melfort hadn't burnt and blasted to shreds.

A nuclear explosion only miles away had been . . . negatived, neutralized. That wracked woodland over there. . . ! The heart of the sun had barely touched those trees. The blasting wind had brushed – brushed by. Space and time had warped around the village, the surrounding fields, enclosing them. What did that mean? It had no meaning. No sense. A protective blanket had fallen. Or risen. There was no possible protection. And yet there was. She was bleeding. No, she had pissed herself. This wasn't the sequel to a nuclear explosion as she'd ever imagined it. Not the aftermath of nuclear war. There couldn't be any sequel, any aftermath.

Just then she saw the vicar's black cloak lying near the south door. His body sprawled out underneath.

Body, body. Amongst broken ice of shattered glass, which wasn't stained glass. Greenhouse panes, hurled from further away.

Body. Only.

The vicar's sliced-off head had rolled several yards, to end perched upright facing in her direction.

The whipper-in of the church: his head had been whipped off. Jeni giggled in horror. There appeared to be very little blood . . . for a guillotining.

The bodiless head looked at her. *It did look.* The eyes

bulged. To express themselves. The jaw tried to move to open the mouth. Like a sheep grinding grass.

Terribly awfully wrong.

With skin clammy and gooseflesh crawling, Jeni stepped slowly towards the severed head. Her legs were bidding for promotion to the first division of the jelly league.

The head croaked. It was a big burping toad.

She bent, nearly buckling over.

"But you can't talk," she exclaimed crazily, "on account of your chin's upon the ground! The weight of your brain's pushing down, eh?"

Croak.

The vicar's eyes blinked. One for yes, two for no? Partridge had hazel eyes. She'd never really looked into them before. She'd never scrutinized his features quite so closely and, um, detachedly. That slim fastidious nose. Skin-ruts ploughed by the advancing season of middle age. The bald circle at his crown. Always before his thinning black hair had been bouncy and groomed, as if he shampooed it every morning. An eruption of sweat, doubtless due to the shock of decapitation, had plastered the hair to his scalp. Now his bald patch was a monkish tonsure.

On his left cheek grew a little brown mole with a trinity of stiff hairs. A miniature Cavalry. If she had a magnifying glass she might make out three tiny skin mites crucified to those bristles, enacting the passion on the Jerusalem of his cheek.

Plenty of glass lying around. Wrong shape, though.

Oh never so *detachedly*! She felt close to hysteria.

"What are you trying to say, Vicar?"

Croak.

The head appeared agitated – but who wouldn't be? His vocal chords couldn't be in much condition. Maybe they were a few yards away in his neck. Untuned, unstrung. The Reverend Jeremy's voice obviously needed restringing.

But then, its eyes ping-pong balls of effort, the head uttered a single wheezy word, which sounded to Jeni like: "Re . . . lic."

Of course! Why hadn't she thought of it? The martyr's relic, guaranteed to cure any agues or bilious megrims! Such as those caused by loss of body. Warranted to ward off wickedness. To restore amazed speech to the dumb. Roll up and be shrived! A snip at three florins! Only ten groats cost to the poor of the parish!

It was only when she'd carried the vicar's head gingerly into the church and saw the cage door wide open, with the reliquary deposited on the floor below, that she recalled her vile flash of vision on that previous visit.

Partridge had unlocked the cage. Key was still in the lock. He'd lifted out the stone turret. Been praying for a miracle, maybe. Rumbles in the heavens – those Phantoms – had lured him anxiously outside.

The head rocked excitedly in her hands. Perhaps it was desperate to turn *away* from that empty cage? Silly! – how could it move of its own accord? Her hands were shaking, that was all.

Turning Partridge's head so that it would face outwards, she put it into the cage. A lot safer in there! Safe from crows and rats – the bars stood close together. Maybe not safe from mice . . . were there any church mice in St Mary's?

Kneeling, she lifted the gabled lid off the turret. In the hollow within on a purple velvet pad lay the anonymous dusty throat bone. A horned hyoid bone, oddly reminiscent of . . . a jaw's harp! *Twang-twang, twang-de-twang . . . de-doo-de-dah-de-twang*. Through the witching medieval forests, just like in Bergman's *Seventh Seal*. . . .

Wasn't it obvious what she had to do? The vicar's eyes goggled either in ghastly protest or in welcome – welcoming the communion wafer – as she prised his lips apart and thrust the throat bone into his mouth. His teeth closed on her fingers painfully. With a cry she snatched her hand away to suck at the hurt. He'd almost drawn blood. Then other dead muscles convulsed; the bone was gulped back inside him. Jeni slammed the cage door, locked it, pocketed the key.

The mouth began to gasp. Tongue jutted. Teeth clamped. Some dark maroon blood welled sluggishly, seeming already half coagulated.

Then the mouth opened wide and vomited a torrent of brown lumpy filth. Flecks squitted on to Jeni's anorak and hands. She smelled shit.

She'd often thought the vicar talked a load of crap.

Where could the filth have come from?

Terribly, ghastly wrong.

At last Jeni shrieked. She fled from the stony echo of her squeals out into the porch. She noticed the big old church key still in its keyhole, locked the main door, pocketed that key too – and continued her flight out into the graveyard, into that eerie quiet greyness, where a roast sheep grazed. Staggered. Grazed.

PART THREE

Nineteen

"Gar-eth – *Jones*!" he exclaimed to himself over and over.

Verbal equivalent of a limp. Ideal marching tune to propel himself, when his own dead body lurched and shambled so.

"Gar-eth – *Jones*!" Hup-one-two. Or in his case: huppity one-and-a-half.

Must keep going. Get there. (Where? And where had he been? He forgot.)

"Gar-eth – " How many times had he said those words? A hundred? Ten hundred? And what did they mean?

Just then a black cloud rolled away from the sun in his mind, and he could think clearly for a while. So he halted.

He was standing by the lamp post in the middle of the green, facing towards Green Street. The goat sat, chained, its Uncle Ho beard tickling the dingy grass. Milky cataracts blinded both its eyes, and most of the hair had fallen out of its sagging flanks, where a few open sores gleamed slickly. Otherwise it seemed content to munch meditatively on nothing in particular, going through the motions. Curved handles of its horns were two question marks of bone.

The ducks on the pond were also on auto-pilot, swimming in circles like wind-up bath toys. Two looked plucked for the oven. The others, which had kept their feathers, could well have stuck *in* the oven for a while before being snatched out again hastily and dunked. Somehow one duck swam upside down, its orange webs wagging in the air. Semaphoring monotonously, "Turn me right way up!" Its nervous system had been scrambled worse than –

Gar-eth – *Jones's*!

"Stop it," he told himself. Now that he'd woken out of his Gar-eth trance he could think some new thoughts. He could remember the warhead exploding. Got up early, he did. Furnace doors opened to spill white-hot steel all over him. He wasn't sure what happened afterwards except that he'd been very badly dead for a time.

A half-life: that's what he was living now. There's an improvement, boyo. A few moments ago he'd been as badly off as that duck.

As badly off as the other villagers. Putrescent puppets, that's what. Rotten bodies with automaton brains. He'd been that, too. Wasn't even a half-life.

Was he genuinely better off now, all of a sudden? Much about "life" remained a mystery. He could feel loss, grief, resentment, and torment at what he was missing. He knew who the living ones were. They were Jack and Bert. Jeni and Nell and Mitzi. And Sheri Diamond. A disproportion of females. Why *them*? Why not himself? Bloody unfair.

He should be able to remember what life was all about – except that it was a state of existence almost as far beyond his own as a human being is beyond a sheep. Difference between a live performance and a recording, eh? He felt he was brightening up. Yes, he was a sort of flexible recording – interactive – which could join in a duet with the living. After a fashion; if the living let him. Otherwise the disc, the tape merely repeated itself automatically, to itself. Some discs were scratched and warped worse than others. Some tapes were half blank, and tied in knots.

How long had he been in his Gar-eth trance? How long since doomsday? Time appeared meaningless. He knew it remained light for hours on end, in a gloomy grey way, but he couldn't recall noticing a sun. It also remained black for hours on end; he couldn't recall moon or stars. Maybe days had passed, maybe weeks.

Was he really getting well again? Might he even become *alive*? Like Jack and Jeni? Whatever "alive" had been.

No. Or not yet. Something had cranked him up, filled

him with missing purpose, to do . . . what? Why, to force Jeni to go to St Mary's; that was it.

(And something more, too.)

Outside the wooden bus shelter three dead girls stood in mute vigil, juvenile dummies from a bombed shop window. The trio must be waiting for the school bus, which would never arrive, to take them off to . . . Churtington, yes, that's where. First Years, by the size of them. Names? No idea. Their mostly hairless heads were covered in mouldy scabs and their exposed legs were suppurating with gummy ulcers. The eyes of one girl were of ground glass hooded in purple oozing lids. Nevertheless they'd put on their school uniforms: the cherry-red blouse, the serge navy skirt. That's how he knew they were girls. The blouses were stained by slimy leakage from the slow rot of flesh beneath. Oddly, it was the girl who looked blind who had managed to put on both of her black shoes. Routine memories must have stirred in those three girls that morning. How long would they wait before trudging back home? All day, till the hour when the bus ought to have returned with them?

That was how the dead mostly lived, unless the village hall committee stirred them up. Gave them a kind of physiotherapy, animated them, wound them up like faltering clocks. Just as he'd been stirred up by the committee from time to time, he recollected, though at the time he hadn't understood; he'd only responded.

The village hall committee! Anguish spiked his heart. *He'd been animated. . . .*

For a moment he peaked, so it seemed, into genuine full life, and marvelled as on a high mountain at a vista of memory, understanding – and terror. *Oh my God, I was dead, what is operating me? Like a glove puppet. What is operating those schoolgirls?*

If his mind was a fruit machine like the one in the White Lion, then the jackpot line had just tumbled into place.

However, this winning line wasn't three golden bells. It was three grinning skulls, each with a snake sliding through the open jaws like an amorous tongue.

Yes, he saw this clearly in his mind's eye. Instead of the fruit machine playing a victory tune, the three skulls spoke:

"And to her was given the key of the bottomless pit," they chorused.

"And she opened the bottomless pit.

"And in those days shall men seek death, and shall not find it. . .

"And shall desire to die, and death shall flee from them. . .

"And shall not suffer their dead bodies to be put into graves."

And instead of coins clanking into the silver tray, shit spewed into it.

A moment later the black cloud covered his inner sun again. But by now he knew what he had to do. *Both* the things he had to do.

A tug at his ankle almost unbalanced him.

The goat was munching the soiled tatters of his trouser leg, perhaps a flap of skin too, though he felt nothing, thought nothing about it. Tearing free indifferently, he stumbled on his way, past the three fouled mannequins of schoolgirls.

The marching tune in his mind was different now.

"Je-ni – *Church*!"

Twenty

The village committee were meeting at Jeni's place. Of the six people who had survived the end of the world intact and

126

entire, Bert Morris had not only been a member of the former village hall committee but also a parish councillor. Since the Parish was the last ditch authority when the final chips were down, by rights Bert had become chairman of the new committee.

Its members were all too aware that a different, invisible authority ruled the village of the dead now. Something unbelievable, mischievous, foul; something which could animate the dead and could spin out their terminal dying interminably, and keep corpses abominably on their feet, rotting, shuffling, and mumbling. The village was plasticene, play-dough in its vicious idiot hands. A hell for its amusement.

Melfort and surrounding farms was a necroquarium, an aquarium of living death. Some power had encapsulated the village, putting an unseen wall around it, and in the sky too a grey blank ceiling.

Outside of Melfort and its environs, out in the burned, blasted, poisoned wasteland of nuclear winter, snow might be tumbling, icy radioactive gales could be howling over ruins and dead land. It could have been *The Revelation* come true.

Sheri had pointed this out. She'd had to study that book of the Bible in school. The sun had probably become black, the heavens would have vanished like a scroll behind smoke, wormwood would have polluted the waters, the soil itself would have been sickled from the rock. Yet of the scorching with great heat, they'd experienced only half a second. Of the smoke of torment, barely a sniff. The village was locked as if with seven seals. They were closed away inside the village and surrounding land, within a grey fog. And Melfort had no need of the sun, neither of the moon.

And the repulsive dead continued to amble about, or stand in the same familiar spot for hours, or loll about at home in foul armchairs, or lie in reeking beds. Never quite sleeping. Rarely eating much at all, drinking sparingly, if eating or drinking occurred to them.

Oh yes, and Bess the labrador was alive, unlike other pet animals and deadstock which wandered around stunned or stayed still. Catatonic cats, dog derelicts, cadaver cows. Bess couldn't be a member of the new committee, though.

Amazingly so to the others, in spite of her son's hideous murder the very night before the nuclear war, Sheri Diamond had rallied and pitched in on organizing – to the extent that they could – this foul farce of Melfort's post-mortem existence. Sheri now saw Felix's agonizingly sordid death as a preliminary tentacle from the evil power which had grabbed hold of the whole village as its plaything. Once it had tormented them all sufficiently to satisfy its taste, once it had tuned this torture of a false, mad survival to the point where they actually began to hope . . . *then*, Sheri suspected, would be the time when *it* laughed and hitched up its cloak to let in the cold and the darkness, the radiation, and the last despairing eternal end. Meanwhile, there was something in a person – a defiant, exploitable *animal* something, or spiritual something maybe – which made them try to continue. This was in her; that's why *it* had let her survive, the more to enjoy her final defeat, when the time came and the last drop had been squeezed. But she'd sure as hell go down fighting, as Ron would have done. At least she thought so. Hoped so. And hope could so easily be her betrayer. So easily.

As Jeni sorted through the minutes of the last meeting, her mind was more on Sheri, wondering how fragile Sheri's strength might be. Yes, Jeni had become minutes secretary. How chuffed Gareth, whom she had once known, would have been. . . .

Poor brave Sheri was ample proof of how the Power would play its games of clever cruelty. Perhaps it murdered and

128

mutilated Felix just so that it could keep his mommy fully alive and fully aware.

On the morning when the war began (and probably ended too) it hadn't taken the few survivors too long to find each other. Jeni had met up with Nell, Mitzi, and Jack – and Bess – back in Green Street.

There, Sheri had seen them. She'd been staying overnight at the Kuzkas, numb with grief, and had finally wept herself to sleep assisted by several large bourbons. She'd been roused by a zombie Mary Kuzka blundering into the bedroom, her nightdress stained with piss and diarrhoea, her blotched limbs jerking, her face a mess of dripping sores, only tufts of her hair remaining. The smell of her was foul.

Sheri had screamed wildly but couldn't wake herself up from the nightmare, since she was already wide awake. As Mary glugged at her incomprehensibly, Sheri fled past her to find Ed swaying in the corridor, his arms hanging flaccidly. Dressed in candy-striped shorts, his body also was striped with puffy, livid weals. His face twitched with palsy. A Staffordshire dog had tumbled from a shelf and lay smashed. A water-colour had fallen, cracking its glass.

Still screaming, Sheri fled to Carol's room and found the girl rocking feebly from side to side on her bed, wearing only rags of pyjamas. Her body was as palely pink and soft and drippy as a bad side of slaughtered pork. Except for her left arm; this was twisted in stiff rigor, a claw of a hand clutching a much-loved stuffed toy, a Snoopy hound.

Carol's eyes, like two burnt-out pearl light bulbs, fixed on Sheri. Goitrous cancers adorned her neck.

"Gurgle, gurgle," said the girl.

Then Sheri had really gone nuts, till she met the others.

And this, Jeni remembered, was how it had been by and large throughout the village. In their shaken, though undemolished, houses, people had become week-old, month-old living corpses as if time had been tied into knots. Some had been sliced as though by flying glass, some crushed and battered as by collapsing masonry, or badly burnt. Many had been rotted by radiation, and then rotted rather more by death's tenderizing, stinking, maggoty touch – this was true of all the living dead.

But as Galileo remarked slyly a few hundred years before, once he'd recanted:

Epour si muove. "Yes, it moves."

Yet the corpses moved. Dead, but they couldn't lie down. Not in oblivion, not in peace. The best they could do in that line was slump exhaustedly, pretty much in a trance; not that there was anything pretty about it.

For his part Bert Morris was already up and about collecting eggs in the deep litter hen house, prior to helping George with the morning milking. No caged battery birds for Farmer Vaux; he was even talking of going fully free-range for the sake of his hens almost as much as for the extra price premium. The world had lit up, and Bert had thrown himself into chaff and shavings. Briefly parts of the hen house became a microwave oven. Several birds flopped, sizzling, from perches. Others staggered with advanced foul pest. Then with a sickening twist came the sudden grey silence.

Bert had rushed outside just in time to see George Vaux turn into instant-corpse, rotten with maggots. And begin to shuffle in a circle.

Unable to help the boss – unable to think *how*, since the horror he saw made no sense at first – Bert had dashed the few hundred yards home, spying a broken window and slates dislodged from his cottage roof. Half way there, it had come to him that there must have been some kind of nuclear explosion such as Jeni Wallis was forever going on about, and quite right too after the latest terrifying news, though she did rather go over the top (*pant, pant*), and the country probably needed credible defences the way the world was these days (*pant*), but how could the bomb have been dropped and farm and buildings still be standing? – unless it was one of those neutron bombs (*pant*) which only destroyed people and other living things; but in that case how was everything so still, why was there nothing but a grey overcast?

Back at Farm Cottage he'd found his missus Pauline in the kitchen, a mouldering carcass standing at the sink in soiled skirt and sweater, who responded to her hubby with the dribbly, reeking affection of a cow for its calf, so that he shrank back revolted.

"Hel-p me, Ber-t," she'd spluttered. "We'll be laaaate for June's wed-ding."

It was ten years since daughter Jane had been wed. Mastering his nausea and the pluckings of insanity, he'd guided her through into their little sitting room, sat her down, and tried to clean her up a bit, but carefully so as not to knock any parts off. In case the dead felt the cold, he put a rug over her.

Afterwards he'd gone up the village and met Sheri Diamond who desperately needed comfort, almost more than he did himself; and then the others.

Twenty-one

It was early evening of that same war day when, led by window climbing Jack with a flashlight, they broke into a dismally dim White Lion to find Tom Tate at his usual post behind the bar.

Tom's head was glutinous, coated in dark jelly. His lips had fallen away, exposing long discoloured teeth in gums like blancmange. One eye was a pit of maggots like an eggcup of fisherman's bait. One dangling, viscous hand had lost all the flesh from two fingers. The man wore slacks and shirt and carpet slippers, soiled by the corrupting of his body. Bulges pressed against the stained shirt as though his innards had broken loose through his belly.

Eppur si muove. Still, he moved.

Tom's other, bleary eye regarded them, and he grunted like a wistful pig whose sty had been peered into.

Fortunately the light was very poor, even later when they fetched candles from the pub kitchen, where Tom's wife slouched confusedly in a state marginally worse than her husband. She smelled even fouler than him.

Too much to expect a corpse to think of unlatching the door at opening time. Too much to expect him to find candles or light them. Too much to expect old Tom to serve any drinks without spilling most of them, though he looked disposed to try, if he could remember how. Jack had gently eased Tom aside to do the honours.

By then they'd mostly come to terms with the truth that all the other villagers weren't so much *dying* of the blast or burning or radiation that had seriously injured them, shocked them into near-idiocy, scrambled their nervous systems. The villagers were already dead, kaput, finito, *had* been corpses from the start. Yet they continued to exist in a foul hangover of their previous lives, a sick parody.

Gareth, too, and Nancy; they'd left that pair at Old Roses looking like two *papier mâché* people who'd been left out in an acid rainfall.

Andy was another of the living dead. But then, he had already given up the struggle . . . in a way. Hadn't he?

As the evening wore on a few dead regulars wended their way clumsily into their habitual watering hole and stood or slumped about in a mockery of their usual custom, failing to drink, failing to talk, but present nevertheless. As was their odour.

Half a dozen candles burned.

132

Sheri had been nursing a Southern Comfort. "If these guys are all, well, *continuing* even though they're all dead. . . ." Her voice shook as much as her glass. "Do you s'pose . . . my Felix might have . . . come back to life? I got to know where he is! I got to see him *now*! He might be . . . saved." The word sounded flat and foul as last week's slop tray.

Jack exchanged glances with the others.

"I got to! Don't you see? Whatever kinda shape he's in. You've no *right* to – " She tailed off, then her jaw jutted. "To keep him from me."

Bert was shaking his head firmly at Jack. But Jack grinned, ghastly.

"Wey, Ha'll just gan doonstairs an' take a look, pet."

"He's *here*?"

"We put your poor bairn doon in the cellar, where it's cool. Howay, Landlord, gee us some scissors."

"Scissors?" cried Sheri. "What are they for?"

"He's inside some plastic bags."

"*Different* . . . bags?"

"Na, he was all in one piece. Aw, I'll take that lemon slicer." So saying, Jack snatched the knife and a candle and departed.

"What . . . what was done to him?" Sheri asked. "I think I can take it. I guess I probably saw worse today."

"Better wait till Jack gets back," advised Bert.

Which wasn't many minutes, though in the meantime Jeni experienced a mounting dread that Felix might be alive after all. Maybe the Power would have repaired the boy after a fashion by stuffing some guts back inside him. Down there in the beer cellar cupboard, wrapped in rubbish bags, Felix might have been whimpering for his mommy: a scarecrow corpse whom Sheri would still try to cuddle and console irrespective of his condition so that she would be like an ape mother at the zoo, insane and lost to them, toting her dead rotting bundle of baby, a corpse which might point a little pinkie at Jeni. . . No!

In came Jack with knife and candle.

"Na hinny, I a's sorry to say your lad's still deed. I a wad imagine that's cos he died last noot, so he couldna benefit like everyone else. I a'm really sorry, Missus Diamond."

"You *are* telling the truth? Felix isn't alive again but. . . ."

"Too fettled to be much of an athlete, ye mean? Na. We'll bury him decent in the chorchyard – tomorrow or the day after, eh? Can't leave him lyin' doon there. Listen, Missus, what wes done to him wes his tripes wes aal drawn ot an' tied in a knot roond his gizzard. That was nay human crime. It was done by whitever power's in charge now, gettin' its hand in afore havin' its fun with everyone else."

"Yes. Of course." Sheri frowned. "Thank you for telling me."

Oddly she seemed to accept this atrocious account coming from Jack's lips. It occured to Jeni to wonder whether the American woman could have understood half of what Jack said. Jack might as well have told her in Norwegian. The *fact* that he'd told her was what counted. The manner of Felix's murder wasn't too abominable even to be uttered: that relieved her mind, just a bit. And Sheri visibly made up her mind to accept this, and ask no other details. Jack, who'd been watching her reaction circumspectly, nodded to himself. He must have chosen his words intentionally. Jeni felt a surge of gratitude and warmth towards him.

Good thing that Sheri hailed from somewhere in the Mid-West, not from Appalachia or New England or wherever they still spoke vintage English, otherwise she might have understood. Might have.

Where was Appalachia now? Where was the Mid-West? Burnt, blasted, poisoned, frozen. They must be. Along

134

with Russia and Europe and everywhere else. Could Sheri somehow suffer a larger loss because she came from a larger country?

Dead Ned Boxall tottered towards the bar, wagging an empty dimple mug which had never been full. Dead Tom Tate focused his functioning eye foggily on it.

"Pint of," said Ned indistinctly, and set down his glass an inch short of the bar top. The mug crashed on to the floor, though the thick glass didn't break. Mitzi giggled hysterically.

"Wey," said Jack, "we should organize worsels. These lads needs supervizin'. The haal village does. We mustn't shork."

"You're right," said Sheri. "We'll *work*, together. We'll survive. We'll keep . . . the wounded . . . walking. Give them a purpose."

Bert nodded. "Let's form ourselves into a proper committee. Let's do that tomorrow. I . . . I must go back and see to Pauline."

Nell asked him hesitantly, "You aren't planning to stay at home, are you?"

"With my dead wife in the house? Is that what you mean?"

Nell nodded.

"What else should I do?"

Nell laid a hand on Sheri's. "Can I come and stay with *you*, for company?"

"Oh yes. Yes!"

"Me too," Mitzi chipped in. "Okay? I couldn't sleep on my own at that Gareth's. I know it sounds silly, but I wouldn't feel safe."

"You're more than welcome."

"We'd best shift wor Andy in with yor neighbours, hadn't we, Jen?" said Jack. "Aa cuddn't exactly fyace sharin' a room wiv the lad."

*

That night while Jack kipped downstairs on the sofa – with the durrah rug hauled over Jeni's sleeping bag "as a hap to keep worm", since there was no longer any electricity supply – up in the Dolly Mixture nursery every now and then Jeni hove into wakeful awareness in her bed like some sea mammal, a seal, surfacing for air, as though in the meantime of unconsciousness Melfort might have moved back to what it was before the war, and before the Power gripped the village; as though she might find herself in sight of some headland of sanity.

In vain.

At least no dreams came to her, nor nightmares.

No need. Nightmares had already taken up residence in all the houses round about.

Twenty-two

So the next morning at Jeni's the committee had got down to business for the first time, most wearing thick sweaters against the March chill. Bert Morris, chairing. Jeni, as secretary. Jack volunteered himself as treasurer and proposed Sheri as bookings officer.

"Or ye could call Sheri social secretary," he explained, "cos we have to organize events, divven't we? To keep the corpses tickin' over. Rouse them oot o' their houses, into yor hall an' the boozer. An' the dead bairns need their play, an' maybe a bit of edicatin'."

Bert stared at him. "Gareth was supposed to be organizing a wine and cheese evening. But surely you aren't proposing –?"

"Gannin' on wiv it? Wey not, man? Wey not a darts toornament? Then there's them skittles. An' folks as gans

136

to chorch could try a bit o' singin', te remind them. Wey, we could whip up a congregation for the funeral."

"No!" cried Jeni. "Not in church!"

She'd almost managed to forget about the vicar. She must never go back inside St Mary's, ever again. That church should be out of bounds. Nobody should enter it. Because. If they did. She glanced in panic at the bare pine planks of her floor, but of course Jack had rolled the durrah up and stuck it away out of sight behind the sofa to stop the rug from getting dirty if any of Jeni's visitors trod mud in without thinking to wipe their feet. You couldn't blame someone for forgetting. Not in the circumstances, coming in out of that eerie grey pall.

Jack oughtn't to have lain asleep under that rug with its tree of doves. The rug could creep, and change! It could hide a yawning pit.

The floor was perfectly solid, and Jack had assured her the sofa was comfortable.

"Not in the church," she improvised. "That would be a parody, like holding a black mass."

"Wey, Aa didn't knaa ye were religious, Jen."

It would seem like a service to propitiate the Power, to worship it. Since what other power was there? And *that* Power certainly existed; whatever its nature.

"Sheri here might be religious," went on Jack. "She may appreciate a service even if it's of wor own devisin'."

"No, no, not there! In the graveyard, yes, but not inside the church. Don't you see how the Power might enjoy that?"

"It could equally relish us stuffin' him in the groond without a service. Let's come back to the Power under any other business, or whatnot? Aa've some notions."

"I don't see anything irreverent about simply laying a body in the good soil," said Nell. Jeni quickly nodded agreement.

137

"Quaker-style might be best," suggested Mitzi. "A time of silence."

"Whoa!" Bert held up his hand. "We need to take things one at a time, or we'll get nowhere. We need a proper agenda. Jack's right about tabling certain items under any other business. As to your little boy's funeral, Mrs Diamond, it's surely your wishes that count."

"I don't have . . . wishes for Felix. Not any more. I daren't have wishes."

Bert nodded his sympathy. "I'd better add one note of caution. Our vicar kept St Mary's locked up a lot of the time. He worried himself about vandals. Naturally the churchwarden and the caretaker and the flower rota held keys too, but we mightn't be able to lay hands on those if the church happens to be locked. We can't exactly break into the church the way we bust into the White Lion."

"Of course not!" agreed Jeni.

"Aa'll gan an' see if it's locked. Later on."

"You do that, Jack," said Bert. "Now, if our pro-tem secretary has her pen poised, let's work out a proper agenda."

Jeni poised her biro over a largely unused John Clare exercise book from which she had torn out the essay on the non-existent British Revolution. How about an essay for next week, class, on the causes of the Third World War? *That* happened. That wasn't imaginary history. Only, no one would ever write a book about it. Or print one. Or read one. Ever.

"Hang on a mo," interrupted Nell, "why should we need a treasurer? Money means nothing any more."

"Money's nowt, pet, you're reet. But we have te inventory aal the canned food in the village, an' drinks. The deed mightn't be peckish but we've got to eat. The power's off, so freezers is buggered. Aa divven't see any falls of manna from the heavens."

"Oh God, so we're going to starve."

"Na, Nell, there's the village shop, an' folks's larders, an' the pub. Likely there's enough bait for a year or two. We also got te dee something aboot the animals an' chickens an' things."

"Right," said Bert, "we'll table the inventory straight after the election of officers. Come to think of it, maybe Jack ought to be in the chair."

"Na, man, you're the properly constituted authority. An' once we get wor hoosekeepin' sorted oot, someone's got te take a trip by bike doon the road to see what's outside Melfort, if anythin'. That's a job for the treasurer."

"By bike?" echoed Mitzi. "That's crazy. You'd need a car for protection."

"The electromagnetic pulse from the bomb could have fettled any car electrics, pet. Besides, Aa'm thinkin' that maybe we'd not get very far afore the Power stopped us somehow. Aa suspect that's what we'll find. Ye divven't suppose any bugger as pleases can traipse in an' oot of a paranormal village of the deed, dee ye? Though Aa'm curious te knaa for sure. . . ."

For lunch following the meeting they grazed on perishables from Jeni's dead fridge. As Jeni had been dreading, Jack then took himself off for a quick sortie to the church.

Why should she worry? He wouldn't get in.

While Jack was gone, they sat drinking Nicaraguan coffee made with water boiled on Nell's gaz camping stove which she kept in the boot of her VW. They sorted out the afternoon's tasks: make a start on the inventory – then animal welfare – then social work. Rather than wine and cheese in the village hall they had resolved to kick off the season's events with a skittles tournament held in the White Lion, ordinarily a popular item.

Ten minutes later Jack returned out of breath.

"Chorch is locked aal reet . . . body lyin' ootside as looks like the vicar . . . ye knaa, black cloak an' paraphernalia – "

"That's Partridge," Bert confirmed.

"His bloody heed's missin' – "

Oh yes, *that's* why she had been worrying.

"Aa couldn't see his heed nowhere. An' he's plain deed. He ain't up an' aboot like aal the other corpses."

"How could he be, without a head?" Bert asked wearily.

Sheri shivered. "Maybe the Power hates men of God. It *would*, if it's the opposite. Maybe it got rid of his head so that the church would have no head, no voice." (And Jeni kept quiet as a mouse.)

"Aye, to make him had his gob. Aa wonder if we should bury his body incomplete? That might be a mistake. How aboot we just hump him back to his vicarage an' stow him there?"

"His bungalow?" Jeni agreed vigorously. "That's the best place. That's where he belongs."

"Dee we aal concur?"

"I'll help you shift him," offered Bert, "but let's pop down to my place first. We'll probably need a barrow. And I'd like to look in on my Pauline."

That wasn't, as yet, the particular committee meeting towards which Gareth would be stumbling. . . .

Twenty-three

A congregation for Felix's funeral! They hadn't even tried to drum up an audience. Yet by the time they had privately scheduled – three o'clock – a dozen and more walking corpses had wandered into the overcast graveyard as if by homing instinct. These were the better class of walking corpses, such as Harry Blesworth's old Dad and Ned Boxall, Marianne Bennett thickly caked in face powder now, and snoopy Enid Jackson whose goitre looked almost fashionable these days; not to mention Nancy and Gareth. They were still a piteous, soiled, decaying bunch, exhibiting sores and swellings, discolouration, drippage, and nervous disorders. Enough maggots and mould were in evidence.

Jack had dug a small grave that morning, about three feet deep. No coffin had been fashioned out of boards or pallet wood; there was just too much else to do, and the result might have been tatty. So Felix was wheeled to the churchyard by barrow and lowered into the grave still in his black rubbish bags.

They stood in silence for a while, the way Mitzi had advised. Jeni stared away into the grey haze which had once been a view of fields unrolling towards Kerthrop. Now there was nothing at all, just a consuming emptiness. The dead pressed closer round her.

"Would anyone mind terribly?" Sheri quavered, "if I sang . . . the Star-Spangled Banner over him?"

"Wey, ye dee what ye need te dee, Missus."

So Sheri began to sing. Her voice rose clear and proud, and to her own amazement Jeni found herself humming along. "Dum-ti-dum-dum-dum-dum – " Her throat puckered, and her eyes were wet with tears. How could she possibly weep at the American national anthem? Oh it wasn't merely the music, the emotive music. And the emotive words. She could as easily have wept for the Marseillaise just then. "Da-*da*-dada-*da* – " No, that was a lie. She was weeping for all the human hope and energy and glory embodied in that particular anthem. The dawn's early glow. The twilight's last gleaming. She wept for all that had been lost. For the future, for space and the stars which human beings would never now touch. For cities of endless light and freeways. For freeways which had been warped by

141

military men and mega-money corporations and media preachers and patriotic politicians and secret agencies until a great society became a sort of lethal octopus squeezing the world and finally crushing it – by accident or by mistake or by the design of plausible madmen who believed in a personal God and a fetishised flag and crusades for their own version of freedom.

As Sheri sang, Jeni realized that she quite loved America deep down, in a gut way in which she couldn't really love Russia or China, but the America that she loved had been deeply submerged like some wonderful Atlantis by its own visible and invisible leaders under the waves of destructive power. In a way America had been ruining its own inner self years before the greater, nuclear ruination. Yet its people, when they weren't pointing an M-16 at you, were usually as wonderful individuals as Sheri was right now. Even though Sheri was a nuclear bomber's wife, widow. Even though.

So Jeni wept.

When Sheri stopped singing, she smiled lamely.

"Sorry, you guys," she said, "but it's part of me. Jesus, I'm so lonely."

Mitzi moved to touch her. "We're your family now, Sheri. We're all each other's family."

"You know, when I used to go to summer camp as a kid to do the frontiersman routine . . . how to cook on an open fire, pitch a tent, handle a canoe . . . I was always scared of touching the flag in case I let it fall. There's a special way of folding it, into a pocket handkerchief. There's a whole art. Whenever it started to rain we'd rush to haul down the flag and fold it, and if it even touched the ground I used to think the earth would open." She looked at the open earth of the grave where her son lay inside rubbish bags. "If that happened, you'd have to kneel next to the flag and kiss it forty times. Some girls said twenty times would do." She looked as though she might sink on her knees by the grave and kiss the soil, but then she stiffened. "One girl said you wouldn't have to kiss it, but you'd never see that same flag again. It would have to be hidden away in shame because it had been dishonoured. Hidden." She kicked some soil down on to the shapeless black lump; then some more. Mitzi led her aside. Bert took over, with a spade. Soon the grave was a modest hump.

Somehow the dead had hemmed Jeni round, separating her from the others. The dead were nudging her, trying to herd her – towards the church door! Gareth was in the forefront of this moribund mini-mob. He gargled incomprehensibly at her. So did Enid Jackson, her suppurating goitre wobbling like a huge turkey's wattle. Gareth's skin was bright pink with leaky sores as an ape's bum.

What did they want? She feared she knew too well. They wanted her to unlock the church and go into it to confront . . . what they knew was there. But they were feeble and unco-ordinated in their attack. It was almost an attack. How they stank.

She broke free roughly and ran to join her friends. Behind, the dead milled slowly, confused. Wondering where she'd gone to, like a rabbit who has a juicy apple leaf snatched away from in front of its nose and can't work out where the thing went to. Filling its universe one moment; vanished the next. You'd never fool a cat the same way. But the dead weren't cats, they were skinned twitching simple-minded bunnies. Their re-animated minds chewed thoughts that were dead grass.

It must have been the close proximity of the church that afternoon which made the dead try to crowd her and manipulate her. When, a few evenings after, the White Lion was jam-packed with corpses for the skittles tournament Jeni felt in no way pressured by any of them, only by the smell. It was she and the other survivors who had to do the manipulating, urging the dead to the pub like cows at milking time, like sheep to a new pasture; and once players and audience were assembled in the bar you had to wind their body clockwork up now and then by timely nudges and reminders.

But prior to that tournament, which was itself well before Gar-eth's shambling approach to a subsequent committee meeting, Jack had ridden out of the village by bike to test the extent of the grey blanket, their protection and their prison wall, as well as to check on the state of any deadstock in more distant fields. . . .

And even as all these various events were unwinding, it seemed to Jeni that time wound round and around on itself. Time had become dreamlike and nightmarish, following a dream logic of associations rather than straightforward sequence. That was rather the way time had behaved, or misbehaved, during her LSD trip back in Oxford. On the morning after the funeral Jeni remembered sitting and thinking very hard indeed about this treachery of time. Or the treachery of her perception of time.

It became clear to her that she no longer knew in what order events were occurring; could no longer quite capture the correct order. Some incidents, when they took place, already seemed to have occurred once before. The memory of other incidents, when Jack or Mitzi or Sheri referred to these, took her by surprise as if they couldn't possibly have happened yet but sprang into being right then for the first time ever. Yet she did know about these events. She fished them from the future, to become instant memories.

"I'm going insane," she thought to herself. "I'm going four-dimensional. Or something."

She remembered thinking. She'd already done so once; or would do so.

"Are we set loose from time?" she wondered. "Are we in some sort of eternity?" While outside of their grey bubble the poisoned snows of the nuclear winter fell from a black sky upon a dead land in a dead world . . . where forests and cities might still be burning, only their failing flames lighting the stygian scene.

Twenty-four

"Wey, Aa freewheels doonhill a way, then Aa peddles a bit. Nowt te be seen but the road an' hedges an' a few deed cows standin' lookin' tatty an' stupid. Their teats was drippin' a bit. But it worn't milk, Bert. More like thin yellow pus. Their udders didn't look as if they'd split, more like shrivelled up, ye knaa. Wasted away."

Bert nodded. "It's the same on my farm. George's farm. They look as if they're grazing, but they aren't really. Just going through the motions. Like George himself, and my Pauline."

"Mebbe that's as weel, what wiv no sun and no rain!" Jack eyed the grey overcast and tinkled his bell a couple of times as if this might summon a shower or sunshine.

They . . . that's Jack, perched on the bike he'd borrowed from the Blakelocks whose boy used to deliver the papers, and Bert and Nell and Jeni, and Bess who'd accompanied Jack on his expedition into the unknown . . . were outside the shop and sub post-office in the High Street, from which he'd set out, and to which he'd returned.

Through the plate glass frontage proprietress Mrs Yates was visible standing numb as a huge anaesthetized maggot in soggy floral print dress behind her postal counter, face blotched with mould. While she waited perplexed to sell stamps for letters to no possible destination or to cash post mortem pensions, the inventory team had passed busily through her store, hauling out all sour milk and defrosted ice cream and hamburgers and lollies to dump in the tiny apple orchard behind her house. Since nominally this was just the start of April there were no house flies, bluebottles, or clegs to cluster on the festering faces of the dead, to tramp their excremental feet on spongy tissue and paddle in pulpy skin. So where did maggots come from? Presumably they came with the package of death, part of the time-shunt. You could bet there would be a feast of flies soon enough; and *they* wouldn't be disabled.

As to other winged creatures – excluding the aimless chickens and dotty ducks – rather less than the usual number of wild birds were about. None seemed capable of flying with any assurance of success. A couple of pecking pigeons were staggering in the street, and some sparrows were hopping and falling and hopping like cripples on matchstick crutches. The birds were half blind.

"After a bit it gets real foggy, clarty as a coalhoose. Soon Aa starts gannin' uphill again. Presently Aa finds mcsel comin' back into the village from the other direction. It's as Aa expected."

"I do hope you haven't made yourself sick," Nell said, "if you exposed yourself to any radiation."

"Aa don't think so. Ye canna gan far enough to run into the aftermath. About a mile, Aa'd say. Couple o' miles radius: that's wor lot."

Bess trundled towards the pigeons. Smelling them, she whined and backed off. *Bad* birds.

"Melfort's under an emergency power, ye might say. Aa'm thinkin' though, that we haven't met any more monsters like we did that neet. An' it hasn't pulled any more really dorty tricks like killin' Sheri's lad."

"Does it need to?" Jeni asked bitterly. "Do we have to

146

meet monsters, when Mrs Yates is standing in there dead and alive? Huh! Too many shocks, and it might drive us totally mad. We wouldn't be in any fit state to be able to suffer. But don't let's count our chickens. Just wait for the next turn of the screw. It has plenty of time in hand, if the food'll last out for a couple of years. I've always heard that *waiting* is an essential part of torture. Recovering just sufficiently, then being dragged screaming again, to the pain. Maybe we're all co-operating nicely by staging capers like the tournament tonight. Setting ourselves up."

"Divven't say that, Jen. We're responsible for folks' welfare."

"Responsible. Just as we were responsible for world peace."

"In wor own little way."

"Maybe this is a Hades for the helpful. If you're always trying to help people whether they want it or not, maybe you have to go on helping them – even when they're bloody dead! Why us?" Jeni had started quietly, as though dead Mrs Yates might overhear and call out the answer mockingly. But her voice rose to a howl. "Why? Why? *Why*?"

"Keep yor hair on, pet. Mebbe there's places like this aal over the globe. Sanctuaries."

"*Do you really think so?* Our world's done in. Just this tiny part of it's been kept ticking over to amuse something that's vile and evil. The vic – "

"What's that?" Bert asked her.

"Nothing."

Such an outcry could only attract some attention. Three wretched corpse-toddlers came hobbling from a gateway, two scrawny girls with open foul wounds, not red but greenly gangrenous, and one bloated ulcerated boy. They approached.

"Wey, mebbe the simple bairns knaa more aboot it then worsels?" Jack dismounted, dropping the cycle. He

147

crouched, holding out his arms as the kids came closer; and Jeni was so glad of this distraction.

The girls hung back but the boy wobbled onward to halt before Jack.

"Wey, there's me bonny lad. Will ye tell me, son? What dee ye think's happened te yor village? An' yor sisters an' Mam and Dad? An' you?"

The swollen boy opened his puffy mouth, and vomited a brown mass of what looked like soaked cat biscuits. Jack knifed hastily out of the way as the mess hit the tarmac.

"Aa think," he said unsteadily, "this lad's a bit of a fatty. He's been stuffin' hisself oot o' habit." Jack leaned over. "That's nay good for yor constitution, son. Not when yor in this state."

The pub that evening was straight out of Goya. Or maybe the bar was the *Raft of the Medusa?* "Far worse!" thought Jeni, fighting an initial urge to spew, to run screaming. Paraffin lamps let her see too much.

How could they possibly have organized *this*? They must already be mad without realizing. This was like holding a ball in Belsen, a gala at Nagasaki, a fête in fire-bombed Dresden; in miniature. It wasn't even a modern horror any longer; it was medieval. A *totentanz* . . . almost as had happened once in the muddy street of the old village . . . worse, really.

The White Lion was packed with shuffling, decaying corpses, young and old. Maggots squirmed in waxy craters. Green flesh hung loose from hands like shucked-off mittens still attached by a cord to the wrist. Noses and cheeks unravelled like fraying balaclavas. Faces were lumps of blue-vein or Gorgonzola or Dolcelatte cheese a week past their prime. Eyes were soft-boiled eggs. Tongues and lips were offal.

Eppur si muove.

148

Clothes – trousers, frocks, and blouses – were blemished by the deliquescence of the flesh and slow leakage from within: of bile, rheum, liquid chocolate leaking from the bowels, yellow bladder drippage, mushroom juice seeping from lungs. . . .

Why should she be thinking of these abominations in terms of the contents of restaurant dustbins? Was it to make the ghastly dead a fraction more palatable? Though not appetizing. Let's pretend the slowly putrefying tissue's something else, soft sculptures assembled by a lunatic, a *merde* artist working in filth. It was said you could get used to most things; and as the minutes went by, and no one actually *oppressed* her, she felt more capable. At least there wasn't any dramatic vomiting or diarrhoea. The dead had their token quarter-pints of this and that, but the occasional sip was ample to wet the whistle, to top up the drips of fluid that leaked out. Their metabolisms were all drastically slowed down, as retarded as their minds.

There, for instance, sat Pauline Morris, the stains on her ballooning frock almost lost amongst a loud flower pattern. Bare arms and swollen ankles suppurated, and her broad face looked coated in damp dough. She'd lost her left ear and most of her hair. She wheezed as she sat there, a slow creaky bellows, perhaps humming to herself. Occasionally she raised her lemonade to her puffy lips and sweet slaver dribbled down her chin.

The committee had organized teams to toss, as best they could, the yellow wooden "cheeses" at the skittles table. With its iron-hooped net, this resembled a football goal.

Bert, who was a grand master of the arcane if elementary rules, was stationed by the scoreboard with a stick of chalk. Sheri was in charge of the elimination chart. Jack hovered near the net to set tumbled skittles upright again, and to wipe the greasy cheeses with a towel when they became too slippery for rotting fingers to grip effectively.

Of course some cheeses flew askew, while others didn't even reach the table. It was amazing that any of the shambolic players did hit their targets. Yet this happened as often as not. Skittles fell; scores accumulated. As the night wore on the "Duffers" knocked out the "Fluff Balls". (Bert had told Sheri the usual team titles.) The ladies of "WI-1" trounced the "Munch Bunch". The "Likely Lads" fell to the "Invalids".

Corpses who weren't playing crowded the rest of the room, either eyeing the bout in progress with a browsing, cattle-like gaze, mooing approval or condolence, or else conversing after a fashion, making mumbling, bubbling sounds. Nell presided behind the bar alongside Tom Tate, who belched out incoherent comments that went unheeded; he seemed worked up with excitement at the half-remembered phenomenon of busy trade. Mitzi often cheered encouragingly, as did Jack and Sheri. Bess scoffed up spilled, unwanted crisps.

Jack took care not to return the stack of cheeses too vigorously to the next player in case he knocked off loose flesh or even whole fingers. Stout Mrs Boxall had already lost a thumb, which stuck to the cheese when she threw it.

"Gi's a hand settin' 'em up, Jen!"

Yes, she could do that. Corpses didn't touch the actual skittles.

And so the night wore on till the final presentation – by Sheri, to the morosely triumphant "Duffers" – of the Whatsit Trophy. Which was a wooden spanner, painted silver, nailed to a chunk of oak. By that time Jeni had downed several whiskies and felt almost casual amidst the crush of walking corpses – until one gripped her by the wrist.

"Gareth! But . . . let go of me!"

He hadn't been here earlier. He and Nancy had remained at Old Roses, along with Andy. Jeni had seen to that, arguing that you couldn't fit the whole village in the pub, that Gareth was no skittles ace, that the evening might upset him because he'd nursed ambitions and here he'd be ordered around by a committee of which he wasn't and couldn't be a member. He might feel humiliated and aggrieved.

Excuses, excuses; though the others had swallowed them. At Felix's funeral Gareth had tried to lead a pressure group against her – to oppress her, dominate her. She was sure of it.

Now here he was, holding on to her, fixing her with rheumy eyes set in a face that was all one single drippy acne-splotch. It must have taken most of the evening for his dimmed intelligence to suss out her whereabouts – like someone picking at a scab till it comes loose – but finally he had.

"What do you want? Get off, will you! Please?"

Maybe Gareth was feeling betrayed and wretched. His tenant and client, Jeni, had suddenly evolved to a higher state of intelligence leaving him stuck behind in the condition of an ape. He had devolved; it came to the same thing.

"Awoo-glaaaa," he said. Like a slowed-down tape recording.

She owed him something, didn't she? Just as she owed all of them something.

"Head and bed," he said, leering closer. "Lock and cock. Cage and dong. Ring-a-ding-dong. Wedding bells ring." He sang, soft and slobbery, "Bell of – Saint Mary – let's feel you a-balling!" An enflamed eyelid drooped as if in a wink. "Belle of the ball, Jeneeee."

"Help me," she whispered as random words oozed out of him – but were they quite so random? An obscene theme seemed to link them.

"Necrophily's the scene, Jeneeee. If Shereeee's from Philadelphia – "

"She isn't. I'm sure she isn't."

"Then I'm from Necrophilia. Nice new name for Mal-fort, boyos! Increase and multiply, ye dead! We'll keep a welcome – "

He'd gone insane. As well as being dead he was insane.

"Listen Gareth, there's been a nuclear war – "

"War, score. Let's try to score. Score a try. Put the balls in touch. Try for a conversion. My tackle's in good order. Must get to the church first, girl! Ding-dong-ball, pussy's in the wall. Vicar'll marry us, quite contrarious, how does my hardening grow? With silver balls and cockle hells and pussy maids all aglow." Memories of the game of rugby; obscenely twisted songs and nursery rhymes. All converging on a theme which she didn't wish to, which she dared not know about. Fortunately no one else would be able to understand him.

"You've been awfully injured, Gareth, but you're being kept alive by some perverse – "

"Reverse! First stage is a cage. Second rung is a tongue. Dung dung dung. Toilet-creature."

"*What?* How do you know about – ? Jack!" she shrieked, as the dead skittle teams began heading homeward, surging, bearing her along in their flow towards the pub door, adding their pressure to Gareth's tuggings.

Jack breasted the tide of shuffling corpses and dragged her clear. Gareth's hand slid off her like a cold eel, a boneless thing. Like the appendage that had killed Felix. In her dream, that was, only in her dream! Gareth was leaving along with the dead, a passive automaton once again.

"Wey, what's wrong?"

She breathed deeply, despite the stench in the White Lion.

"Gareth seized hold of me. He was acting weirdly."

"That's to be expected, pet."

"Threateningly. Sexually."

"Aa see."

"Maybe the Power's planning something."

"Ye'll be safe wiv me, Jen. Divven't take on."

Later, back in the granny flat, she felt light-headed from the whiskies, and Jack kept bumping into things, particularly herself. Particularly. Holding on to her, touching her.

Yet somehow she couldn't accept going upstairs with him, to sleep with him. Even if all that they did was sleep, and keep yor feet still, Geordie hinny. Which – she doubted – wouldn't have been all that they did if they went upstairs together.

"Gareth," she thought, "has laid his mark on me. His prohibition. For tonight, at any rate."

Twenty-five

Some twenty juniors of assorted size sat limply on dwarf chairs in the school hall, which doubled as a gym as well as a classroom for first years and rising fives. Wall bars, ladder, and climbing ropes were mounted along one side. The opposite wall was mostly windows, with jagged cracks in two, giving on to the concrete schoolyard fringed with its railing of iron spears.

Posters of farming through the ages papered the other walls, along with kiddy artwork of the village duckpond, golden Guernseys in an emerald field, a dingy medieval ploughman, a combine harvester crayoned like a futuristic, bloodstained battle-tank. Behind the school piano hung a giant, dog-eared, calendar-like pad the size of a Sunday newspaper with verses of hymns printed large upon it. Cases and tables displayed cardboard farms with paper animals, model tractors, and old photographs of pre-First World War harvesting time. The whole school had been busy on a farm project, up until the war, the final war.

A few dead John Clare first years had been dragooned into class too. Twelve year olds; these were just a spit away from the oldest of the juniors, though to them that might once have seemed a giant spit.

Mitzi was presiding, with Miss Samuels slumped moribundly at her desk up front looking and smelling like a dead rock salmon. Since Mitzi knew nothing agricultural and the head teacher was no longer a fount of any sort of wisdom, Mitzi had invited Bert in to talk to the class of corpses.

Maybe something would penetrate – something familiar – to stir their expired, robotic minds. Continuity!

Bert wasn't exactly an organized talker working to any plan, and his audience had brain-rot besides tics and palsies. The glassy-eyed, festering kids seemed half comatose, half deranged. But once he got launched, Bert spoke with a muted passion which suggested that he was mainly talking to himself, rehearsing something which was preying on his own mind. He'd never been quite so garrulous as chairman of the committee. Perhaps now he had the ideal audience to bounce his thoughts off, an audience of dummies; and after a while Mitzi cottoned on.

". . . In my own Dad's or Grandad's day all you children would have had to do farm work, you see? In May or June you'd have been hand-weeding the corn and scaring off birds, and later on you'd be gleaning and threshing grass against hurdles to get the seed for replanting. In the old days we didn't have tractors and combines or weedkillers and fertilizers, right? To make hay you used scythes and handrakes and pitchforks. You started off as a raker, then a pitcher of sheaves, then you had to learn to load on to a wagon, swan-back so the stuff wouldn't fall off, and only after years' experience could you be trusted to build a rick. . . .

"Those old-fashioned stooks and ricks were a lot better at drying what you'd cut. With combining there's a lot more moisture left in the grain. That's why you see grain-driers and storage bins on farms these days. The seed merchants won't take the stuff straight off. . . .

"Talking of *hay*, grass is the crop that Britain grows best. I mean naturally best, without using chemicals and stuff. You know all that ridgy land down along the valley? Them fields like corrugated roofs?"

Mitzi wondered what valley; then decided he must be meaning the area in between Melfort and Hobby Hill.

"Anyone know how them ridges came about?"

No one knew anything.

"Well, those were water meadows made by ridging the land and diverting the Thrush, using dams and wooden hatches. You flooded your grassland in the winter. That was mainly to protect the grass against hard winter frosts that would knock it back. Come March, you'd close your hatches to let the meadows drain, the grass would shoot up, and you could put your animals out to pasture a good month earlier than otherwise. . . .

"The big challenge is, you had to grow enough food in half a year or so to last your cows and sheep a full twelve months. Apart from your hay and straw you'd need mangolds and kale for cattle, and turnips to carry the sheep through, and barley and buckwheat and stuff for the pigs and chickens. And protein peas, and what else? Keep and carrots for horses. Lots of modern cattle cake's got imported things in it, and pig and chicken food's usually bought in these days. That's to say . . . used to be.

"You'd have to feed yourself through the winter too. Oats for porridge, vegetables, barley for beer. Come the autumn, you'd have to work out how many animals you had surplus to the provisions you'd managed to store. You'd have to slaughter all the extra mouths. . . ."

Miss Samuels stood up, as if triggered. Ah yes, *she* had been slaughtered, thought Mitzi; and so had all her pupils. The woman shuffled over to the cue-sheets of hymns. Class over? Time to praise? She just stood there lamely.

"Getting back to the subject of grass," said Bert, "it used to be a proverb: to break a pasture makes a man, but to make a pasture breaks him. What that meant was, if you ploughed up a pasture you'd get rich harvests for the next few years – but to resow a decent pasture's a back-breaking task. There's getting the seed, for a start. It's not just grass seed. Leafy perennial rye is fine for your grazing and silage, but it isn't deep-rooting so it misses the minerals. Nowadays we'd top-dress with nitrogen and stuff. Our forefathers would mix in clover that fixes nitrogen and herbs like chicory and yarrow and dandelion that root deep; or else you'd soon have an exhausted pasture."

So Nell's "good earth" wasn't all that good, unless you in turn knew how to be good to it. Mitzi stuck her hand up.

"Can I ask a question?"

"It'd be nice if someone does."

"Could a village like this one become self-sufficient, and organic and whatnot?"

"Aside from its people and animals being corpses, you mean? Aside from nothing green showing signs of growing?" Bert sighed. "Can you turn back the clock?"

"If things were more normal?"

"I'd like to know how! Self-sufficient's a bit of romantic moonshine, to my mind. It's an idea that townsfolk have. No bit of the country has been really *that* for the last fifty years. What you're talking is subsistence, like in a mud hut village in Africa. I'm afraid we're going over the heads of this lot here." He snorted.

"We used to grow lettuce easily enough at the peace camp."

"Rabbit food! You can't digest lettuce!"

"Nonsense. We ate a lot of lettuce."

"Surprised you didn't starve, then. Lettuce is cellulose. People don't have the right chemicals inside them to break it down and get any nourishment. It goes straight through and out the backside."

Miss Samuels began to sing wheezingly:

"Let us with a gladsome mind

"Praise the Lord for he is kind –"

No one joined in.

Twenty-six

And at last (and at first) Gareth stomped to his rendezvous with the village committee. . . .

"Wey, we could organize a beauty contest, Aa suppose!"

"Us in our knickers, is that it?" Mitzi tugged a loop in her sweater. "Sorry, I didn't bring my bikini to this holiday camp. I quite forgot."

"Na, not youse lasses. The *deed*. A contest o'corpses."

"That's sick." Sheri wrinkled her little nose and jutted her jaw, an insulted high school cheerleader. "Gross gross *gross*."

"It wouldn't be wor criteria of beauty, pet. What Aa'm gettin' at is, mebbe we could excite the Power to show us what's on its mind. Aa had a sort o' dream aboot this. How we'd have a parade in front of yor hall, with lots o' bunting, an' the dead would choose the Queen o' the village an' they'd crown her, then everyone would dance the conga roond the houses wavin' crêpe streamers, an' –" He shut up.

To Jeni, this dream of Jack's bore a hideous similarity . . . *to what else*?

To that goosing chain of degraded nude bodies prancing out of the church of the medieval village in her video-vision! Led by that inhuman monk. Once long ago.

"Did you dream something more?" she asked Jack urgently.

"Wey . . . now that Aa recall, the deed was like geet big squashy maggots or caterpillar chrysalises, an' as they danced their pattern roond aboot the lanes an' over the green, gannin' this way an' that, they started . . . splittin' an' peelin' open . . . an' oot of the corpses skipped bairns fresh as daisies! Aye, that was it. An' Aa heerd music." Jack whistled the opening bars of *Boys and Girls Come out to Play*. "Played on a squeeze-box."

Bert frowned. "That's what used to happen every May Day. Did Jeni tell you?"

"Na. So what used te happen?"

"Old Mr Donaldson; he retired last year, and moved to Thrushby –"

"That's how the school house went vacant," interrupted Jeni.

"Very traditional chap, Raymond Donaldson –"

"You aren't kidding."

Donaldson had been headmaster for going on thirty years, running the little primary school as though the date was still 1950-something. Or even 1940. He believed in rote teaching of the 3 Rs, and pupil politeness, and was passionate about music. Increasingly out of date! – though that could sometimes be a strength as much as a shortcoming.

" – even if he did sometimes hold May Day in June on account of the weather. The school maypole was always set up on the green. The kids would march through the streets with posies. He'd play his accordion while they danced the ribbons round the pole, after they'd crowned the King and

Queen. *Boys and Girls. Amo Amas.* Then there'd be dancing up and down the green for kids and parents too. The eightsome reel, the Dashing White Sergeant – just like fifty years ago, I'd say. That new Miss Samuels was planning to have the kids do some pageant in the school instead. Robin Hood or King Arthur. That's because she couldn't play the accordion, and you can hardly push the school piano all the way to the green."

"So Aa was dreamin' aboot reality."

"Yes, and I wonder why." Bert mused. "Our new vicar always gave Donaldson's May Days the cold shoulder. Boycotted them, he did. He'd never bless the crowd the way old Ashley-Usher used to before him. Now *he* was a character, was Ashley-Usher. He'd join in the dances, kicking up his skirts."

"When Bert says 'new'," explained Jeni, "he means six or seven years gone by."

During her own years in Melfort she had never noticed that Partridge was opposed to the school's May Day celebration. He never said a word about the subject at governors' meetings; none she attended, anyway. She couldn't recall him showing a flicker of interest, which was perhaps significant. Donaldson must have squashed the vicar's objections flat, well before her own time, and Partridge knew he would get nowhere till Donaldson retired. Might Miss Samuels' pageant owe as much to some Christian words from the vicar as to her own incapacity on the accordion? Could Partridge have leaned on the new head teacher?

Partridge was deadly scared of pagan evils, right? And May Day was an innocent, gentle hangover from paganism; the rural May Day, not the red flag May Day. May Day was a tame residue from the time of earth spirits and corn gods, sacrifices and lusty ritual matings to fructify the fields, the time of witches . . . and dark power.

Mustn't concentrate on the vicar!

159

"Weel, it occurs te me that mebbe wor gettin' some sort o' message from this Power, so mebbe if we was te –"

"To have the corpses crown their beauty queen?" cried Nell. "Their princess of ugliness and pus and worms and disfigurement? A Monarch of muck? The rightful ruler of this village – is that it? For what purpose, Jack, *for what purpose*? Did your dream tell you that too?"

"Mebbe we'd be giving *it* a message. A one-finger message. Aa divven't knaa. Aa'm just followin' an instinct . . . but mebbe Aa'm sick meself, like Sheri says. Sick in the heed. It was only a suggestion."

If only, thought Jeni, she had started sleeping with Jack; maybe he would never have dreamt such a thing. His nocturnal energies might have been drained. Apparently the Power was getting to Jack, winkling its way into his imagination while he lay at a three a.m. low ebb. She felt a surge of paranoia.

No need, no need! Jack was made of stouter stuff than dead Gareth. Self-centered, and now soft-centered Gareth. Rotten-centered.

Just then, came a series of thumps upon Jeni's front door. In the next moment everyone must have glanced at everyone else, counting heads.

"Ye knaa that joke aboot the last man in the world? He was sittin' in his room twiddlin' his thumbs, an' he heard this knock on the door –"

"Ta-dee! And it was the last *woman* in the world," said Sheri brightly.

Thump. . . Thump.

"Must be someone from the village," said Bert.

"They divven't have the gumption."

"Maybe," Nell said hesitantly, "it's somebody from outside?"

"They wouldn't use their fist when there's a door knocker," Mitzi pointed out.

Jack stood up. "Aa'll answer if nobody else is willin'. Afore the poor bugger gives up an' gans home, while we're aal still bletherin'."

It was Gareth at the door, his pulpy upraised fist leaking juices.

"Wey, it's just yor landlord cum to collect the rent!"

Corpse-Gareth shambled on into the living room, a gangrenous toe poking through a hole in his thick, torn sock like a green-shelled snail. He turned full circle as if the raised arm was the rudder of a mobile windmill, till he oriented on Jeni; slowly he lowered his arm towards her and opened his fist, palm upward.

He said, "You-bring-the-key-you-took-to-the-door-of-the-church-where-the-iron-cage-that-held–"

"He sounds like that Welsh railway station!" Jeni commented as loudly as she could. "You know the one I mean: Llan-Fair-Pwll-Go-Go-Whatnot! It means something like – how does it go now? – the chapel beside the fountain half way down the hill where the deer, oh I can't remember, they just invented the name to attract tourists, did you know that?"

"Hwisht, pet! He's tryin' te communicate."

"Oh it's any old words pouring out of him. You know these Welsh windbags –"

"Had your gob, will ye?" Jack said roughly. "What's your problem, Taff?"

Gareth's hand jerked. "She-locked-the-church-with-the-vicar-inside-the-cage –"

"Hadaway, man! Aa found the vicar lyin' deed in the chorchyard. We wheeled him to his house."

"Not-his-head-you-didn't. His-head-will-preach-now-he -has-a-new-throat-bone-and- the -shit - is - out-of-his-system –"

"His heed's inside the chorch? An' it's still sermonizin' – is that what ye mean?"

"Jeneeee-must-bring-the-key." Gareth looked distressed, as though those weren't his own words and he knew it. They were the words of an imp with a speech impediment inhabiting his ulcerated tongue, hurting it at every twist.

Jack swung around. "Have ye been straight with us, Jen? Dee ye knaa somethin' Aa divven't knaa?"

Desperately Jeni addressed the dead man. "Is that you talking, Gareth? Or is it the Power?"

Something happened behind Gareth's eyes.

"Who do you think it is; Lloyd George?" replied the corpse. "Bloody shame Swansea thrashed Cardiff, eh boyo?"

"We mustn't let ourselves be manipulated, Jack. It's trying to manipulate you."

"Ye divven't want us te knaa aboot something in the chorch. Give us the key, Jen. Now."

"I agree," said Bert. "We're a committee. We can't keep secrets from each other, even if they're awful ones."

"You've kept secrets from us," echoed Mitzi. "*Why?*" She looked about to fly at Jeni.

"You hand the key over," said Nell, "then we can all go to the church together, and see what's going on. Safety in numbers."

Gareth gurgled with what might have been laughter, and chanted encouragingly:

"I prefer the dear vicar,

"He's longer and thicker;

"Besides, he comes quicker than you!"

"What the hell does that mean?" asked Sheri.

Jeni tried to explain, "It's just a limerick – a dirty one. Rugby locker room stuff."

"Uh-uh." Sheri shook her head. "Vicar. Come quick. What is it with you and the vicar?"

"Well," said Jeni, losing heart, and afraid of losing her

162

only friends, the only friends there could be for her in the world ever again. "Well —"

Twenty-seven

The people had hooked the mesh door back and the heavy main door, unlocked, yawned wide; but Bess the labrador refused to sneak inside. She hung about the porch, growling quietly and fretfully, waiting for her people to quit this pursuit of the awful smell of death, hoping that they would rush out again soon. If they started floundering in the cold vibrating sea of air in this grim stone place she doubted if she could dive in to haul them to safety.

For under the waves in the gloom lurked vast ghastly things.

As Bess blinked into that gloom, in her mind's eye suddenly she glimpsed the hounds of Cromwell's men peeing interestingly against the ends of pews. Even when the tang of their urine tickled her nose, she wouldn't be lured.

Another blink. This time she saw a nativity: a thatched wooden manger with straw and stiff white paper angels. Chicks cheeped in a wire cage. A spindly lamb a-baaing and a rompy puppy, which might have been one of her own, were tethered to the manger. In the crib, the basket for the human pup, a china doll lay wrapped in a lacework shawl. A crowd of people all in their best clothes were singing, while a man in a black robe with the collar of a dog presided from the little stone tower up front. The puppy whined to attract Bess, but she wouldn't be drawn. She wouldn't be invited.

For beneath the scene, beneath the stone floor and the crust of the world: vast black ghastly things.

She shied away.

The visitors barely glanced at the vases of withered daffodils, the commonplace stained glass, memorial plaques like dull golden slices through some solid eternity.

The reliquary upon the shit-stained floor . . . the padlocked cage . . . staring from the gloom, the mad impossible head.

Which began to churn its jaw about, to ungum its lips.

Gareth had been left way behind; maybe he was no longer following.

"Kneel!" the head shrieked.

Bert immediately got down on his knees, either out of obedience or because that way he felt he presented less of a target. Shari copied him, though she looked distressed at her reduced ability to escape. The others ignored the order. Enough clerks of court had told peace people to stand up when they were being charged with obstruction, criminal damage, or whatever else had been pulled out of the lucky dip of the law. In a court of oppression you stayed sitting down. If this cleric wanted them on their knees, they'd stand.

The head spoke in a more reasonable tone. "My message is uncomfortable. And so am I. Why should you be comfortable?"

"Why not kneel?" muttered Bert. "And hear what it has to say. No point in irritating it."

"Oh very well." With a sigh Nell lowered herself. Glancing at her, Mitzi followed suit.

"I'm waiting."

"Yer bugger." Jack tugged Jeni down beside him. It seemed as if they were all now set to worship the head, to receive foul communion from its black swollen tongue.

"Thank you," said the head. "*Thank* you. I have some things to teach you, my children. Some words to say, in a language not my own."

The vicar's head began to address them in that voice which was and wasn't Partridge's; and as it spoke the listeners' knees and then their hearts grew numb.

"Let's speak of language, shall we? There was such a babel of languages till recently – until they all expired abruptly! Those were all essentially the same language under the skin, with the same bones – if in different positions. So much for your human babble.

"Next there's the language of . . . for want of a better word, creation. That's the universe. Its words are matter, such as dust and rocks and gas, stars and worlds. Its syntax is physical law: gravity and electricity and nuclear forces, the play of particles and radiation."

"Is that . . . the language of God?" whispered Sheri.

"Call it so in your human babble, if you care to. Oh how amusing under present circumstances to hear nuclear forces and radiation called by such a name!"

"Which you daren't even pronounce?" she dared to ask.

The only answer to that from the caged head was a chuckle that chilled them.

"And there is, or *was* until recently, a language of the living world: a language of fields and forests, seasons, wind and waves. That's the language which all birds and animals heeded, and were part of. It has now become a dead duck, children, thanks to your nuclear games."

It was on the tip of Jeni's tongue to ask: "How about elsewhere?" How about the southern hemisphere? How about black Africa and Australia and Argentina? Why should the head tell them the truth, even if it did know the answer? What was it: a genuine oracle? Besides, she already knew the answer. Inevitably the nuclear winter would have spread south. The sun would have vanished from the Pacific and Antarctic. Outlook: bleak, and black. By now the whole world seen from space must resemble a dirty version of Venus, cloaked in clouds of muck and poison.

165

"Lastly," said Partridge's head, "there is the language of evil, a language of the dire night. The gibbering, the screaming.

"Its terms are terror, nausea, pain, filth, and worse, always worse. Terms, do I say? Say rather: poisonous seductions, the kiss of the grave, the gropings of insane ghosts, eruptions from under the earth. And always: *power*, twists of twisted power like a clever torturer's knots.

"The language of evil only has a few principal terms: such as ghoul and vampire and zombie, torment and evisceration, genie and damnation. This is the speech in which the nightmare zone, the beast, talks to itself.

"And humans overhear. People heed the language of evil time and again. Madness, cruelty, filth, abomination. The beast in the heart! Here is the swamp from which human genius crawled. Here, the source of power and imagination. Life arises from death, the terrible void. It always remembers its way back."

Sheri broke in. "All art and achievement starts out from filth and vileness, is that it? And that's the bottom line?"

"They certainly ended back there, just a while ago! Where is your precious art now? Floating in the stratosphere. Burnt, fouled, contaminated."

"Yeah, well the war was –"

"Justified? An accident? A misjudgment? Or perhaps the last judgment? *Fools!*"

"It sure ought to please Evil!" she retorted.

"I could turn you inside-out for your folly, Sheri Diamond, and still keep you alive. That would be your true reply, uttered in my own native language. Yes, inside-out! Or I could turn your diamond into coal, a body made of burning coal."

"Why don't you?" she whispered, "Satan."

"For the simple reason that the diaboli of the world have

166

awoken, Sheri, and have joined in me – to survive! To call my power *Satan* is to glamourize. Likewise, to call creation by . . . that other name, which has no place in my vocabulary. The force of evil is stored in the diaboli of the world. Seals are set upon our locked powers. Certain people can learn to break these seals, with our encouragement. They can be taught the language of evil. Even *Satan*," and it mouthed the title sarcastically, "finds a nuclear war . . . unacceptable."

"Unacceptable?" repeated Nell, bewildered.

"Yes. Unacceptable because nuclear war destroys even evil. Utterly. Even *Satan*," and filthy spittle flew from the thing's mouth like snake venom, "revolts against a nuclear war, which annuls everything whatever. Forever."

The temperature in the church had become icy.

"Therefore I set a seal around this village. Therefore I put forth my power to hold off the storm of fire and poison. Therefore I cause some light and warmth. Therefore I preserve you and this place and its beasts and birds and plants."

"Preserve?" cried Jack. "This gang o' corpses? Ye must be havin' us on! You're playin' wiv us. Jeni tried to warn us."

"You fool!" wailed the head. "Jeneeee is the person whom I taught to unlock the seals. She is my agent. Do you not realize this, Jack? Jeneeee is the genie-summoner."

"No – !" Even as Jeni opened her mouth to protest, the gates of memory burst wide spewing out ancient silt, sluicing forth pickled bitter brine and fury.

Fury in the ancient meaning – as in Furies, those bloody avenging demons from hell. . . . She was in Donna's room again, and time had melted.

"Let me bring you to orgasm," the heavy nurse ordered, pinioning her with one hand while the other hand groped between her thighs and pressed flesh into her secret flesh.

Fingers stretched the flimsy membrane of her brief lace knickers which she'd bought specially to wear for deflowering by Phil Daniels and had worn again that day; dress light and loose. Donna manipulated her rhythmically, massaging in a way that Phil certainly hadn't known how to, but which Jeni herself knew so familiarly.

"I'll scream," Jeni had gasped. Panted. Whatever.

"No you won't," murmured Donna. "You'll enjoy. The armour will snap."

Devilishly familiar! Unsummoned by her, images arose of black-uniformed Nazis crowding around a gypsy girl, of black-robed Inquisitioners ripping the rags off a beautiful young witch, hunting for devil-marks on her flesh, poking and prying – and in Jeni's mind, in a language she didn't speak yet somehow understood, the witch called out to her Master for assistance to strike her captors and tormentors, to blast them, burn them, hurl them against the stone walls so violently that they would become clinging tapestries. Or else to please spirit her away out of their midst. But please hurry, keep your promises. Not promises exactly. Implied promises, hints, inducements, allurements. Hadn't the shaggy Horned One shagged her, in her dreams at least? Hadn't he shown her another land on the backside of the Earth? Hadn't he kissed her backside hotly, hadn't she put her tongue into his backside, the key to unlock him?

Jeni knew this witch utterly. The girl was in rebellion against the powers of the Earth, against the hated dominators with their crosses and swords and tools of torture and their cruel hypocritical goodness and their taxes and bibles and laws to oppress the poor folk and outcast womenfolk.

No help would reach the girl; not in that life which climaxed in anguish and agony.

Had Jeni once lived that life, which was so real to her while she lay underneath Donna? Did the witch's dying agony imprint a roving ghost upon the world, impose a signal upon the waves of time which her brain picked up now that it was unbound from time, stripped of its censor filters by the drug? At that moment did she assemble a motley of memories from films and novels and history to make a kind of golem girl in her mind, which was only an image for an unknown power in her, a potential, a way of believing in it, a symbol code to gain access? By that means, by that token, did she empower her body to some feat of Zen Judo where all of her muscles were totally in key, where her apparent strength increased severalfold, where she was capable of uttermost effortless exertion as if hypnotized then triggered to action by a code-image?

Whatever, the golem or ghost in her mind cried out its conjuration, and she spat the words out too into Donna's face. Donna was slammed back bloody-nosed half way across the room.

And then at Kerthrop when the Hunt neared the wire, she had filled with fury again – there at Kerthrop where the diabolus had slumbered sealed and locked but dreaming of the world while it slept, dreaming of Jeni tapping its power in Oxford, dreaming her restlessness in Reading as her fingertip descended on Hobby Hill, perhaps guided there, her finger and her, dreaming her all the while for she had formed a tenuous link which could be strengthened, and she was suitable, dreaming of the USAF base that pressed upon part of its slumbering place where once it had destroyed a village in its play, invited by a monk eager for unearthly power, and whom it transformed, where now nuclear weapons sat close by, which it came to understand, and which appalled even Evil. For evil was of the earth and of human evolution; it was the cruel crazy tormenting dark streak, power-hungry, luring, destroying. And earth and evolution would end, and evil too. . . .

Sheri whimpered, "Did you . . . kill my boy?" And Jeni

realized that the American woman was addressing her, not the head. "Did you . . . sacrifice Felix *to this*? So horribly, because it had to be horrible. And inhuman and filthy. Did you, Jeni?"

Twenty-eight

Still down on their numb knees they were all gazing at Jeni, Sheri with awful suspicion in her eyes. Meanwhile the head had fallen silent.

"No," Jeni whispered, "I couldn't have done, don't you see? Dennis Ainsworth said it was physically impossible! No human being could have killed Felix."

"Not even with a devil's help?" Bert asked softly.

"No! I didn't do it. But I know what did. It was a . . . limb . . . a limb of the Power that did it! I know because I dreamt that after you found the body."

"What do ye mean, a limb?"

"An arm of the Power. Like a snake. Squirming muscles, soft but so strong." Jeni was weeping helplessly but this time Mitzi didn't shuffle closer to touch and console.

"An' ye dreamt that?"

"I didn't just dream it. I . . . I gave birth to it."

"Ye *what*?"

"Days ago, weeks ago, I don't know. . . . The morning after the Hunt, after the wire exploded, that's when. I went to the toilet, and it was inside me. It came out . . . like a long, long turd, only it wasn't any turd. It swam away before I could even flush it – "

"Ye gave borth te an *arm* doon the netty?"

"Yes!" She stared back at Jack blurredly. "It hid in the drains, and it killed little Felix."

Yet in her dream of the boy's death, hadn't it been her own arm that killed him? Her arm, mutating into that toilet-thing?

That dream hadn't been reality! It had been a message, a communiqué, couched in the language of evil. A statement by the Power. Which, naturally, would twist the truth, and even twist the person it addressed. Contaminate them by association. Befoul them.

Who could stand witness that she was innocent? Why, Bess the labrador! Who now skulked outside, refusing to set paw in the church. Bess had been with her on her walk that day, approximately when the boy was murdered. Bess would have reacted differently towards her, becoming over-excited and savage – or else shying away, scared.

A dog, as witness: that's what you were reduced to in the court of evil. Pray that the Power didn't warp the poor fat bitch so that she could stand up on her hind legs and speak, and lie!

"Weel, where's that arm got off to nowadays, Aa wonder?"

Jeni shook her head helplessly.

However, it was Nell who rescued her: troubled, yet solid Nell. "Our friend's pretty quiet," she observed, sneaking a look at the cage. "Maybe it's enjoying this."

"You're reet! Aa think it's tryin' to set us at odds. An' it's succeedin'."

Jeni nodded vigorously. "Yes, that's it. I feel like I'm being trapped. Tied up in knots."

Jack eyed her doubtfully. "Ye've still told us some funny old things, hinny." He snapped his fingers. "It said ye unlocked the seals. But ye didn't, did ye? Ye locked it in that cage!"

"Yes, yes, that's true – I did."

Jack shouted at the head, "Ye liar! They talk aboot seven seals in the Bible, divven't they? There's one seal left at least! You're locked in that cage. So bugger yor shen-anigans." He stood up defiantly.

"Wrong," said the head. "You came here freely and opened up the church. That is all I needed. This cage is my place of honour, my pulpit. Thanks to the holy throat bone with which Jeneeee provided me" – her name was a wind from hell – "I have a human voice."

"Eh?"

"I stuffed the relic in the vicar's mouth," confessed Jeni. "It seemed . . . the right thing to do at the time. I was in shock. The warhead had just detonated."

"Such nonsense, about my being caged! Has it not pen-etrated your thick skulls? My power is already extended. It already encloses Melfort thoroughly. So you shall not close the church door again. You shall find the hinges far too stiff. Stiff as a sword stuck in a stone. I need to be available . . . to my congregation. There are certain *rituals* yet to perform."

Bert groaned, perhaps involuntarily, a groan of dread.

"Stand up, little man. Your joints are creaking. Stand up, all of you. But do not hurry away!" (For the others had all scrambled up.) "Not yet. If you do not come here every day . . . to commune . . . then I shall be obliged to com-municate in the language I know best, that of happenings such as your son's death, Sheri. I might even need to ani-mate Felix – to have him claw his way out of the grave to re-enact that death."

Sheri went white. Her fingernails bit into her palms.

"You would not enjoy that greatly; though it would add some vivid variety to your present grey monotony. 'Suffer little children to come unto me!' Yes, that *might* be the most appropriate event."

"No," gasped Sheri.

"It might fit the pattern. The pattern feeds the power,

you see. The pattern determines the outcome. Well, a pattern can be made in more ways than one. From roast toad and virgin's blood at full moon, from dancing widdershins round a pentacle of silver rods made from stolen altar plate, whilst cackling such-and-such. . . . How ludicrous most conjurations have always been! They must needs be ludicrous as well as hideous, since evil comprises nonsense and lunacy. It's the reign of the absurd, my dears, of disorder so strong it becomes a new, unstable order – of triumphant discord and ugliness.

"Equally, a pattern can be made from a noose of wire, a holy relic, a dead horse, a virgin boy whose entrails are drawn out of him. Once a particular successful pattern starts to form, the initial elements constrain the later elements. They select as increasingly inevitable those later elements which will complete it.

"Such is magic, my children, such is witchery. Such as the summoning of the diabolus. Every child knows this principle when it assembles its collections of fetish objects – a victory conker, a dead mouse, a broken bracelet of Mummy's, a sparkling stone it found – and injects cunning cruelty: the spider with its legs torn off. That child is lisping in the language of evil. Most children lose the knack as they grow up. If only *babies* had more skill! There's nothing more savage in the world than a baby human child. It tries to grab everything it wants. It screams with rage when it can't get it. But most patterns go askew. Most people haven't enough knack. Unlike Jeneeee."

"Aye, ta for the lesson," sneered Jack, "but what's aal this leadin' up to?"

The lips and cheeks of the head twisted in a smile.

"A final ingredient remains."

"What would that be? A beauty contest o' the corpses? With us presentin' a golden delicious apple to the ugliest?"

"Not exactly, Jack."

"Hey, if your power's aaready extended, why do ye need another ingredient?"

"To maintain and cement. Otherwise this sanctuary might fail. Then you would all be dead as doornails. I'm all that you have left now. Equally you are all that I have left, to sustain the life of evil. So I shall not let you fail me. If necessary I shall open the boy's grave, and we'll see what we hook out."

Sheri moaned.

"What is this ingredient?"

"Dead Gareth will show Jeneeee. It is up to him and her."

"Whatever it is," cried Sheri, "you got to do it, Jeni! You got to! I don't know if you did hurt Felix, but you mustn't do this to him too! You mustn't let him be pulled out of his grave and . . . and butchered all over again. Whatever *does* come out of his grave, whatever mad bad mockery."

"I'm being trapped," Jeni repeated in misery.

"Swear to me you'll do it! You caused all this. You made it happen. I wish I was dead. I wish we all were. I wish the war had wiped out everything. But there's this instead, this hell. Because you're a witch!"

"Wey, that's not a very amiable way to ask a favour, Sheri. We must keep friends. After aal, the war was more yor doin' than wor fault – ye might say that."

"Her people shot Mal," muttered Mitzi.

"Whisht, pet. Under the corcumstances we best forgive an' forget. Nay use cryin' over spilt milk."

"Sour milk," said Nell. "Very sour."

"We're aal in the same boat."

Sheri smiled in a tight, brittle way. She looked close to hysteria.

"That'll be the bottom line, hmm? *I* caused all this – not her. I'm to blame because I'm American." Desperately she

174

controlled herself. "I'm losing it, aren't I?" She went to Jeni. "I beg you, by everything you hold dear. I didn't think I could be hurt any more; but it's thought of a way. It doesn't matter about me. Beat up on me. Go ahead, I won't fight back. Punish me all you like. Disfigure me. Just leave my baby's grave alone. In peace. Maybe I oughtn't to use words like peace." She jutted her jaw. "Take a swipe at me for saying peace. Knock my teeth out. Hurt me. I'm only begging peace for my boy."

"Yor gannin' a bit over the top, pet."

"Can't do anything right, can I? Cain't say anything." Sheri sagged. "Maybe that's what Jeni and Gareth gotta do anyway, between them. Maybe that's the last line of the recipe. Tie me to the altar and . . . do things. As a sacrifice to *that*."

The head in the cage chuckled.

"Oh fuck you!" she screamed.

"Not exactly, Sheri. But close."

"Let's get oot o' here, Sheri. An' you, Jen. Let's lowse worsels over to the boozer. Aa could do with a liquid lunch. An' if we bump inte Gareth, well, we'll see what's cookin'. Once we knaa, we can make wor minds up. Ye canna promise blind, Jen. She canna, Sheri – though Aa see your point."

"Oh I *can*," declared Jeni, haunted by her dream. Haunted by the threat of that dream repeating itself, wide awake, when the American boy's grave might break open like the crust of an oozing scab, when her own arm might melt into inhuman yellow boneless muscle. "I can. I promise you, Sheri."

"That's reckless talk, pet. Though Aa respect ye for it."

"Why should I care?" And Jeni also shouted at the vicar's head, "Fuck you!"

"Getting warmer," came the reply. Smarmy, gloating.

Twenty-nine

The shambles of Gareth was waiting in the churchyard. He was idling by Felix's grave, poking the soil with one rotten-socked foot so much as to say: It's me – or him. It's the boyo or else –

Or else Sheri's boy, resurrected as a bewildered parody carrying his guts in his hands until he could be destroyed disgustingly again. Jeni heard Sheri catch her breath. Mitzi slipped an arm around the American, whispering reassurance.

Jack was making to accompany Jeni, but Gareth jerked a gangrenous hand to dismiss him as well as the others.

"Jeneeee. Only Jeneeee."

She asked, "Wait for me in Church Lane, will you?"

"Aye, pet."

She wasn't sure whether she was better off being alone with Gareth, or worse off. Better, on account of what he might say or do to drive an alienating wedge deeper between herself and her only friends. Worse, because she would have no witnesses. None of her friends would know for certain what ghastly bargain Gareth forced her to make – or even whether she made one at all.

Only when the others had gone did she continue towards Gareth.

This, surely, was part of the game of evil: eventually to isolate each survivor in his or her own hell. Although she knew that she hadn't, *couldn't* possibly have murdered the little boy, the Power made it seem even to herself that she had done so. Only Bess still fully trusted her; the labrador had nuzzled her hand for comfort on the way out of the church. Jeni had flinched from that wet snuffly reassurance in case she brought harm to the pooch by association. If she seemed to rely on Bess as a steadfast point of reference she might cause the dog worse havoc than any road accident. Bess had wagged her rudder once and capered aside, almost in friendly complicity, accepting the minor rejection as no rejection at all.

And that was part of hell too. Anything you relied on might be damaged or vilely warped. Any carpet could be pulled from under your feet. Commencing with a numdah rug woven with a tree of peace, under which a pit yawned.

"Well, Gareth?"

"You-gave-birth-to-the-arm-of-power. Now-you-must-conceive-it-in-your-womb. Time-runs-sideways-backwards-inside-out-so-that-sanctuary-can-shelter-you. So-birth-precedes-conception-and-conception-follows-birth. We-must-screw. Balls-tackle-touch-cockle-pussy. I-love-you."

Not a statement of love, oh no. No way. A declaration of an action to be performed, a ritual ingredient. Gareth's was the voice of the Power.

She stared at the corpse, which at least was still clad tattily, and wondered what sort of foul body those rags covered.

"You want to go to *bed* with me?"

The blotchy, hairless head nodded.

So it's goodbye love, she thought. And goodbye sex. She'd never be able to sleep with Jack ever after, or even sleep with herself. Supposing Jack still wanted her, which she doubted, if he found out about this he'd never get it up. And supposing miracles followed, but afterwards he found out that she'd copulated with a rotting corpse as hors d'oeuvre, well . . . hardly the best basis for a relationship, unless Jack was a fucking saint as well as randy as a rabbit. If you could pass on VD and AIDS caught from a diseased lover, what could you pass on from a zombie-corpse?

Why figure on Jack? She almost giggled giddily. It was

Gareth who wanted her, not Jack. Gareth was making sheep's eyes at her. Boiled mutton eyes.

Soiled, soiled she'd be, worse than a rape. She would feel so, anyway, even though she offered herself willingly as a sacrifice to the lips of death. She would never be able to touch *herself*, except perhaps to wash maniacally. She would certainly never touch herself with any awakening pleasure, in case something decaying reached down from inside her to catch hold of her fingers.

In a sense this was the climax of her darkest masturbation fantasies from long ago. For she would be fucked by Evil. This was nemesis. And it was hell, the destruction of love, sex, touch, the transformation of herself into a kind of conscious robot, a zombie made of dead unfeeling flesh. She would never dare feel again. Her last memory, before she switched off her nerves: a dog's amiable kindly kiss on the hand. A dog's love.

"Your place, or mine?" she asked. "Or shall we do it in some other corpse's cottage? They'd hardly notice, hardly raise a finger. Unless you need an audience. Do you? Maybe we ought to get married properly seeing as your Nancy's defunct. Can't fancy Nancy. How about getting spliced in church with the vicar's head presiding? A congregation of cadavers, a couple of dead daughters of the village who aren't too badly decayed, for bridesmaids? The bells would ring out if we tied a bellringer to the ropes. Confetti and loose flesh could fly like apple blossom. Reception in the village hall afterwards. Honeymoon in the White Lion, upstairs."

Again she had begun to cry – as though she had ever wanted such a thing as a wedding! She was babbling, delaying. The horror was reducing her to banality. Once the Gareth-corpse had possessed her, she knew that she must surely have lost her own self, and any freedom, any proprietorship of her own body. To herself she would be dead tissue.

"No," she whispered, "I won't do it."

Gareth stamped petulantly upon Felix's grave.

"Will! Or-the-little-boy-will-rise-to-the-occasion. No-choice-eh?"

"You won't be able to fuck me. You'll burst like a bad tomato."

"I-will-have-assistance. A-power-tool. If-we-don't-make-love-soon-Jeneeee – "

"Love!" She spat.

"If-we-don't-I'll-be-much-messier-next-week. So-will-every-villager-be. You'll-spoil-the-pattern-speed-the-rot." Suddenly, as if he was making a supreme effort, the real Gareth seemed to look out from those corpse eyes, a human Gareth. "Go on, Jan, be a sport! Nancy wouldn't mind. We're liberated. She won't even know about it. Please! Then I'll feel better."

"Will you? How about me?"

"Keep your eyes shut if you like. Don't look at the mantelpiece while the fire's being poked, eh? It'll feel the same. We can both enjoy it if we try. Please!" A small spoilt boy wheedling for a sweetie, insisting on a sweetie. To make him feel better.

His ulcerated lips looked disgusting. And his pulpy gums, his slack teeth coated with yellow fur. He needn't kiss her on the mouth or anywhere else. But he probably would, slobbering all over her.

"Look you, girl, no one's using the vicar's house. That's not far to go."

"The vicar's. Right. Agreed. I must tell the others not to wait for me."

"Jeneeee – !" he wailed after her.

"Don't worry," she shouted back, "I'll not run away."

For where was there to run to?

Out in Church Lane, Sheri stared wide-eyed.

"Yes?"

179

Jeni told her "friends": "Go to the pub without me. Gareth and I have something to do."

"What is it, pet?"

"I'd rather not say."

"You aren't going to dig up – ?"

"No, Sheri. I dig nothing . . . about what's going to happen to me. I'll be dug a bit though. I'll be dug."

"What dee ye mean?"

Jeni shook her head. "Go on, go away. And don't ever ask me."

"You look blanked out," said Mitzi.

"Good. I want to be blank. I hope I can be blank. I'll be blank afterwards. Always blank."

They went, looking totally distrustful. Soon Gareth caught up.

Thirty

A modest bungalow built of red brick at the end of tiny Dryden Close. No TV aerial. Net curtains at all the windows, the frames needing a lick of paint. Pruned stumps of roses in the well-weeded border, showing a few red sprouts of halted growth. An idiot blackbird, blind in one eye, stood in the middle of the patch of lawn immobile as a clay ornament.

If the bird had been waiting for a worm, it could wait forever. Nancy had told Jeni that the vicar dosed his pocket handkerchief of grass with Chlordane poison to wipe out the worm population. She caught him at it, on a walk last year. When she accused him of unecological behaviour, Partridge argued that he was guarding his lawn against moles. Moles could burrow from the Pattersons' paddock which closed off the little road (and where a Welsh cob and a Shetland now mouldered on in a half-life). Moles ate worms; kill the worms and you'd keep the moles away.

Jeni recalled Gareth sucking portentously on his pipe before pronouncing diagnosis: "Our vicar's *scared* of worms. Worms mean the corruption of the mortal body; death without resurrection. He can't bear to have them in his garden of Eden." "But the soil needs its worms," Nancy had insisted. Gareth nodded. "I wonder if he doses the graveyard too? Cost too much, I suppose. Did you know that Darwin's first book was a treatise on earthworms? I don't suppose that would endear worms to the vicar either, ho ho." "Worms can't get into coffins," Jeni had said reasonably. . . .

Worms: that's what she was going to find inside the bungalow. Worms still spilling in an endless stream from the vicar's sliced windpipe, carpeting the place. A bathful of worms. A whole bedful. A mattress of wriggling white worms. That's why the Power had prompted Gareth to name this place as their love nest. And the biggest, whitest worm of all: Gareth's own tackle.

Incidentally, where *had* Bert and Jack stowed the vicar's body, dead from the neck down, after they wheeled it here in the barrow?

Had they tucked it up in bed? That would be lovely. Or had they popped it in the bath? Next best thing to a coffin, with drainage laid on. Or sat it in a chair? Jeni concentrated on this puzzle so as not to think of other things as she walked slowly, and as Gareth staggered, up the concrete path to the vicar's front door, a door that certainly wasn't locked.

She pushed the door open, and almost spewed upon the mat. The toilet-thing was stretched out along the hall, a hosepipe of a worm lying in wait.

No it wasn't. That was the wheel-track of the barrow printed in the pile of the carpet.

Leading to . . . the kitchen? She followed the ribbed line till it met lino. Partridge's shrouded body lay full length with the collar of his cloak squeezed up against the fridge door as though demonstrating some trick of stage magic. See, Magnificent Mandrake has his head inside a closed fridge keeping cool, while the rest of his body's outside on the floor! How does he do it? (Actually, he retracts his head inside his shoulders like a tortoise, a knack that every member of the Magic Circle masters. Now you see it, now you don't!) A rancid smell hung about the fridge.

The power was off; the smell was of perishables, well perished even though the kitchen was chilly.

Come to think of it, it would be pretty chilly stripping clothes off to copulate with a corpse. How much could she decently keep on? Sweater? T-shirt? Bra? Socks? Maybe Gareth would be a demanding Casanova. A roué of debauchery. Pity she hadn't worn a skirt instead of jeans; she could simply have hoisted it like a two-quid dockland whore.

She glanced out of the back window into the little rear garden of grass and more rose beds surrounded by a larch-lap fence. Then she went to check the pantry. The shelves were all bare. Unless Partridge had been carrying fasting to extremes, Jack and Bert must have loaded up their wheelbarrow after they dropped the vicar off.

A grunty snuffling flipped her attention to the kitchen door, and Gareth.

"Bedroom, boyo, bedroom!" She surged past him in search of the right door.

Wrong one: this was a little study so crowded that only one pilot of the soul could ever fit into its single carved oak seat. Result of squeezing the ample study of the old vicarage into the spare room of a modern bungalow. Her glance took in the old desk, the filing cabinets, the topheavy bookshelves and table crammed with silver-framed photos of churches and Madonnas and crucifixion prints.

Next door: bingo.

The bed was unmade. Its bedspread, which had been tossed to one side, was jumble-sale craftwork crochetted in ruby, black, and gold, giving it an ecclesiastical appearance. Partridge had obviously exited in haste. After comforting Sheri and handing custodianship over to Mary Kuzka he must have caught a few hours sleep before rushing out towards dawn to unlock the reliquary cage. So as to ward off abomination with the help of Saint Anonymous. An alarm clock with brass bells stood by the bed. Other things she noticed: a white surplice peeping out of the large wardrobe; the silver hair brush and bottle of Cotswold Rosegarden aftershave on the lady-like dressing table.

"Aha!" Gareth blundered through the doorway after her.

His irregular gait was determined partly by the derelictions of his body but also by the priapic erection pressing at his stained cords. His puffy green fingers worked the zip down and the frayed trousers parted to fall about his knees. His cod-flesh thighs were embedded with pustules like fishes' eyes all staring at her. As for the cod itself . . . he dragged down browned, fouled underpants, and a smegmic organ also stared stiffly at her through its glue-drippy meatus. A purple chancroidal ulcer decorated the side of his glans. Cysts distorted his scrotum like knobbly fungi trying to burst out of the sac of tightened skin.

He managed, clumsily, to step out of trousers and rocked to and fro, the diseased swollen penis twitching metronomically. His tongue lapped through his ulcerated lips, a panting dog's, smooth and magenta.

Shrugging, Jeni kicked off her trainers then unzipped her

jeans and hauled them off. Next, her knickers. She lay upon the lavender sheet with her knees drawn up, turned her head aside and shut her eyes, imagining blankness.

Soon Gareth covered her, squashing her, stifling her in sweet foetid decay. His mouth slobbered on her cheek. A soft hand forced her face round to meet his. His tongue thrust into her mouth to butt hers. And his loins lunged. Lubricated with pus, his ulcerated glans entered. As his whole shaft impaled her, cysts thudded against her sex like a bag of marbles.

Blankness. Blank as death. Death was fucking her. Evil was fucking her. Be blank. Freeze up. Feel nothing, hide inside.

Inside was where the toilet-thing came from. No, not there. Vacate that part, go numb, be dead, a corpse yourself, dead from the waist down, dead from the neck up. Heart thumps. Hide in your heart, the red living heart pulsing away like a bird in the hand. But the thing fucking her had a pulse of its own, its penis. And birds were squirming in her bush.

"Respond," panted Gareth. "Move yourself. Make love to me. Stroke me. Excite me. Or I can't finish. I can only go on and on. Do it to me, girl. Stimulate me. Love me."

"*How? How?*"

Use your imagination, girl. Just disconnect your senses first. Like smell and taste and touch. Touch without touching.

Think uniforms. No.

Think Gerry Healey. No.

Think Jack? No, don't be a fool.

Think . . . Donna? Think that *you* are Donna raping Jeni, raping yourself. Compelling her (and you) to orgasm.

Think that evening in Oxford. Think of the witch who made a devil come to her, who made him come.

Let the witch take over, let her do it. Let her operate the

Jeni body. Yes, yes! Let *her* lust after abomination, the shaggy stinking sabbath goat. Let her lick its bum, let her suck it off, and this time she'd survive, this time she'd be helped, this time she'd win . . . the world or what was left of it. Waves of power, waves of times washed her beneath the surface of herself as if she was drowning. Yet now her body was thrusting for the shore, stroking, squeezing, and convulsing, her legs dancing, her feet drumming a devil's tattoo.

When Gareth came, he didn't cry. He screamed in pain. This sound, so close to her ears, shattered the surface beneath which her Jeni-self lay deep – yanking her suddenly into the air, light, now-time, and awareness.

The Gareth corpse rolled aside, gasping and writhing. Jeni saw blood dripping out of the head of his ulcerated, wilting penis. She sensed that this wasn't her own blood, but his. To bleed fresh sacramental blood – that was something new for a corpse!

And to feel pain was something new for him too. To feel any intense sensation, when you were dead.

He grimaced at her through slack teeth and lurid, suppurating lips. Was he actually trying to *smile*?

"It's done," he rasped. "The pattern's perfect."

"Is it? I wouldn't know." As she propped herself on her elbow to scrutinize him, dimly she sensed someone else – who was herself, a witchy girl – falling away down a deep dark well clutching on to a bucketful of pain and filth and debasement as the rope between her and Jeni unravelled longer and longer. The witch had taken a load of the mess which was this experience, along with her. Not the whole of it, just a load. A lot was still left, but Jeni didn't feel insane or annihilated. Just somewhat so. So she could bear to scrutinize the living cadaver beside her.

Gareth's cold puppet passion was spent; it had climaxed

185

in a scream and blood. Yet he seemed somehow . . . more human, more alive, more normal.

"Gareth?"

"Christ in a chipshop, Jen, that hurt!"

She clutched his shoulder.

"Are you feeling better? Do you know who you are? Do you know what's been happening? Gareth?"

For a few moments he stared back at her glazedly, then his rotten lips said:

"*Get-ting warm-er.*"

That was when *she* screamed – louder than he had screamed and longer. The witch-girl with her bucket of mad filth was rushing up the well-shaft towards her at breakneck speed. The well-shaft was her own throat. Her screams were choked as she vomited her breakfast of corn-flakes and lemonade all over the lavender sheets and the corpse which had mated her – to give birth, in twisted time, to the toilet-thing.

PART FOUR

Thirty-one

Perhaps the toilet-thing was still lurking in the drains and sewers under the village, but perhaps not. None of the true survivors apart from Jeni had ever caught a glimpse of it, either wriggling over blighted grass or rearing itself up out of a stagnant, disused toilet bowl.

Since there was no mains water – only what was left in tanks and the motionless brook at the bottom of Green Street, plus a cattle trough fed by a spring which still bubbled up – Jack had long since dug a latrine pit on the green, which was an exact duplicate of the one at the peace camp. A sign: SHIT PIT. A bender, an igloo of tarpaulin over hooped branches, for privacy and to keep the rain off. If it ever rained again. Inside, a torn-off wooden toilet seat resting on crossed planks almost flush with the turf.

Bert had suggested mounting the seat on an open box with the bottom knocked out so that they wouldn't need to squat so low, but Sheri with her summer camp experience pointed out that waste matter would flick on to the sides, which was unhygienic. Unpersuaded, Bert preferred to add his own waste to the slurry already on the farm. Jeni never used the shit pit either; she couldn't trust what might be hiding down it. She used a field or a paddock instead. But Nell and Mitzi and Jack happily continued the old peace camp routine, and though Sheri could presumably have dug holes in her own back garden she too visited the pit out of some stubborn, self-punishing solidarity.

The sprightlier of the dead sometimes wandered up to the latrine as if attracted to it and stood outside the bender for a while, purposelessly since they only ate and drank enough to feed a sparrow, and farted into their clothes.

Perhaps, reasoned Jeni, the toilet-thing had indeed come

189

to the end of its perverted, and inverted, existence when Gareth mated her. Now that the Power's lips were unsealed, and now that it had been reinforced thanks to her, such an arm of the new law was unnecessary.

And no one but herself, and dead Felix, had ever seen the arm. How much credence had the others placed in her "outburst"? Jack hadn't pursued the theme; nor Sheri. Nor had Jack asked what she and Gareth got up to together. He must have been waiting for her to tell him of her own free will. Within a few days of the event Jeni had stopped feeling quite so annihilated; by then she hadn't wanted to tell him. And so time passed by.

If any of the dead had come across the toilet-thing, they weren't saying. They made no better sense than the residents of a senile dementia ward. Gareth likewise; clarity had abandoned him.

How lonely Jeni felt; yet couldn't share her loneliness. She was aware that loneliness might be another trap, leading her to confide and betray. Particularly she rejected the snuffly, dumb overtures of Bess. And this was perhaps the true content of the blankness she had begged for: an untrusting void in the heart. How it ached, this hollow wound that Gareth had been driven to inflict in her. Whenever Jeni was about, Nell also acted pretty blank these days; Jeni couldn't help noticing that. Thus blankness mutiplied itself as in an empty mirror.

Of course, there were all the projects of the committee to keep one busy. The Old Folk Patrol. Animal welfare; keeping an eye on the deadstock. The afternoon youth club in the village hall, which was as bashful and tongue-tied as ever it had been in the past, with the added ingredients of decay and morbidity; at least, while the batteries lasted, the dead kids could hear cassettes of their onetime favourites, a-ha!, Amazulu, Whitney Houston, Madonna. Some zombie "lessons" in the school. Blundering, sluggish games. A playgroup of cancerous mothers and stunned corpse-toddlers. A random number of the dead would usually turn up for such events; spontaneously wasn't exactly the word. Other torpid participants could be rousted out.

And there was Church.

For the living were obliged to attend a morning "service" every day without fail. If not, then evil might opt to speak with a different voice than the vicar's, with a voice of vile incidents. The dead came too, without any prompting from the living. First a handful, soon a score, presently many more.

Sometimes the vicar's head simply harangued his congregation in the style of a hell-fire preacher, as if St Mary's had regressed into an earlier age. Partridge raved in the accents of *Revelation*. Open the bottomless pit! A flying eagle full of eyes. A red dragon casting down suns. Fire from heaven, smoke of torment. In one hour made desolate. Gnaw your tongues for pain. Plague, poison.

He was merely describing what had happened everywhere else on Earth, either immediately or lingeringly. But not in Melfort – where ye shall seek death and shall not find it! The vicar lashed them with his black tongue furiously, for the lunatic folly of the nuclear war. During such rants the Power's attention often seemed elsewhere, as though the head was running on autopilot while the Power concentrated . . . upon what? Maintaining the time-twisted envelope around the village. Adjusting, balancing, tuning . . . whatever. Keeping the house of cards from tumbling, keeping the corpses feebly kicking.

On other occasions the vicar insisted upon a Quaker-like silence. These times were almost more daunting, which was perhaps the intention. Was the Power about to fail, unless they added their will to his? Were the black freezing nuclear winter and the hot radiation about to flood in over the village? Unless they all concentrated, unless they all prayed. . . .

Other times, he demanded praise like some petulant child who had performed an exemplary antic.

". . . And the deadly wound was healed. And they worshipped the power of the beast! Amen! That's what the pernicious book of rubbish prophesies – the book that led the world to disaster. What an embittered, vengeful, paranoid fellow old John of Patmos was, to be sure. Classic nut case, eh congregation? All please shout, 'Oh yes he is!'"

And the dead groaned out, "Oh – yez – ee – iz."

"Sexual frustrate, to boot. I gave Jezebel space to repent her fornications; and she repented not. Behold, I will cast her into a bed. John wants to screw her, right? And he lusts after riches. Pearls and pure gold as clear as glass and all manner of precious stones which he never owned. Emeralds and topazes, the compleat potentate's treasure chest, eh? So how about some worship? Let's hear it for the power of the beast! Praise me, praise me, praise me!"

And the dead praised the Power raggedly, automatically, till the vicar's head chortled with satisfaction.

The living coped with these praise sessions variously, since the Power didn't seem to object to parody. The more of a mockery, the better, as they discovered. The sooner it was all over.

Mitzi and Nell ululated – *woo-woo-woo-woo-woo-woo* – like the Greenham wimmin. Sheri adopted a cheer-leader approach, bouncing up and down, waving her arms, twirling an imaginary baton, bawling for her grid-iron gladiator in his helmet of rusty bars. Jack would bellow out, "Wey, you're a canny bugger!" Then he'd launch into the gloom-song about the Aberfan pit-heap disaster, made all the more lugubrious by his Geordie rendition. Putting in whatever words took his fancy and as many extra vowels as he could manage, he wrung out his heart like a dirty wash leather.

"Wey, close the cyoal-hoose door, lads,

"It's treacherous insyide,

"There's dort an' cancer an' starvyation –"

Bert took up this lead. In a joke rustic voice – or maybe this was Bert's notion of a black and white minstrel, since he rolled his eyes – he murdered various hymns.

"Oh Power aar 'elp in ages parst,

"Aar 'ope fur years to coom – "

Jeni adapted the labour anthem, which wasn't really too wide of the mark with all its martyred dead:

"The Power's flag is deepest black,

"It flies upon a heap of cack – "

Welcome to the monkey house. Or the raucous tropical aviary. The further over the top they went, the more tolerable these lunatic rites of worship.

But that particular morning the mood in church was different to other days. . . .

More of the dead were present than ever, even some corpses who were totally lethargic at any other time, never stirring unless frog-marched. They all seemed . . . expectant? Like dogs hoping for a bone from the butcher's van.

The vicar's head made a speech.

"Dearly beloveds! What if the nuclear evil is so much greater than ordinary evil that, set against the nuclear darkness, evil is light? Not a bright light. But light enough. The only illumination left.

"Evil rules, now. Evil is all that protects you. All that cherishes. Because it has the sense to want to survive. Because that's all there is left now. Oh, evil has always loved people – with the lust of a spider that feasts on its mate! Or like some other creepy-crawly joke of nature that eats up its paralysed parent! You're the parent of evil. You're its creator and its lover, its victim and its slave. It is your very own monster, your mistress, your master, your clever torturer.

It is the friend of the filth in your heart which now covers the world so thickly that everything stifled and died. And evil itself would die thus. How could evil not cherish you, so as to protect its own existence?

"Well, my kiddies . . . my mums and dads . . . ye must become as children, eh? Boys and girls shall come out to play. May Day will be your holiday of horror. Just harken to the celebration I have planned. There'll be presents for almost everyone, and a big big surprise!"

Thirty-two

However, Partridge's head had not enlarged on the precise nature of the surprise. Else how would it be a surprise? He had merely instructed them to prepare a traditional May Day celebration. A procession round the streets. Music and maypole dances on the green. Those ancient rituals: of the merry freshening of spring into summer, of fertility, of the leaping of beasts and the singing of birds and springing of leaves from all the darling swelling depraved sticky buds.

This knowledge was certainly in the vicar's skull even if he had always abominated the practice. If any residue of Partridge's intelligence remained in that rotten head, how he must be howling inside.

After the service the mouldering dead trudged out of the church and away. Did they have a slightly nimbler spring to their steps, especially the dead children? Hardly, hardly.

The living had already escaped into the churchyard. So where was spring or summer? What could be seen of fields and trees and hedgerows through the grey pall presented the same unchanging silent sight, of nothing happening. A countryside in coma. That half-roasted and now half-rotten sheep watched them as numbly as if stuffed, though maggots seethed. Although weeks had gone by, it came as a surprise to be told that May Day was just around the corner; a surprise in several ways.

"Do ye knaa what date it is?" Jack asked Bert.

"I haven't been paying much heed to calendars lately. Been neglecting my weedkiller diary."

"The Power must've been keepin' track o' what passes for time. Only, it occurs te *me* – "

"I'd have thought it's closer to mid May by now."

"Or even June," said Mitzi.

"Never!" Nell exclaimed. "It can't be later than the end of April."

"Wey, what a bunch we are. It's got us aal confused. We divven't even knaa what month it is. We should'ha kept count."

"So who cares?" said Sheri. "If the Power wants it to be May Day next week, *that's* May Day."

Jeni spoke. "I think we've been experiencing time differently."

"Wey, we've all been livin' through the same days, pet."

"Yeah," agreed Sheri, "day after day after lousy day."

"We don't *feel* them the same way. They add up differently. Don't you see what I mean? Nell feels as if it's still April. Mitzi thinks it could be June."

"How aboot yourself?"

Jeni shook her head. "I don't know. But I want to cycle out of the village. No one's been outside since you went, Jack, weeks ago. I want to feel for myself the way the road . . . bends back on itself – because there's been a wrinkle in time. Maybe now it's ironed out." Now that the toilet-thing had completed its reverse life cycle, from Gareth's ejaculation to Felix's death.

"I'll come with you," Sheri said suddenly and firmly.

Did Sheri sense that Jeni's proposed expedition wasn't

merely an exploration of twisted space and bent time but also a probing of something intensely personal to Sheri herself, something intensely hurtful – her son's nasty murder?

Did something in Jeni's eyes short-circuit to Sheri in a flash of understanding, giving birth to a crazy hope that Felix's death might somehow be undone? Undone, not by a Gareth stamping on the boy's grave until the disembowelled little corpse heeded the call and rose writhing ghastly through the soil to clutch at its mother – but in some other magical way?

Did Sheri fear that if she failed to go along she might miss out on something vitally important? The American stared at Jeni.

"I will, too!"

Jeni nodded, though she felt sick at heart.

"Wey, that's aal very fine an' dandy, traipsin' off for a picnic, but ye hoard the Power. We've to coach the bairns for May Day. We've rehearsals to arrange."

"I'll only be gone an hour, if that. Then I'll help," promised Jeni. "I need to experience for myself what's beyond the village."

"Yes, *we* have to," Sheri said.

"It's all right, I want you to come." That electric spark between them. . . .

"Aye, but how long's an hour oot there these days?"

They could as easily have walked. However, on a bicycle you felt that you could get away from things quicker, supposing you needed to get away from something.

All of the village's decent bikes were stored under cover at dead Fred Briggs's garage. This had been Nell's idea. Bikes were an unrepeatable resource, and a low technology one. One day she had collected all machines that were in good repair and had ridden them to the village garage, or in the case of kids' bikes pushed them there.

Not that there was any weather to rust the bikes. It neither rained, nor did it shine. Still, you never could tell.

This initiative by Nell was her version of rural socialism, a pigeon which Jeni ought to have plucked by rights if other worries hadn't been on her mind, or blankly absent from it. All means of transport which still worked should be centralized for the use of all. Not that anybody actually rode a bike nowadays. The dead lacked motive and coordination. And as for the living, Nell's garaging project seemed to have effectively quarantined the bicycles, out of sight and out of mind.

Out of mind, until Jeni and Sheri walked to Briggs's garage to equip themselves: with a smart, small-wheeled, red Moulton for Sheri, and an old black single-speed job of thirty or forty years' vintage for Jeni. Wicker basket strapped to the handlebars – the bike reminded Jeni of Oxford, all those male and female penguins pedalling to lectures with flapping gowns. Oxford, Donna, the Trots, the chestnut tree, that first experience of the Power. . . .

The streets and hard-standing continued to harbour immobilized cars and vans, and farm yards housed dead tractors – dozens of defunct vehicles with their batteries all going flat. Jeni was determined to check a bike out of the central depot to give her stamp of approval. She should have thought of this herself. At least she could demonstrate the concept in action. Why, Nell had almost *stolen* the scheme from her. "Mustn't think ill of Nell. Mustn't think ill."

Sheri and Jeni bowled downhill past forlorn cottages into a grey vaguery walled by hedges. A scraggy black and white bird standing at the edge of the tarmac cocked its head at the hiss of tyres and staggered drunkenly.

"Hullo, Mister Magpie!" Jeni shouted at it, imitating the village kids. Unlucky not to greet magpies when you met them. One for sorrow, two for joy. There was only one magpie visible.

197

Barks pursued them, and Jeni squeezed her brakes. Bess was lolloping in hot pursuit. The labrador skirted the confused bird. Even so, Mr Magpie fell over. Bess licked the leg of Jeni's jeans.

"Go back!" She pointed, flapped her hand. "Back!"

"Woof," remarked Bess.

"*Go away!*" Jeni's cry, almost of frustrated rage, drew an odd look from Sheri.

"Go home, there's a good mutt."

Bess ambled ahead, determined this time to ignore rebuffs. So they pedalled on, while the dog kept pace. A glance back showed Jeni the magpie struggling ineffectively to stand up again.

The road twisted this way, that way. Then the surface began to break up. A pox of potholes soon joined together, so that what had been a perfectly decent road was reduced to a riverbed of loose stones, cratered and rutted.

"Hey!" Sheri was having a rough ride on her Moulton's small wheels; her bike kept trying to skid. So they stopped to consult, while Bess went sniffing about interestedly.

Sheri massaged her bum. "Jack didn't mention any of this mess, did he? Do you figure the blast-wave could have caused it? Blast wouldn't tear up hardtop like this, would it? Looks like it's been this way for years."

"I think we've got further than Jack did – and without being turned round."

"How's that?"

"It's letting us go further."

"Into . . . radiation?"

For answer Jeni gestured at the hedge, and the oak tree looming over it. The hedge was greening, the oak almost in leaf.

"Not radiation."

Just then a thin russet blur rushed across the wreck of a road, a snake on legs, hardly more than an inch from the ground. Into view, out of view, diving into the grass verge. The dog hadn't even noticed.

"What was *that*?"

"Weasel or stoat. I never know the difference. It was alive, Sheri! Really alive, full of beans. Extraordinary."

"You don't suppose . . . maybe there wasn't any war at all? That it's all normal further out? But the Power wrapped the village up tight in some kinda forcefield where time stands still? And now we're escaping back to the real world? Uh?"

"Who are you kidding? After Damascus, and the *Enterprise*? After your base went ape, and shot Mal? After a sun exploded in the sky – just before the shutters got slammed!"

"So where's this, then? Why does it smell so fresh?"

"Look at the state of this road. Then look up, Sheri, look up."

A black pall loomed overhead. The sky ahead wasn't even the grey they'd become accustomed to, but an oppressive black.

"Thunderclouds," Sheri said feebly.

"We'd better wheel the bikes."

Around the next bend, the road was only dry, gouged mud. Presently the hedgerows degenerated into a tangle of undergrowth backed by foggy forest which seemed to wear that eerie blackness like a drooping blanket draped over the crowns of all the trees. Behind branches, looming vaguely through the gloom, a squat tower.

"I don't like it, Jeni. These woods were never here before."

"Maybe they were. Once."

"What do you mean?"

That tower – in the Norman style! Something foul was seeping from the woodland, turning the road surface to greasy, smelly mud. The bike tracks were like snakes. At the next bend the way broadened, and those old oaks drew right back from it, to reveal. . .

. . . the church, riven by cracks, about to collapse. Its door yawned open. Burnt-out shell of the Manor and cremated outhouses; a few sly wisps of smoke still slunk up from there. Ravished cottages behind their strips of kitchen garden. . . .

Along the churned-up filthy road lay maybe a dozen corpses. One was badly charred. Another wore armour, which Jeni recognized. That pointy helmet, those chain-mail tails. Other bodies were naked, smeared with mud and with dried blood from the mutilations of their bums and sex organs. As though pigs had taken half-moon bites. Or people performing like pigs. The place seemed devoid of life, almost too devoid. Bess suddenly fled, back the way they had come.

"Oh my God," muttered Sheri. "Where *is* this?"

"It's the old medieval village of Melfort. Hundreds of years ago. The Power ravaged this place. I saw it happen. Just like this, in a sort of vision. I mean, this is how it would have looked afterwards. The day after, or a few hours after."

"Jeni, did you live here in some previous life?"

The directness of the question horrified Jeni.

"No, no, I couldn't have done." No, because she'd been a witch. Because inquisitors had tortured her and burned her. That must have happened in Europe. They hanged witches in England. Usually they hanged them after torturing them. She had no idea what language the witch and her persecutors had been speaking. When the witch cried out, her voice had seemed native, natural. No Power had come to *her* aid at the end. Whereas here . . . the Power arose and had its way with the villagers, and with the family in the manor house and the knight.

Yet Jeni sensed the young witch lying in wait close by,

waiting her opportunity. The witch inside her was only a little bitty way down the well-shaft, the inner pit. She was rising up, just as she'd risen to take control when Gareth demanded stimulation.

"Let's get out of here, quietly," Jeni whispered.

A cackle of laughter rang within the shattered church.

"Jen-eeee!" cried a banshee voice.

Her legs were paralysed, her feet were rooted. Beside her, Sheri was panting fast as if running, though she wasn't actually going anywhere.

Through the church doorway stepped the brown-robed monk.

"Oh no."

The creature might once have been a man, or maybe it was only an imitation of a man, a twisted parody. Its hands . . . its claws . . . were stretching, flexing emptily. If only they had been encumbered with that brass cross, whatever its potency! But they weren't, they were free.

The monk's cowl was thrown back, and the head – part gleaming bone, part ebony, part stiff jelly – was more horselike than ever as if some terrible living chess-piece rose curving from the creature's shoulders. The nose and the huge-toothed mouth flowed into one another, jutting and predatory. The eyes were balls of blood. Its very look was paralysing. Yet one had to look at it, couldn't look away.

Was Sheri whimpering, or was it herself?

The unhuman thing in monk's robes walked down the graveyard path.

"Stay and playyyy!" it whinnied. "Girl and girl come out to play, eh?"

"Come on, come *out*," Jeni begged the self inside herself. "Come out of me, witch. Take charge."

Now the monster had reached the lych gate, and was setting foot on the road. Foot or hoof or claw; the robe hid this detail.

Within herself just below the surface surged someone who knew this beast, someone struggling to emerge as if from a cauldron of boiling water where she was trussed. And just before her other self burst free – it would be easier and easier each time, wouldn't it? – Jeni realized the awful truth, too late. Of course, too late. To realize just a little too late is an exquisite part of torment.

There was no weird young woman who had lived previously, and died previously. No elder, junior witch. There was only herself – sane, and insane. There was only sanity, and madness. Madness was her own mind turned inside out, tortured into another, alien shape.

As the creature neared them, Jeni started to giggle and turned towards Sheri.

Thirty-three

To betray: that was the worst. To betray your friend, your family, or your pet animal, or your life or yourself. To betray *meaning* – the meaning that you'd accumulated within yourself, the meaning of your own person as bound up with the world of others, with living things, with life.

Of course life always betrayed itself in the end – with death, the clawed shadow that waited to rip you and snuff you. This shadow followed everything that lived, and every living person cast this same shadow over others in the form of cruel words and cruel actions, of promises betrayed and hopes betrayed, of woundings and lost love, of the creation of grief as if grief was an art.

This was the shadow that capered beside the pig on its panic truck-ride to the slaughterhouse. It was the gin trap that closed on the rabbit's leg. It was the gunshot and the poison bait. It was the hook through the writhing worm that ripped the mouth of the trout. It was the napalm and the phosphorus. It was the machine-gunning of elephants from helicopters for their ivory. It was the bomb packed with ball bearings tossed into the playground or the supermarket. It was the electrodes on raped genitals. It was the beakless, clawless, bald chicken in its cage, the cage around the heart. It was the screaming vivisected monkeys, the nerve-gassed dogs, bleach-blinded bunnies, butchered whales, the human head in a cage for rats.

Oh aren't we sensitive today! In this world of deaths and living deaths! And is sensitivity, is guilt, enough of a penance? Especially when it's best to ignore, to forget, to look the other way. Otherwise you might easily overload with horror – for pain runs implacably through an enormous subtle network. Otherwise you might go mad, with madness your only safety valve and final excuse, last exit from responsibility.

Jeni wept. She wept. She let her body grieve, to drown her thoughts in tears. Grief consumed her.

People had already betrayed the human race, including all the unborn. All possible significance had died. For a while the few survivors had continued to do things, pretending that a thread of meaning survived. They had counted cans of beans, garaged bikes, organized the parody lives of dead people and dead animals. Pretending.

But no; no meaning.

The Power would take them one by one. One by one it would splatter them, snap them like some vicious animate idol that liked to bite off a head now and then, enjoying the music of the screams, the hot rum of the blood. The Power was merely spinning out its narrowed range of choices.

So it had revolted against the nuclear holocaust? Why should they believe a word that its mouthpiece, Partridge, said?

Obviously they'd harboured a little hope. People are made that way. If the torturer says that you'll be set free, or even granted a few days' reprieve from pain to recover in your cell, you can't help but hope, hopelessly. You can't help but believe, however disbelievingly. And the Power knew this.

Oh she wept. She wept for brave Sheri and for herself and for her other friends. She even wept for the goitered, ulcerated, blind goat on the green, and for that poor rotting sheep in the churchyard. And for the duck that swam in circles upside down, drowned but still driven onward.

Words penetrated her own personal dense grey dripping fog. Faces loomed distorted. Jack's. Mitzi's.

"Where's Sheri, pet?"

Jeni shook her head. Where was Jeni, for that matter? As the world became clearer she discovered the school-yard. A maypole stuck up from a cross-base of timber like a candy-striped stake for a witch. A dozen raggy junior kids stood about, sick beyond death, mouldering, maggoty, squelchy-skinned, hair fallen out. She averted her gaze from the blinded eye, the scrofulous skull, the burnt match-stick legs.

"Sheri went with you," Mitzi reminded, and Jeni noticed her own big-wheeled old bike lying on its side on the concrete. "Is she all right?"

"I don't know," said Jeni.

"How come you don't know?"

"What did ye find?" Jack asked her.

"We found another village, a medieval one. It was the original Melfort. It had been pillaged. Ruined. Just dead bodies there. Something came out of the church. The Power. I blacked out."

Oh no she didn't. She gave herself over to . . . somebody else, who was Jeni twisted in a crazy-house mirror. She went into the crazy house inside herself and hid there. Behind the warped mirror.

"Next thing I know I'm here."

Jack eyed her with deep suspicion. Of course he would. How could any human being trust another?

Mitzi nibbled her lip. "I like Sheri. I pray she's all right."

Nothing to pray to except a fiend. No one to turn to. Nothing to trust. Only grief. Grief be my guide, to further grief.

"She'll torn up." Jack's reassurance sounded unconvincing.

"Shouldn't we mount a search, down that road?"

"No, pet." Was he scared? "Aa think we'd best get on doing what the Power told us to. Are ye gannin' to pitch in, Jen? It'll keep yor mind off worryin'."

Off grief? No, grief was the air she breathed.

But Sheri didn't turn up until the next day; and she certainly didn't turn up alive. Only Bess had turned up, tail between her legs, avoiding everyone. The next morning when the survivors pushed their way through the flock of corpses into St Mary's, what had been Sheri lay on the altar.

What had been her.

"You stinking shit!" Mitzi screamed at the head in the cage. Jack had to restrain her from rushing at it. Nell was being sick in the aisle, and Bert stood ashen, trying to understand what he saw.

"At least," Jeni thought frozenly, "I couldn't have murdered Sheri that way. Could I? – even with a fiend's assistance?"

Sheri, and the bike she had been riding, both occupied exactly the same space on the altar. The Moulton cycle had been inserted impossibly into her torn stretched naked body, crucifying her mechanically. Her bloody hands hung limply from the ends of handlebars which must run right through her arms, as bones. The grips stuck out of her palms like extra fingers. One wheel necklaced her, spokes needling inward to pierce her neck in a bastard halo. The top tube must be bracing her spine, as the saddle jutted out from her bottom. The down-tube and the seat-tube emerged behind her knees. Pedals poked from her ankles, the wings of Mercury, velocipede-style. Her right ear had been stretched to accommodate the bell. Her mouth gaped, lockjawed by the lamp.

"Shit, shit!" shrieked Mitzi over and over till she was gasping for breath, and couldn't shriek any longer.

In the general silence that followed, the vicar enquired, "Would you rather bury her – or just ride her to the garage?"

At first Nell insisted that only a woman should touch the other woman's body to try to disentangle her, so as to lay her out decently and wrap the soiled altar cloth around her as a shroud. Only then could the men act as pall-bearers. Meanwhile they could employ themselves digging a grave. Right next to Felix.

A shaking Mitzi offered to help. Jeni didn't offer; the others were ignoring her. Not so the vicar. He winked at her repeatedly with a floppy, mouldy eyelid, a grotesque stooge's semaphore signal designed to incriminate her. She went and stood with her back to the cage to hide this display, and now had to contend with a string of stage whispers, hoping that no one else heard. Thankfully the dead congregation were mumbling and glugging to themselves like gas shifting in bowels. Of course the vicar could have spoken louder but at the moment the Power favoured a nightmare of half-audible accusations in a whole cast of voices impersonating her one-time friends, as though these were all gossiping about her in some malicious limbo. Her head buzzed with the vile babble.

Disentangling proved impossible. Sheri and the Moulton were part and parcel of each other as though an insane surgeon-magician had decided to create a new hybrid, of machine and human. After tugging and twisting futilely for ten minutes till she was as filthy with clotted blood and juice and oil and grease as a butcher-mechanic, Nell gave up. Obviously the Power had noted her garaging project and felt obliged to comment. The vicar had been busily imitating Nell's voice behind Jeni's back. "Hmm! So you should have been commissar of bikes? Resented my initiative, is that it? Thought you'd put a spanner in the works, hmm?"

By then a shallow grave was ready, dug with spades from neighbouring garden sheds. When Jack and Bert had manhandled Sheri out to it, however, they had to lay her on the turf and broaden the hole considerably to take her outstretched, metal-braced arms.

"I'm going to pop down to Sheri's house," announced Mitzi. "I'll see if I can find a US flag to stick in the soil. She'd have liked that."

"Good idea," agreed Bert, wiping sweat from his eyes. "She didn't deserve this."

Bess ambled up, sniffed the crater in the soil with Sheri and the bicycle lying cupped in it, cocked a leg and peed. Oddly, this seemed like respect, a marking of Sheri and her resting place as part of acceptable animal territory, a recuperation of that body tortured into something mechanical, as true flesh once more – and a keep-off warning to anything that might disturb it.

Thirty-four

Jack, Bert, Mitzi, Nell, and Bess.

And Jeni.

Four survivors. A dog. And one more.

They could hardly give her the cold shoulder for too long
. . . or was it Jeni who was giving *them* the cold face?

Five survivors in a village of rotting zombies in a world
destroyed had to try to get on together. That only made
sense. (In a world ruled by nonsense triumphant? By
vicious nonsense?) In fact they could hardly meet Jeni's
eyes – or she theirs – without the question arising, "Who's
next?"

And yet, what had she done?

They were all in the White Lion that same noon for
another liquid lunch. Tom Tate, returned from church,
manned his bar like some performing seal which had been
coated in drippy, reeking grey glue; not much of a performance. With a nod to him, Jack squeezed past to collect a
four-pack of Fosters, which were the last cans left in the
pub, and to pour a Captain Morgan for Bert from an almost
empty bottle. After a few moments' heart-searching and
internal struggle he thrust one can at Jeni, who accepted it
gratefully.

"Er, Jen, divven't take this the wrong way, but Aa'm
shiftin' oot o' yor place. Aa'll move in with Bert."

"Yes. Of course. I understand." She'd lost his affection,
been robbed of it. How could a man feel any trust or liking
for a woman who might destroy him fiendishly? Might
cause his death in some novel, nauseating fashion.

"We're aal vulnerable now," Jack remarked to no one in
particular. "One by one. Eenie meenie mynie mo."

"I didn't. . . .," began Jeni.

Mitzi glared at her with hatred and sick fear. The hatred was a clothing for the fear.

"We all still have to work together," Nell said firmly. "We must get May Day properly organized. You'd think the Power might have considered that!"

"Did the Nazis consider the comfort of the fiddlers at the gates of Auschwitz?" Mitzi asked. "If part of a quartet dropped dead that still left a trio. Then a duet. Finally a soloist. Who'll be the soloist in this little concert of ours, I wonder? Who will applaud her? What will her reward be? Maybe I wouldn't want her sort of reward."

Shaking helplessly, Jeni snapped, "Maybe you wouldn't want to be fucked by a corpse!"

Mitzi recoiled as if a curse had been slapped on her. It was Bert who recognized the distress – not the venom – written on Jeni's face.

"Is that what happened between you and Gareth? Is that what the Power made you do?"

"Yes, yes! Or else it would have dragged Felix out of his grave. *That's* what I did for Sheri."

"And maybe it made you hate her," murmured Nell.

Mitzi recovered herself. "Oh great! A ritual fuck," she sneered. "A filthy black magic rite – part of its frigging pattern – and you went along with it. Naturally!"

"What do you suggest? I should let the boy burrow out of his grave with his guts round his neck?"

At least Mitzi was speaking to her. Perhaps it would have been better if she wasn't, for the skinny blonde girl retorted with hideous, offbeam insight:

"So here's the ritual climax: Sheri crucified on a bicycle! Climax, did I say? Oh ho. Frigging foreplay, more likely. Us next. Or will it be," and she cast around, "will it be Bess for a spot of lezzy bestiality and disembowelment?"

"No! Not Bess! Never!"

Mitzi peered at her. "You *can* choose your victims, can

you? That's interesting. What a remarkable change from Jeni the Red bustling around our peace camp, buzzing off to meetings, mounting demos, blaring about emergency powers! Satan and his sister joined the peace movement, but they couldn't behave like members of the human race forever. Oh no. The sham broke down."

Jeni felt that Mitzi had opened a hole into her head, into her heart, and had stuck a microscope inside to reveal the surging virulent microbes of her memories and the imps that hid behind those memories.

"Hang on a minute," said Bert. "Felix and his mum were both American. I think something had it in for Americans. Well, there aren't any more Americans left to pick on. Not live ones, anyway. So why should we be next?"

"Why shouldn't we be?" Mitzi asked softly; she seemed to have run out of steam.

"I . . . I honestly don't know how Sheri died," said Jeni. "I respected her. I almost loved her."

But she *did* know. In general terms she knew. She could well imagine Sheri's torment in that medieval village at the hands or claws of that thing dressed as a monk, assisted by a witch fully familiar with the devil's ways, the terms of service. Sheri's son had his insides pulled out. She had been stuffed – with a bike. How symmetrical her death had been. Pray that Sheri had died quickly.

Pray to what?

Lies. Betrayal. She had loved Sheri – *in what style*?

Mitzi was guessing the truth. Did that mean Mitzi was in danger now? But what *was* the truth? That Jeni contained her own private fiend? Or that she was being led to believe this? Lured, and hoodwinked? And this was just one more twist of the Power's torture. If she accepted this "truth" she would finally and entirely betray herself.

"Could I have a rum too, Jack?"

"Pirate's parrot-juice? Wey aye, pet. Looks like the last

'un." He sounded glad to be asked. Glad because she was reacting within normal human bounds? Glad because he had escaped from her immediate clutches?

Accepting the shot of Captain Morgan, she said, "You don't need to walk on eggs with me."

"Eh?"

"You don't need to watch your step when I'm around. If anyone cracks it'll be me." But was that *true*?

Mitzi licked her lips. "And when you crack, what'll be inside? What'll hatch out?"

Jack said loudly, "Let's talk aboot these rehearsals, shall we?"

Thirty-five

Came the day which the Power identified as May Day, the procession of dead schoolkids shambled in reasonable order around the streets and lanes of Melfort, shepherded by Nell and Mitzi, with Bess woofing and pretending to nip heels. The boys and girls had been decorated with bright ribbons pillaged from a dozen sewing baskets. By way of song they managed to hum like bees or moan like distant cattle.

Jeni trudged along too, feeling as though a rope was around her neck, choking her onward towards faggots which awaited.

The procession started from the school. En route a score of dead grown-ups and teenagers joined the march, which ended circuitously at the green. There, the rest of the population all awaited. Even the most decayed and doddery had dragged themselves or somehow prevailed on a fellow corpse to act as crutch, to lend an arm. Jack and Bert, as marshals, hardly had a thing to do beyond maintaining a large clear circle around the pole which now dangled its plastic streamers loosely, a tall anorexic's skirt. The dead villagers pressed together patiently. When the juvenile troop entered the circle, Bert switched on the cassette tape – of folk dances, folk songs.

Clutched in the numb hands of lurching children, the red, green, blue, and yellow streamers unwound in and out one more time, till a dozen dead girls and boys came to a halt. They stood like numbers on a clock dial designed by Dali: twelve slumped, mouldering hours linked by floppy plastic hands to the central spike so that it was everything o'clock. Never o'clock. The crowd moaned. The cassette player seemed to have stopped, just like the child dancers.

Jeni's mind itched and her calves twitched to kick her forward; a frog's legs galvanized by an electric wire.

"Wrong number!" she exclaimed. "Must dial a different number."

"What's that, pet?"

"Thirteen o'clock! That's the hour of the coven. The hour of the Power." Helplessly Jeni advanced across the grass, ducking under a yellow streamer held by the youngest Boxall girl whose face was almost unrecognizably rotted.

"Don't let her!" cried Mitzi. Bert held Mitzi. Mitzi struggled.

"We have to let this happen," Jeni heard Bert saying fiercely. "Whatever it is! Otherwise it'll be something else another day. Something worse. It could happen to you next – don't you understand?"

Jeni stood with her back up against the naked wooden pole, the stake stripped bare. The throng of dead sighed – and music recommenced. A recorded voice began to sing lustily:

"I had four sisters sailed across the sea
    Pery mery winkle domome
And each of them sent a present unto me
    Partrum quartrum paradise lostum
    Pery mery winkle domome!"

Could this song really be on the tape? The dead kids stumbled in and out around the pole, loosely wrapping the top with their streamers. One circuit.

"The first brought a chicken without a bone
The second brought a cherry without a stone
    Partrum quartrum paradise lostum
    Pery mery winkle domome!"

The second circuit brought the plastic streamers down to touch Jeni's hair.

"How can there be a chicken without a bone?
How can there be a cherry without a stone?
    Partrum quartrum paradise lostum
    Pery mery winkle domome!"

As the streamers covered Jeni's face she knew she was posed exactly like some Joan of Arc in any of a dozen old films, being bound round by the executioners with coil after coil of rope or chain in fetishistic bondage, as prelude to those men setting fire to the faggots piled at her feet to roast her alive, the witch. She could no longer see because of the bandages, could only just breathe, couldn't cry out through the gag. The cocoon of streamers still let her hear the song.

"When the chicken's in the egg it has no bone –'

One streamer held her by the throat. Another crossed her breast, pulling her tight.

"When the cherry's in the flower it has no stone – "

Now her waist! She tried to shuffle her feet to kick away

faggots if any were piled around them now, but she could hardly move – her legs were paralysed.

The music slowed to a stately largo, and each word of the dog-Latin chorus came out like ecclesiastic plain-chant . . . or like an invocation.

"Par–trum!
Quart–rum!
Par–ad–ise!
Lost–um – "

What was this chorus? Some parody Latin hymn? Some . . . exorcism?

"Per–y!
Mery–y!
Win–kle!
Dom–om–e!"

She could hear things ripping – but what? The fabric of the world sounded as though it was tearing, thread by thread. She felt hot. Burning hot. Just as utter panic was about to seize her she felt the lowest ribbon unwind, to begin to release her.

Many other distorted voices took up the chorus – the dead villagers were singing. Only, they were singing the words in reverse order:

"Domome winkle mery pery
Lostum paradise quartrum partrum!"

Her chest was loose, her throat was free, her mouth un-bound.

And now the dead were singing nonsense.

"Emomod!
"Elkwin – !"

No, they weren't. They were reversing the words themselves. They were chanting the dog-Latin and bits of English backwards.

"Yrem!
Yrep!"

How could they manage to sing backwards? The new words sounded like the names of demons.

The plastic band across her eyes flew away, and she saw: the corpse kids hobbling rottenly in and out around her, unwinding their long streamers from her head, from the pole – as the massed dead of Melfort mooed out powerfully:

"MUT–SOL!
ES–IDA–RAP!
MUR-TRAK!
MUR-*TRAP*!"

Ghastly sinister words suggesting trap and murder, or *mur* for wall and *sol* for sun or soil and mutant and rape and *meurt* for dying. Death trap. Wall of death.

That wasn't the worst. During the time while her eyes had been blindfolded the dead had done their best to tear off their own rotten garments, or each other's. That was the noise she had heard. The green was littered with torn soiled rags and tatters, discarded shoes. Now the villagers only wore stray loops, patches of cloth which had adhered to them, half-sleeves, quarter vests, odd socks, knickers stained brown and yellow ripped into holes. Even the kids with the streamers in one hand had managed mostly to denude themselves. The near nakedness of these dead people was so much more monstrous than the piggish nudity of those other villagers, crazed and lustful and compelled, capering behind that monk before rooting in the mud. At least those had been whole, sound bodies to begin with. This flabby nudity was foul with sores and cancers, inflammations, skin diseases, peeling rotting seeping flesh, squirming nests of maggots.

As the dead child dancers reached the limits of their streamers they began to flop down one by one – not at all gracefully as in a curtsey, but like puppets whose strings have suddenly been dropped. Yet those strings still jerked their fallen bodies spasmodically.

One by one, then two by two, then three by three the dead villagers began to groan, to cry out bestially, and tumble to the ground – where they did not lie still, oh no; they writhed, contorted, wallowed. Within a minute only Jeni herself and her fellow survivors were left standing, surrounded by a mass of jerking, shuddering, heaving corrupted cadavers. Ghastly nude. A great herd of seals being slaughtered by an invisible, acid-spraying hand.

Then one of the corpses – was that Harry Blesworth? – began to split open. His blotched codfish legs and his poxed trunk and his raddled arms: they crevassed as though a butcher's knife had sliced deep along them. Foul liquids welled as the man burst apart in an oozing of ichor. His skull cracked open.

Struggling out of the corpse, fumbling free, came an arm, a leg, a head. . .

. . . of a naked boy.

The boy crawled free, stood up, and wailed – from the shock and terror of it? or to be able to breathe?

Seven years old, maybe eight. The boy was smeared with the stains of his emergence from that . . . chrysalis of rot and death. But that was only superficial mess. In other respects he looked sound in wind and limb. His features bore a strong resemblance to Harry Blesworth; Harry as the boy he must once have been.

"Hoorah!" cried the boy.

As if his cry was a signal, the other dead burst open, disgorging boys and girls from inside themselves. The stench was appalling, the noise a chaos. Most of those emerging sounded joyful. How they shouted with glee – whoopee! – and skipped about amidst the discarded piles of blubber and offal, milling, giggling at each other's nakedness. None appeared stupid . . . unless they'd been stupid originally. None seemed mad or damaged. They looked perfect again. Boyish, girlish perfect. They had become as little children.

And the maypole dancers and all the other dead *kids* were also splitting open where they lay – to reveal wailing, fist-flapping babies.

Oh yes, a grown-up body could contain, could hatch, a boy or a girl. A boy or girl could only hatch an infant.

"Get them babbies free!" bellowed Jack. "Afore they stifle!"

His shout broke the spell which had fallen over the original survivors. Within moments the five of them were burrowing into the oozing, cleaved carcasses of those dead kids like a team gutting plucked turkeys to bring out the babies and lay them safely on the side-lines. A stretch of free grass became a squalling maternity ward. None too soon – for the heaps of foul discarded body tissue and organs were already becoming no firmer than beached jellyfish, great bruised purple jellyfish that dripped, melted, flowed, slowly drained into the ground, even the bones dissolving waxily. Very soon the rescuers were wading ankle-deep through an amorphous stinking gluey pond to snatch the last babies. Boys and girls were joining in, to help. They were conscious, bright again! "Mister, can I help?" "Here, give it me!" "Turn her over!" "Hold him upside down!"

A few babies, they failed to save. Nostrils and throats had clogged. The lungs had stopped breathing, the faces gone blue. No amount of thumping or sucking or kiss of life helped.

The tethered goat-corpse had also collapsed. Even now it was giving birth to its younger self – in the shape of a frisky kid. . . .

217

Thirty-six

"Please all keep together!" cried Mitzi. "And please stop asking things! Please let us sort out what's best!"

"I'm hungry," complained wee George Vaux, "and I'm chairman of the Parish Council too."

"There's a new committee nowadays, of public security!" snapped Jack.

"Says who?" demanded little Dennis Ainsworth. "I need to see to my porkers. I could have two hundred piglets squealing for feed, and fighting and biting. With all the filth, they'll catch pneumonia."

"Yes! Wait!"

"The goat got reborn, didn't it? Why shouldn't I have piglets?"

And the dead ducks on the pond had also been reborn as ducklings.

The babies were squalling for attention. Enid Jackson, girl again, with the merest hint of a goitre now, clutched her hands over her crotch.

"Those poor mites *have* to be wrapped and fed. And so do I. It's shameful, this. I don't know how I'll hold up my head. Babies come before piglets, any day. Right now – not in half an hour, either."

"Yes! Hold on!"

Enid Jackson indeed held on, to her crotch.

"We must all get some clothes on," she insisted.

"In time!"

"What a wonderful miracle," enthused Clare Fox, a mere mouse of a girl though with a light of glory in her eyes.

"Oh god, oh god," groaned Nell, "how can we cope?"

Voices babbled from all around.

"Quiet, *please*!" Mitzi shrieked. "Patience!"

"Wey, at least they aren't aal reborn as what the philosopher called tabulous razors – with no notions in their heeds!"

"Apart from the babies," Bert observed. "Missus J's right on their account. Girls! Girls!" He clapped his hands. "You, you, and you – yes, yes. Start carrying the babies inside the White Lion. Carefully, mind – one at a time. Get them swaddled. Wrap them in curtains, pillowcases, anything to keep them warm. Please be in charge of that, Missus Jackson." Unable to help himself, he giggled at the title.

"Don't you mock me, Bert Morris."

"No. I'm sorry. Do it, will you?"

"Since it stands to reason, certainly. Would you kindly tell me how you propose to feed the little ones? Typical of a man to forget *that*."

"There's a few tins o' powdered milk in the inventory," Jack called over, "an' some cans of evaporated."

"Almost useless," little girl Enid retorted. "Babies need proper milk. Good rich fresh milk. Will there be any of that, if the cows are all little calves?"

Bert slapped his brow. "We'll use sheep formula milk. There'll be enough stocks on the different farms."

"Are you out of your mind?"

"No! Orphan lambs thrive on it. Sheep milk's richer than cows' milk. The powder will need diluting more, and it'll go further."

"We'll see about that." And little Enid Jackson began browbeating a squad of baby-nurses from amongst the crowd of naked girls.

"I'll pitch in," piped an American voice. That must be Mary Kuzka. Girl, again. "Where'd Ed? Where are you, Ed?" she called.

"Right here, honey." A gangly boy approached.

And their daughter Carol too; she'd been old enough

219

and big enough to become a little girl. She ran up and hugged . . . what could have been her sister and her brother.

Enid Jackson frowned. "No *men* are needed, thank you."

Carol Kuzka planted hands on hips. "You gonna be sexist about this? Kids and kitchen for the women?"

"Bloody hell," said Bert, "the last thing we need is a political discussion."

Enid Jackson smirked. "*I've* been put in charge, so we'll do it my way. Girls! Get *on* with it!" And, miraculously, girls began to carry the screaming babies away.

"We need aboot a hunderd discussions," said Jack dully, "in five seconds flat."

"What do you mean?" asked Nell, who had just caught the tail end. "Everything's coming back to life. What's wrong?"

"Wey, isn't it obvious? Does the Power give free lunches? Eh, Jeni, does it?"

"How should I know?"

"Aa think yor more likely to knaa than any other bugger, since ye knew what to do at the maypole to bring aal this aboot!"

"I didn't know – oh never mind."

"Listen, an' aal tell youse." He ushered them a few paces away from curious ears. "How we gannin' te eat now there's hundreds o' mouths to feed, eh? Unless ye have any devil-manna laid on, Jen, we can aal storve te death inside a month or so. Oh, Aa suppose we can kill aal the piglets an' whatnot te spin it oot longer – providin' they've been reborn like that pushy little snot thinks."

"He's Dennis Ainsworth," said Bert, who looked distinctly unhappy.

"An' what dee we torn to afterwards? Cannibalism?"

"Chicks'll grow into hens, and lay," Bert muttered.

"Wey aye, an' how do we look after aal these *livin'* animals?"

"I know, I know."

"We had wor work cut oot when they were deed! Aa'll tell ye: we'll have slave labour, that's what." He swung round on Jeni. "Yor goovernment emergency powers was gannin' to involve child labour gangs, worn't they? Well, we'd best stort learnin' to be slave-masters pretty quick. Good thing we're twice the size of any o' the slaves! It's gannin' to be a dictatorship here, just like it would have been after a normal bloody nuclear war. Slavery, dawn to bloody dusk – it's not gannin' to be any picnic, an' we'll probably still starve. Suffer little children, eh? We'll need te make them suffer to keep them in line, an' aal for nothin' in the long run likely. The Power must be laughin' its heed off. Ye dangle a smidgeon o' hope, an' as soon as ye gulp it doon it's shit in yor gob."

Nell turned to Bert for another opinion, but he didn't have one.

Even so, she began, "We *must* believe that the Power genuinely wants to help. That it's doing its best to save nature, because it's part of nature. That – "

"Aye, exactly," Jack interrupted, "but would ye buy a used car from it?"

Jeni cleared her throat. "We should ask. Ask the vicar. What its intentions are."

A couple of naked boys were loitering close by, contriving to eavesdrop. She realized that one was Gareth, visibly bubbling with intentions, schemes. A chunky lad. His companion – a skinny lad overtopping him – was familiar too; he just had to be Andy. Andy's face twitched as if a colony of fleas inhabited it. He looked way over the edge. Nuts. He'd been losing his marbles before the war; death hadn't given any marbles back to him.

"Jen!" Not "Jen-eeee," now, but plain Jen. Gareth the boyo stepped forward, accompanied by his batty batman Andy. So where was Nancy? Ferrying babies and swaddling them, perhaps? At long last, a baby in her arms!

"Old comrades stick together, don't they now?" said Gareth. "Right through thick and thin. Old comrades share political know-how, that's why. I'll help you sort out the work in a proper socialist style. *Won't I?*" he demanded.

An image invaded her mind of Trotsky, when he was in power before the old Party comrades quarrelled, using the Red Army as a rod of iron to control dissenting farmers and others.

"Gareth . . . do you remember what you did to me?"

"Now there's a good one! What *I* did to you? With you and the Power calling the tune between the two of you?" Thus further to hammer the wedge between herself and the others – and into that gap to insert himself. "I was used, girl. Used, and *hurt*. You hurt me. Andy here's been hurt too – by closeness to you, Jen."

"In that case, maybe the greater the distance between you and me the better!"

Andy stared at Jeni maniacally.

"Oh god god god," moaned Nell. "We can't start fighting over who's to be a chief and who's to be an Indian."

"You listen to me, Gareth," Mitzi cut through loud and clear. "You might be an old comrade – that doesn't matter a shit. You're a kid. So's Andy. We can't make this village work if we show any favouritism."

"You . . . bitch. No wonder you couldn't stay at Greenham in a genuine collective. Oh yes, I heard how you finked out. Jeni told me."

"I didn't tell it *that* way!"

Mitzi jabbed a finger at the boy. "You shut your cake-hole. I'm not interested in dredging muck. That's all *before*. Now's now. Those who are physically adult have to be in charge."

"I fail to see why. The best thinkers should be – "

"Cut it, titch!"

"Oh, so we're a cupboard Stalinist, too?"

"Don't know what you mean. Just don't push it." Mitzi's hand had balled into a fist. She glanced at Jack for vindication. "Isn't this what you meant, a minute ago?"

"Aye, an' it's startin' aalready."

"There could be another way," Gareth resumed slyly. "All together under one banner with strong leadership and something like shop stewards to represent the work force – against management, in other words the Power. I'd gladly help out as a shop steward or convenor. Mediate with the labour force. Organize it."

"Rabble-rouse, ye mean," growled Jack. "An' what yor talkin' aboot is bein' an overseer, not a bloody union official."

"Oh well it would be a *bloody* union man, to you. Never unionized, were you? Blackleg carpenter, wasn't it? Trucking around the whole country undercutting other workers' jobs. Jeni told me."

"Piss off!" Mitzi shrieked at Gareth, on the very brink of attack.

"You'll regret this," he warned softly. But he did back off. He melted away with crazy mute Andy into the naked juvenile mob.

"Right!" Mitzi hurled her words like skittles at the children. "The rest of you! Go to houses where real kids used to live! You know which houses. Get yourselves kitted out in kids' clothes and footwear. Everyone report back to the village hall in half an hour. Sorry if this sounds brusque, but we've all got work to do if we're to survive."

"Brusque?" shouted out Ainsworth. "It's downright sodding impertinent. Who do you think you are? This is our village, not yours. And we aren't sodding children."

"Oh but we *are*," a young girl declared, stepping

forward. Surely that was Mrs Vanderzee, who had taught part-time at the school. She sounded utterly authoritative. "We are all going to *act obediently*, just like children should. We are going to have to accept discipline just as if we are children. For the moment." She turned around. "Is that perfectly clear to everyone?"

A few voices agreed, then a few more.

"Good! Now *I* shall collect clothes for Mrs Jackson and for those other girls who are looking after the babies. You'll help me, Mrs Bennett. You too, Mrs Yardley. Now let's *all* go and make ourselves decent."

Nell sighed. "Thank goodness for that."

Jeni asked, "Shall we go and see the vicar now?"

"What about them?" Bert jerked a thumb at where the babies they'd failed to save lay amidst the deliquescing sludge.

"Later," said Jack. "Whether we like it or not, we'd best nip up te the chorch. Mebbe wor vicar's heed's given birth te a talkin' canary, full o' riddles an' who's-a-pretty-boy."

Thirty-seven

Dire apprehension, worse than she'd ever felt, clutched Jeni as she forced herself to walk towards the porch of St Mary's. The "miracle" was going to be blown away as lightly as any dandelion seed; she was sure of it.

Jack and Mitzi were putting on a bold, defiant face for the forthcoming interview, while Nell, who wanted to trust in some inherent natural goodness, had opted to stay behind to supervise the nursery in the pub. Bert's doubts were

224

audible. He was arguing softly with himself, hardly aware –
or hardly caring – if the others heard his mumbles.

"May, isn't it supposed to be? Not too late to sow main-
crop spuds . . . the way the weather's been lately . . . have
to *hand-sow* the bloody seed tubers, Christ. Harvest in
October . . . have to store 'em in clamps, I reckon. . . ."

Yes, he was trying to compute their chances as parents
and providers for the resurrected village.

"Hmm, swedes and turnips'll wait till late June, July."
He cast a glance at the grey overcast. "Oh, what's the use?
Winter wheat'll never get into ear.

"Still, on the other hand – "

Hand-sowing of potatoes. And of anything else. Harvesting by hand. Hard labour dawn till dusk, on starvation
rations. How to conserve their food stocks? Employ a
better-fed guard with a shotgun? And who would that be?
Flog anyone who steals a potato? Thus ensuring a serfs' rebellion. . . Half a dozen kids armed with tools could take
on an adult and kill her, or him.

How long before someone like Mrs Jackson, with Gareth
whispering in her ear, decided that the destruction of the
world had been caused by adults; but she and the other
villagers had been reborn as little children, innocent and
presexual – therefore Melfort and the Earth should be
purged of the last remaining grown-ups?

Perhaps the Power, the elder God, would accept a few
human sacrifices with good grace and repay with fruitful
fields, sleek cattle, plump hens. In another generation
Jesus, Marx and company would have vanished forever.
The demon-God would squat in the driving seat, absolutely
real and present to Its flock.

Grim prospects, grim.

Still, reason might prevail. Civilization might continue.
Apart from the one-time kids reborn as bleating babies, the

Power had resurrected the people of Melfort with their adult memories intact.

Maybe the Power *chose* this course to top up its reservoir of potential pain and horror. With plenty of grown-up passions, traumas, jealousies, delusions, and squabbles on the boil, it could amuse itself quite a bit longer tormenting the population, couldn't it? Until final starvation time, cannibalism time, the last hour of despair. It wouldn't even need the few real grown-ups around to add piquancy. People reborn as children could suffer adult torments just as readily. More so, perhaps. They'd be more vulnerable physically.

"Though on the *other* hand," muttered Bert. He'd need ten hands.

"Shh," hushed Mitzi. She patted Bert, and he looked shamefaced.

"After ye," Jack said to Jeni.

They filed into St Mary's.

Inside the reliquary cage sat a white skull. A vile-smelling gruel had dripped from it; this was already drying, lacquering the base of the cage and the flagstone beneath.

A bare skull, without flesh or eyes or tongue. Just bone. Empty sockets. Grinning teeth. Ostrich egg of a cranium. Which neither saw nor heard nor spoke.

"It's dead," whispered Mitzi.

Jeni stretched a hand half towards the bars. Jack caught her wrist, though her heart wasn't in completing the gesture.

"Leave it be."

"Yes."

"No more sermons. No more rantin'. No more advice. We're on wor own, Aa think. To make and mend. It'll still be aboot, Aa bet – but no more mouthpiece!" A crazy hope gleamed in Jack's eyes. "We'll lock the chorch. Nay bugger'll step inside this cursed place, just in case."

Bert shuffled, shifting his weight from foot to foot.

"On the other hand – "

"Howay, bonny lad! We've work to dee."

Thirty-eight

Just as on the morning of the war, Jeni stood in the churchyard. Her work party were due to meet her in Church Lane, outside the gate. That morning they would proceed to Harry Blesworth's farm to give the boy and his girl-wife a hand, though many hands hardly made light work. Despite a sound sleep from the glooming onwards till grey dawn – keeping good medieval hours – she still felt tired. Everyone felt tired. No tractors, no machines, just manual labour, child labour. Work and sleep. And work; during the past three weeks.

Maybe that was why Gareth hadn't caused any trouble yet. Too tired. He was in her work party; her responsibility, her . . . punishment. Maybe Gareth was biding his time, building his strength, waiting for the inevitable cracks to widen as the remains of fodder and silage and formula feeds ran out, as the fields were picked bare, as more reborn lambs and calves and piglets were slaughtered, as some fowlpest ran riot.

Ah, he hadn't made his move because the eating was still good. Roast runt piglet, barbecued ailing lamb. Problems she had never imagined now occupied her mind. Ainsworth's porkers weren't the hardiest breed for an outdoor life on poor diet. George Vaux had a few Saddlebacks which would have to be cross-bred. At least the majority of baby animals had seemed thoroughly weaned; just as well, seeing as there were no animal parents and human babies were consuming all available forms of milk powder. The lambs especially shouldn't have had to rely on such grotty pasture; already there were victims of scouring and emaciation, sure sign of parasites picked up as larvae in a mouthful of grass. Just wait for the illthrift of summer – if any summer ever came – without much worm drench to administer. Just wait for keds, tics, blow-flies, and scab when the sheep dip ran out.

And what about next winter? Would they even see next winter? Would the Power allow some sort of seasons so that they could freeze as well as starve? Oh the everlasting greyness of it all! Nature had been reborn but sluggishly. Buds became miserable leaves reluctantly. Grass struggled up feebly. Vegetable seeds were producing yellow chlorotic wispy sprouts. Nor had it rained; water had to be hauled back-breakingly from the few sources, pushed in cans on carts to do little but dampen the dry earth. Yet who would wish for radioactive rain?

As she stared from that charnel hilltop beside the forbidden church, into the shrouding veil in the direction where Kerthrop had once been, suddenly there in the east a disc of light blossomed.

As once before, Jeni pissed herself. Terror clutched her heart. No time to run into the shadow of the tower!

The fireball had only been interrupted – frozen in time. Now it was set loose again to blind and blast and melt and burn to ashes. It was the start of the nuclear war all over again, the agonizing wreck of everything – finally this time, finally.

The Power had played its joker. She couldn't see, she was on fire, consciousness was torn from her.

"Hi ho, hi ho, as off to work we go – !"

228

A smelly wet cloth dabbed her cheek. A black mass pushed against her. A rope whacked her leg.

Bess was licking her, nuzzling her to rouse her from her faint.

". . . Hi-ho hi-ho hi-HO!"

She raised her head. Dwarfs were clustered by the churchyard gate. No, those weren't dwarfs; they were her work party, of child villagers, with Gareth giving voice to wake her up. They were all staring at her. No, they weren't. They were staring beyond her, and their faces were no longer glum but lit with joy.

Her jeans pressed the grass damply as if there were a dew. The dew was her own. As she got to her knees, still dizzy, and as Bess sniffed interestedly, she kept the urine patch turned away from their gaze. She hardly need have bothered. No one was looking at her. In the east the grey overcast had parted. The sun was a disc of trembling, dazzling liquid gold – at the end of a long tunnel. The tunnel bored for miles through turbulent dark murk, right up through the dingy poisoned atmosphere and stratosphere.

In the sudden, unfamiliar sunlight headstones and grass and trees and roofs all glowed with forgotten colours as if an old painting had newly been restored, stripped clean of years of muck. Well, maybe the painting was still dusty. Maybe it needed a rinse. Birds were beginning to sing. Lambs were baaing. Satisfied that she was well, Bess left her to run about in doggy ecstasy.

Jeni stood up. She understood.

"Isn't it wonderful?" she called. "Carry on to Church Hill Farm, will you? I'll be along soon."

Her crotch would dry in the sun presently, and she could rub the fabric with grass to confuse the stain.

Like Chinese magic flowers unfolding in a glass of water, buds were making up for lost time on the trees. Daisies were opening white faces in the grass. This, at last, was renewal – true, utter, wholesome renewal. Oh they would work with a will today, would her dwarfs! With nature burgeoning, probably they would be *forced* to work harder; if that was possible. However, now it was worthwhile. She tore up some grass and earth and rubbed at her jeans, which were already grimy. The dwarfs had departed.

She whistled. "Come along, Bess!"

Bess headed to heel. As the dog lumbered over the grave-soil where they had laid Sheri shallowly to rest, the turned earth convulsed. Something erupted from the low mound to grab hold of the labrador's hind leg. Something flexible and yellow – the toilet-thing!

Bess yipped, stumbled, half turned – and howled as the yellow arm dragged with terrible strength, pulling her leg and haunch into the soil as if into quicksand, swallowing her up. Bess wallowed, clawing for purchase. Her frantic eyes locked with Jeni's, begging. Already the dog was up to her midriff in churning dirt.

By the time Jeni reached her, Bess's shoulders were disappearing. Only her head left, howling! Throwing herself down, Jeni gripped the dog's ears uselessly. One ear slid from her grasp, then the other. Bess's muzzle vanished; soil fell inward. As Jeni rolled clear, she heard a few last stifled howls from underground. The earth heaved as if chewing the dog, digesting it as fast as flowers and buds were opening. Now there was no dog.

Sheri's grave belched, burped, was still.

The weather continues favourable, wrote Jeni.

But that was an understatement. The fact that there was weather at all was bliss, a daily blessing. Sunshine by day, sweet soaking rain that fell mostly by night – not to mention some sight of stars and moon. Occasional afternoon showers too. The Power had widened its sky-tunnel so that this looked less like the inside of a tornado. The tunnel swung slowly across the sky to track the sun till it set, then it swung back overnight to arrive in the east for dawn. Presumably the Power laundered and filtered the rain. Maybe it fetched the water from some time before the war, kidnapping clouds and squeezing them dry. Maybe it used water from deep underground or distilled from the depths of the ocean.

She wrote in biro in a school exercise book by the light of a single candle. Perhaps it was important to make a record while there were still pens and paper, dog tired though she was. Dog tired. (Oh Bess.) Maybe after she had filled a book or two the Power would arrange a spot of spontaneous combustion. (Don't think of it.)

Earlier in the day little Celia Touchbrook was torn to shreds by a defunct combine harvester which suddenly roared into life in the yard where she was slaving. The combine became a devouring monster. It chopped Celia up and baled her obscenely as a block of meat and bone. Then it died again, blades dripping with her blood. Reverted to a heap of junk, its electrics buggered by the EM pulse from the Kerthrop warhead.

The Power was trying to resurrect some farm machines?

Oh no.

It killed Celia today, she wrote, *because that's its habit. It's like some sick cunning madman who acts normal most of the time, who's a good father, husband, charity worker, but who goes out now and then and rapes and strangles and mutilates. These are the tics of evil. Its fuel. That's its language, in which it talks to us, its captive audience. Without whom, it would be nothing; so it claims. That's what recharges its battery.*

This is the razor blade buried in the cake of the miracle; but it's the only cake in town.

Who will be cut up next? Who will be destroyed or

231

mutilated or tormented? Someone surely. But not everyone.
Not even many . . . for lives are precious to the Power.

The next victims might be animals. But not all animals.
Not even many.

How soon? Some time. No way to tell.

Maybe in time the Power will learn to talk a different
language; that's Nell's hope. Let's hope for her sake she
doesn't try to teach it how.

How I wish people hadn't learned to speak their own
language of evil so fluently.

A is for Atom. B is for Bomb. C is for Cruise. D is for
Deterrent. E is for Explosion. F is for Firestorm and Fallout.

I saw Mars tonight up the tunnel. I'm sure it was Mars,
that red world which people could have gone to in another
ten or twenty years – Americans and Russians both,
together, challenged by and challenging a dead yet vastly
wealthy universe. We'll never go there now, or anywhere –
except perhaps deeper into the haunted devilish medieval
past.

And we are the lucky ones, the only ones left, sheltered by
Evil from the nuclear storm which was more evil than Evil
itself.

N is for Nuclear weapons. N is for Null, for Nothing, for
Non-existence. And nuclear weapons no longer exist, either.
Neither does life on Earth except in this one bewitched vil-
lage.

I'm tired, I'm cursed, I'm still alive. A thump on the door!
Mars shines, the candle burns, my heart beats fast.

More SF/Fantasy from Headline:

SHADOWS

Darkest fantasies by masters of the macabre including STEPHEN KING

EDITED BY CHARLES L GRANT

Imagine a collection of nightmarish tales as dark as a
freshly opened grave.
So terrifying that they scatter dreams like leaves before
a midnight wind.
So macabre that they freeze the blood. So horrific that
Evil itself turns away.
Imagine. Now open and read.

FICTION   0-7472-3002-1   £2.50

Headline books are available at your book-shop or newsagent, or can be ordered from the following address:

Headline Book Publishing PLC
Cash Sales Department
PO Box 11
Falmouth
Cornwall
TR10 9EN
England

UK customers please send cheque or postal order (no currency), allowing 60p for postage and packing for the first book, plus 25p for the second book and 15p for each additional book ordered up to a maximum charge of £1.90 in UK.

BFPO customers please allow 60p for postage and packing for the first book, plus 25p for the second book and 15p per copy for the next seven books, thereafter 9p per book.

Overseas and Eire customers please allow £1.25 for postage and packing for the first book, plus 75p for the second book and 28p for each subsequent book.